"Birch, darling, what's the matter?" she cried

His body leaden, he turned away from her in the bed. *I'm blind*, he said in his mind, but he had no voice to say the words. *Oh, God! I'm really blind.* Knowing he had taken Julia to the top of the mountain and was leaving her to find her way down as best she could, he groaned inwardly. It seemed the subtlest cruelty of all. But he couldn't help her.

Julia lay stricken, frantically searching her mind for a clue as to what had gone wrong. Had she been too eager, come on too strong? Their lovemaking had always been straightforward, from the heart.

A growing fear that now she had to always be on guard—even when she poured out her love— gave her a stark feeling of loss....

ABOUT THE AUTHOR

Jenny Loring, who resides in California with her husband, Roger, has a long and impressive track record with Superromance. Before becoming a novelist, Jenny was a newspaper reporter and columnist, so it isn't surprising that in her most recent Super, the hero and heroine form a photojournalism team. Nor is it surprising that *Interlude* explores New York and Paris settings, reflecting this author's enjoyment of glamorous locales.

Books by Jenny Loring

HARLEQUIN SUPERROMANCE

Interlude
JENNY LORING

Harlequin Books

TORONTO • NEW YORK • LONDON
AMSTERDAM • PARIS • SYDNEY • HAMBURG
STOCKHOLM • ATHENS • TOKYO • MILAN

Published January 1990

First printing November 1989

ISBN 0-373-70388-0

PROLOGUE

WHEN THE CALL CAME that morning the concierge was feeling disheartened. The new young man at the phones, he feared, lacked the savoir faire necessary to work the communications center of the venerable Paris Ritz. It was not like the old days when he himself had come to work at the hotel. Now they came loaded with references but couldn't handle the simplest problem without calling for help, he thought testily, reaching for his phone in response to its discreet buzz.

"*Le concierge* speaking," he said into the mouthpiece.

"*Pardon, monsieur*, I have a call on the line for Monsieur Birch Cheney from a Monsieur Langley in New York City." It was the new employee, speaking in French.

"Ah, yes. Monsieur Cheney, the American photographer. In *numéro* 662, on the Cambon side."

Automatically calling up information he deemed useful for the young man to have at hand, the concierge continued. "Monsieur Cheney and his wife arrived from the Far East yesterday. Late afternoon. Madame Cheney is *très* beautiful. A journalist, I believe. It is my understanding they publish travel books and articles *à deux*." He paused a moment to let what he'd said sink in, then added, "*Certainement* you know they are not to be disturbed."

"*Oui, monsieur*, but the caller is most insistent."

"You must tell him with the utmost courtesy, but firmly, that Monsieur Cheney has left explicit orders to put no calls through to the room until we are notified otherwise."

"*Mais, monsieur*, I have done so. He says the matter is *très* urgent."

"And you believe him?" the concierge asked with scorn. "You do not know it is something they always say?"

"He demands to speak to the concierge."

Though a small explosion of air escaped the concierge's lips, he tempered his reaction. He hadn't arrived at this station in life by letting whims of impatience rule. "Then by all means let him speak," he said, his words tainted with sarcasm, nonetheless.

"*Oui, monsieur. Merci beaucoup,*" said the young man gratefully and quickly connected the waiting line.

"*Bonjour*, Monsieur Langley," the concierge said in his most unctuous voice when he was sure the connection had been made. "This is the concierge. I am told you wish to speak to Monsieur Cheney. The Cheneys are asleep after a long and arduous flight. I am sure you would not wish to have them disturbed."

From across the Atlantic a chill, authoritative American voice replied, "Under ordinary circumstances, no. But in view of the fact that this call has been trying to catch up with Cheney for three days and concerns a matter of life or death, I'm sure you will want to connect me with him as quickly as possible."

"A matter of life or death?" It was an old ploy, yet in spite of a certain cautious cynicism that came from years of serving the rich and famous, the concierge believed him.

"One moment, *s'il vous plaît*," he said, and realized he had lapsed into French under the pressure of having to make a decision. "I will see that you are connected with Monsieur Cheney *tout de suite*."

CHAPTER ONE

IN THEIR TOP FLOOR CHAMBERS earlier that morning Julia Cheney had dreamed of Birch and awakened to an erotic pulsing deep inside. In the shallow darkness of beginning dawn she lay confused, not sure where she was, not even sure for a moment what hemisphere she was in. Then her mind cleared, and a crystal chandelier hanging from the ceiling across the room took shape. Recognition rushed in.

She was in Paris in the beautiful rococo room at the Ritz where they'd spent their wedding night five years earlier. Last night, just as Birch had promised, she'd fallen asleep in his arms in the same bed.

As they'd closed the door behind them leaving, that last day of their honeymoon, she'd said to him, "Promise me we'll come back."

And Birch had tipped her face to look in her eyes, and said as seriously as he had when he'd repeated their vows, "On our fifth anniversary. I promise."

Closing her eyes, she slipped her hand across the silken sheet to touch him. Finding only emptiness within her immediate reach, she hoisted herself on one elbow and peered into the shadowy grayness around her. The sight of Birch's long body in a tangle of covers on the far side of the huge bed brought her fully awake.

She watched the rhythmic rise and fall of his chest for a second, then scooted across the space between them.

She shaped herself to the curve of his unclad body and pressed her face into his cool flesh, loving the soft, welcoming rumble she heard deep in his throat. He rolled over and gathered her to him. When the full weight of his arm settled across her body, she knew he'd made the move without awakening.

It was an awkward fitting of curves and planes that had her burying her nose in the pocket of one of his shoulders, leaving scarcely enough room to breathe, but she made no effort to improve upon the position. Breathing in the faint, musky scent of their earlier love-making, she lay still, reluctant to disturb him or remove herself from the luxury of his closeness.

Oh, ye of little faith, she chided herself, remembering how let down she'd felt that day weeks ago when Birch had told her about the Thailand assignment for *Passporter* magazine. *Well, there goes our anniversary at the Ritz*, she'd thought resentfully. Knowing how Birch was about promises, she should have known better than to doubt.

They'd made it to Paris on target, though it had meant not going to bed for a week. It had meant spending daylight hours prowling the streets and alleyways of Bangkok for material, and the nights in a borrowed darkroom with an adjoining cubbyhole lighted by a single bare globe, where she'd turned her notes into magazine copy at her typewriter while Birch worked his magic with his day's film in the other room. Without a continuous flow of coffee they would never have made it, she thought reflectively—coffee and memories of the elegant bed-chamber that had cast a magic spell over their wedding night.

But there was no question it had been worth it. The magic was still here. The rich, silk damask draperies still dripped falls of golden fringe. The walls were still festooned with roses, and the moldings and cornices still delicately ornamented with shellwork. The crystal prisms of the chandelier cast the same rainbows of light upon the ceiling overhead.

And through the door beyond, there still waited the alabaster bathroom in all its Roman splendor. Julia took particular delight in the silver swans' head faucets and the inch-thick towels that were kept warm on heated racks. Just last night she'd sat on the rim of the immense sybaritic marble tub they'd just shared and watched Birch towel himself dry.

Remembering, a deep sensual quiver spread through her. She ran her tongue lightly along Birch's neck where her face pressed against his flesh, and the powerful male perfection of his naked body rose vividly to her mind— the torso as splendid as that of Michelangelo's *David*, but the lower half more fully developed. He was more beautiful by far.

Forgotten was all thought of leaving him undisturbed. As she lifted her face from below his chin, her cheek grazed a stubbly cheek. She felt the gentle sough of his breath as her lips found his, parted slightly in sleep. Her fingers moved to comb the soft wiry curls on his chest and to knead the flat plane of his belly.

His lower lip was as smooth and firm as a ripe plum, she thought. She tasted it gently with her tongue until his lips parted enough to draw it into the velvet recess of his mouth. She felt his own tongue spring to life and move teasingly on hers, and she met his awakening with a gasp of delight.

Sensitive still with memories of passion from their earlier lovemaking, their bodies were impatient. Their lips clung eagerly for a moment. Her thighs parted in involuntary welcome, hips thrusting to meet him as he came down.

"WAKE UP, my Juliet. The lark's on the wing."

It was midmorning. Birch's blithe misquotation brought Julia struggling her way to consciousness. Eyes closed, she tested her state of being and decided that aside from a certain cranial heaviness, she felt no worse than was normal for one who had flown from another side of the world in the past forty-eight hours. It took a moment to summon the energy required to lift her weighted eyelids and sit up drowsily. As she did so, she pulled the sheet up to cover her partially, leaving one breast bare. Her eyes focused on Birch, now dressed for the day in a casual suede jacket, plaid cotton shirt and corduroy pants. His thick, dark sandy hair was slightly awry.

"Mmm...nice scenery," he said, grinning down at her.

Julia reached under her pillow, where she'd tucked the scrap of silk that was her nightgown some hours before. She pulled it on over her head and emerged, yawning.

"How come I feel like I've spent the night in an opium den, Birch Cheney, and you look healthy enough to go out and wrestle a bear?" she asked fretfully.

"Because I'm the man," he replied with a grin. Reaching, he deftly caught the pillow she threw at him, then let it fall to the bed. In his hand were two letters. He held them up as flags of truce.

"Mail already?" she said in surprise.

"One mailed yesterday here in Paris. The other came air express from Paley, Washington."

"That'll be anniversary greetings from my folks," she guessed, reaching for it. "Who do you suppose is writing us from here in Paris?"

"Jean Paul Plongeon, I expect," he said, slitting the envelope with a slim gold pocketknife she'd once given him, then handing the knife to her.

Julia opened the letter from home and unfolded it absently, her mind on the famous oceanographer whom *Pictorial Geographic* had asked them to see while they were in Paris. The magazine wanted a lavishly illustrated article on Plongeon and *Zephyr*, the small ship from which his diving expeditions were launched. From Bangkok, Birch had written to ask for a meeting.

It was the free-lancer's way of life, she thought wryly. One had to look around for the next job before the present one was done, to hedge against employment gaps. They'd weathered so many of these in the early days of their partnership, Julia now sometimes found herself reviewing their pending assignments like a miser counting his gold.

With satisfaction she thought of the article they'd contracted to do on the great Parisian fashion houses for *Flair* and the one for *Home Gardens* on Monet's water garden at Giverny. For a moment she savored the gratification of having top publishers waiting in line for their services, then she turned her attention to the letter in her hand.

Her mother's tidy Palmer Method handwriting filled the inside of an irreverent anniversary card, making the punch line unreadable while expressing parental love and bringing her up-to-date on affairs of the family and farm.

"Anything new?" asked Birch.

"Not much," she said, holding up the card for him to take. "Dad's planting the garden and Mom's playing lots of bridge. My sister, Marilyn, is running for city council. Mom says the orchards are in full bloom." She reached for the letter in his hand. "What does Plongeon have to say?"

"He'll see us next Thursday at eleven at his home on the Bois de Boulogne."

He gazed into the distance with a familiar look of boyish excitement on his strong, handsome face. It was a look Julia found particularly endearing and at the same time unsettling—it had led them into bold ventures not always to her more circumspect taste. Throwing the covers aside, she scrambled on her knees to the edge of the bed and threw her arms around his waist.

"Dammit, Birch," she said accusingly, peering up at him from somewhere in the neighborhood of his breastbone, "you simply can't wait to go down in that blasted bathysphere of Plongeon's, can you? I can see it in your eyes."

His clear, gray eyes came back to her. "If he'll take us," he admitted. "They say he's not all that hot about having amateurs along on those deep-sea dives. We may have to get the underwater pictures for the article from the crew."

"That suits me just fine," said Julia flatly. "The thought of being shut up like bugs in a bottle at the bottom of the sea doesn't strike me as all that thrilling."

"Does that mean you don't intend to dive?"

"I didn't say that. All I said was it isn't my idea of a good time."

"You don't have to, of course. I can probably cover anything you miss," he said. "It might even be easier to persuade the Frenchman to take me down alone."

"Because I'm a woman, you mean?" she asked, bristling. "You wouldn't let him get away with *that*, Birch Cheney!"

She saw the teasing glint in his eyes as he replied, "Why not? It'd give you an excuse not to go."

It wouldn't be the first time Birch's courtship with adventure had overridden her own inclination to play things safe. At the same time, she knew it was the very thing that had gotten them to the front ranks of the photojournalism profession in little more than four years.

"If you go, I go," she said stubbornly. "Like always."

"That's more like it. I'd hate to think the unflappable Julia would draw the line at anything as safely scientific as a bathysphere," he said.

"Unflappable? Like when?"

"Oh . . . like when the rhino charged you in Tanzania, for instance . . . and then there was the rock slide in Nepal—"

"You call that unflappable? I was scared . . . *spitless*!"

"And the time the hot-air balloon came down with us in the top of the tree."

In her mind she saw the two of them, dangling like a pair of monkeys in a basket from the top of the banyan tree, and laughed—an unexpected carefree giggle—then touched his recently shaved cheek lovingly.

"You, too, have had your moments, lover boy. Let's not forget the day you took off after those two muscle-beach Sicilians who goosed me in Palermo. You were pretty impressive yourself," she said fondly. "Macho— like Rambo but without the posturing. More like David on his way to slay the giant."

Birch gave a derisive snort. "I was scared spitless!" he said.

"Clown!"

He tried to pull her off the bed, but she lunged and caught him around the middle with enough force to throw him off balance. Together they tumbled back onto the bed in a confusion of laughter and endearments and ever-mounting desire that was brought to an untimely halt by the sound of an efficient, purposeful knock at the door. For a moment all action stopped. Birch grunted.

"It's our floor waiter with breakfast."

"Breakfast?" Julia murmured muzzily.

"I ordered coffee and rolls while you were asleep."

Slowly, reluctantly Julia let go of her hold on him. They disentangled. Her feet found the floor. In her scanty silk nightgown, she skimmed across the carpet to the dressing room, closing its door behind her at the same moment the fully dressed Birch opened the door of their room and admitted a young man with a breakfast cart.

Behind the closed door Julia turned back and paused to listen, a smile still playing at one corner of her mouth. She followed the sounds of progress in the next room— the metallic click of silver upon silver, the tinkle of crystal, the silken whisper of fine china eased across starched linen by careful hands. The garçon was taking his time about it, she thought with impatience, staring unseeing at her reflection in the mirror, suddenly awash with happiness to be here again with Birch. And all because of a promise he'd made as their honeymoon drew to a close.

For a moment she harked back to that first lean year of their career, recalling a coveted assignment he'd turned down—an assignment that had money and rec-

ognition written all over it—because it conflicted with
the opening of a home for handicapped children they'd
promised to photograph for free. Remembering, she was
filled with the same loving wonder she'd felt then when
she had realized for the first time just how seriously
Birch took his promises.

From the bedroom he called out to her, "Decent or
not, you can come out. He's gone."

Julia's eyes refocused and she turned from the mirror. Still wearing only the wispy nightgown, she decided
not to change. Instead, she opened the dressing room
door and went eagerly toward the sound of his voice, the
silken texture of the carpet kissing the soles of her bare
feet as she walked. She crossed the room to where Birch
stood by the window looking out, and grabbed him
around the waist in a fierce hug that brought a grunt
from deep in his solar plexus. He turned and drew her to
him.

"Oh Birch, thank God you're *you*!" she said with
breathless fervor.

Her head rose and fell lightly on the eddy of laughter
she could feel generating inside his chest.

"Is that a general endorsement or did you have
something specific in mind?" he asked.

"General, now that you mention it. I can't think of a
thing I'd change," she said, pushing back from him a bit
to gaze earnestly into his eyes. "The hug's because I
suddenly realized you're practically an endangered spe-
cies nowadays."

He feigned alarm. "Good God, woman, you're not
suggesting I've outlived my usefulness?"

Julia frowned reprovingly, refusing to be teased. "I'm
serious, Birch! You're a throwback to the time when a
man's word was his bond. I really *love* that about you,

you know. There aren't all that many of you around anymore.''

For a moment he looked completely undone. He fumbled for words and finally muttered something about promises being the glue that holds civilization together.

Julia was amused at his discomfiture and at the same time somehow pleased. It was so Birch! She might have known the gratuitous praise would embarrass him.

With his next breath he'd regained enough composure to voice a prickly protest. ''Dammit it, Julie, you make me sound like a pompous—''

She cut him off with a soft, derisive hoot. ''Of *course* you are, darling! But on *you* it's adorable.''

In a sudden, unceremonious lunge he swooped her up in his arms and bent his head to capture her mouth with his.

Releasing her, he said gruffly, ''There are some things I love about you, too. Like this...'' His tongue moved lightly across the lobe of her ear. She shivered again and submitted to the titillation of his mouth, his hands. He bent his head again to her upraised face, covering her lips—half-parted in invitation—with his. Her tongue tasted the fresh, heady wine of his mouth, and for a long moment there was nothing else. Then they drew apart, and Birch carried her across the room, past the exquisitely set table where their waiting breakfast was growing cold.

As he laid her down lightly on the unmade bed the phone rang. Birch groaned. ''Dammit, I told them when I picked up the mail not to put through any calls,'' he muttered.

It rang again. Reaching to unfasten his belt, Julia murmured out of a voluptuous haze, ''Don't answer it.''

But the bell was relentless. After the fifth ring Birch grabbed the phone and an armful of pillows from the bed. In the bathroom he buried the bothersome device, then came out, closing the door behind him and leaving a trail of discarded clothing strewn across the floor as he returned to the bed in blissful silence and lifted her nightgown over her head.

THE AIR WAS SWEET with the smells of the Paris spring when they stepped out of the Ritz later that morning, Julia dressed in casual harmony with Birch in loafers, gray flannel pants and a cashmere sweater much the same color as her red-brown hair. Leaving the Place Vendôme, they set out on a pilgrimage of old haunts— small, intimate places of no renown that had been kind to their love in the time of their honeymoon. They walked in companionable silence along the streets of their earlier enchantment, replete with the joy of being together, care-free and in this place. It was a joy that asked for no words.

"You're not going to get us lost?" Julia ventured as they crossed the Seine to the Left Bank.

"Thanks for the vote of confidence, Bride."

"No offense, darling, but letting you navigate is like letting a color-blind decorator redo the living room."

"Trust me. I know how to get where we're going."

Julia sniffed. "*I* should trust a man who can lose his way in a revolving door?"

"Nonsense. I'm as trusty as a compass."

"Some compass! Need I remind you of the time you had to hire one of the villagers to lead us back to our starting point in Luxembourg?"

"Ah yes. A memorable day. Better you should *thank* me for getting us lost."

"Watch it! The gods'll zap you for that kind of hubris," Julia said in an aggrieved tone.

But his words took her back to that day and to the castle they'd happened upon because they'd taken the wrong road in Luxembourg, and she knew secretly that he was right—she did owe him a vote of thanks! She thought of the white-bearded raconteur who owned the castle and asked them to join him for lunch, and of the gregarious bootlegger who'd later plied them with a heady distillation of his own making. In spite of herself, she gave Birch a sheepish grin.

Though she strongly suspected he was devising their course as he went with no actual goal in mind, she played docile and followed his lead. They came in time to a gently curving, tree-lined street flanked by ancient three-story houses, each graced with tall, heavy shutters. In front of a solid square structure of buff-colored masonry Birch came to a stop.

"Voilà!" he said.

On one side was a stone wall and a wrought-iron gate that seemed somehow familiar. Mystified, Julia peered through the gate's fretwork. She drew in her breath. "Oh, Birch!"

"I *thought* you'd remember."

Down the cobbled walkway, half-hidden by flowering shrubs, lay the small, exquisite garden she and Birch had made love in uninvited one splendid, starry night five years earlier.

Grabbing his arm, she hugged it joyously. "I can't believe you found it! I take back all I said." She reached out and gave the iron gate a tug. "It's locked," she said, her voice suddenly flat with disappointment.

"You were thinking of walking in?" he asked, laughing. *"C'est la vie.* The gate was ajar last time, you will

remember. Oh well, no matter." Seizing her in his arms,
he bent her backward in a classic tango stance and kissed
her. The kiss that was begun in play deepened and bal-
anced dizzily on the provocative edge of passion. But
though Julia was aroused by Birch's kiss, she was unwilling to put on a public display.

We must have been crazy back then! she thought.
*Young and crazy and terribly in love. What if we'd been
caught?* "Birch!" she gasped and wriggled free of his
hold. From the corner of her eye she'd caught a glimpse
of a short, red-faced man armed with pruning shears
coming toward them on the walkway from the rear of
the house. Birch turned to see what had caused her fuss,
and when he turned back to her, his eyes were brim-
ming with amusement.

"Don't act so guilty, Bride. You want the man to
think this is an assignation?" he said wickedly in her ear,
then called out in his fearless language-tape French,
"Bonjour, monsieur."

The Frenchman came to a standstill and surveyed
them stolidly as if undecided whether to return the
greeting or challenge them. After a moment he lifted his
shoulders in a Gallic shrug and turned away.

"Ces Américains," they heard him mutter in a tone of
puzzled dismissal. Quickly retracing his steps, he disappeared around the rear corner of the house.

"Friendly sort," remarked Julia.

Birch grinned. "He has no time for small talk with
crazy Americans."

They decided to move off in the general direction of
the Latin Quarter, their goal the cheap hotel where
they'd lived that spring, after they left the Ritz.

It was a quantum leap in reverse from a suite at the
Ritz to a squeaky-springed bed at La Maison Rive

Gauche, Julia decided as they gazed at its smoke-encrusted facade a short time later from across the street.

"I didn't remember it being so shabby," she said.

Birch grinned. "Well, it wasn't exactly the Ritz."

It struck her for the first time that they'd been as blissful in one as they had been in the other. She felt obliged to say in the hotel's defense, "Well, it was cheap and the room was clean and we had a bathroom all to ourselves."

"And a noisy bed," he countered.

"Paid for out of our own funds," she reminded him a bit caustically—lest he forget that the Ritz had been a wedding present from one of his appreciative, well-heeled clients. Birch's father had called the gift a "frivolous extravagance" and had all but ordered them to turn it down. The family's beach house in the Hamptons was a more appropriate honeymoon spot for a man of his son's modest means, Cheney *père* had said; and who could argue with the man who, at that time, paid Birch's salary and knew exactly how modest his son's means were?

Ultimately, it had been Birch's decision to go for the Paris honeymoon, and it rankled that his father had blamed Julia, as he'd blamed her for every other move his son had made since. From that day forth Horace Cheney had pursued a personal vendetta against his daughter-in-law.

Swallowing the bitter taste that rose inside her, Julia consciously closed her mind on Birch's father. She turned her attention back to the hotel across the street where they'd first been sent by her old friend and colleague, Max Eisner. Max, in fact, had been their reason for staying on in Paris after they left the Ritz, thereby further incurring Birch's father's wrath.

In the silence that fell between them as they gazed at the shabby hotel, a shadow of sadness she sensed Birch shared fell upon Julia's spirit.

"Are you thinking of Max?" she asked.

"Yes," Birch replied. "Aren't you?"

She nodded. "I miss him. He was a part of our Paris that's lost forever."

"Right," Birch agreed soberly. "I keep thinking what a lot I owe to him."

Max Eisner had known more about taking pictures than any other photographer she'd ever worked with, Julia thought now in silent tribute to their late friend. When age and illness had forced Max to stop working and retire to Paris, where he'd lived as a young man, she'd lost her cameraman and, with his death, a friend. Until Birch, who had his own special genius for making romance and adventure come alive through his pictures, she hadn't been able to find another cameraman half as good.

When she knew they were coming to Paris, she'd arranged a meeting with Max in the hope that a little shoptalk and gossip would cheer him up. Almost as an afterthought, she remembered, she'd slipped a handful of Birch's pictures into her bag for Max to see.

She could still hear Eisner's gravelly voice with its slight Bogartian lisp saying the words that were to change their lives: "You got the makings of a pro, kid, but you still got a thing or two to learn. Nothing I can't teach you, if you got the time."

After that, Max seemed bent on transferring to Birch his awesome skill as if to keep it working for him after he was gone. By the time they left Paris, Birch was no longer merely a talented amateur shutterbug. He was a skilled photographer who longed to put his craft to test in the marketplace.

"Want to take a look at the hotel inside?"

Julia blinked owlishly and came back to the present as Birch's voice broke in upon her thoughts. She shook her head. "Not particularly. Everything I ever cared about in there is out here with me right now," she said.

Arm in arm they went, caring little where their feet took them. Eventually they arrived at a Left Bank neighborhood of dusty shops offering antiques and used goods—strange jumbles of valuables and junk.

"Mind waiting here a minute? I'll be right back," Julia said suddenly. Without stopping for an answer, she turned into one of the shops, leaving Birch to peer without interest into the shadowy store that swallowed her.

Inside, her eyes adjusted to her dusky surroundings and she saw that the narrow shop was filled to overflowing with every manner of oddity, laid out in a cluttered fashion on every available surface. Things even hung from the ceiling.

From behind a curtain at the far end wafted the enticing smell of well-garlicked soup. After a minute the curtain parted and she caught a glimpse of a solidly built middle-aged woman sampling the contents of a steaming pot on a small iron stove. The man who pulled the curtain closed behind him as he entered the store was pinched-faced, stoop-shouldered and thin. Shrewd eyes took Julia's measure from above a wispy brindle beard.

"*Bonjour, madame,*" he said, coming forward. "*Américaine?*"

Nodding Julia pointed to the item that had caught her eye in the window, a beautifully fashioned antique compass in an ivory-inlaid ebony case.

"How much are you asking for it?" she said when he brought it for her to see.

"Twelve hundred francs," he replied, speaking now in heavily accented English.

"That much?" Instinct told her it was worth perhaps half.

Without a word, the shopkeeper turned and walked back to the window with the compass.

"Wait." She knew she had to have it for Birch, no matter what. "I'll take it."

The shopkeeper turned back. "Twelve hundred francs, *madame*?"

"*Oui.*"

When the compass was tucked safely in her handbag she escaped, blinking, into the brilliant sunlight. Birch was nowhere in sight. *He might have waited,* she thought impatiently, but when he emerged from a shop a few doors away some five minutes later, her reproach died on her lips. Reading his face, she knew that the small package he carried contained a gift for her and that it pleased him immensely, but he wanted her to think it was of no more importance than a package of razor blades.

"Hungry?" he asked when he reached her.

Consumed with curiosity, she lied. "Starved!" she said.

They headed for a remembered bistro, crowded now to overflowing inside and out with carelessly garbed young people from the nearby Sorbonne. Luck led them to an empty table in the dappled shade of a chestnut tree where a white-aproned young man took their order. Left alone, they settled down to sip new ruby-red Beaujolais.

Across the table, Birch took Julia's hand and folded her fingers around a smooth, irregularly formed object about the size of a small biscuit and seemingly weightless. She gazed curiously at a length of supple gold chain that escaped between two of her fingers. Whatever it was, it seemed warm to her palm. Still she kept her hand closed, postponing the moment of surprise.

"Don't hold it too long," Birch advised, half-teasing. "The shopkeeper says it could melt." Julia looked at him round-eyed. Rolling her hand over, she opened her fingers and gave a cry of delight.

"Amber! Oh, Birch! Look! It's got a perfect, lacy-winged insect sealed inside." She was suddenly breathless with pleasure, no more for the gift itself than for the fact that he'd remembered how intrigued she was by the prehistoric resin. The first article she'd ever sold had been about amber.

"A million years ago this bug picked the wrong tree to rest on and got trapped in a blob of pitch," she said, her voice touched with awe. She held the piece of amber up to her nose and with a murmur of sensuous pleasure, handed it to him.

"Don't drop it," she warned him. "It's brittle as glass. But smell! That's what the heat from your hand does. Doesn't it smell good?"

"Like it?"

"It's one of the loveliest gifts I've ever gotten."

Crinkling her nose at him, she smiled and slipped the chain over her head. The bit of amber came to rest just above the parting of her breasts. Raising herself out of her chair she leaned across the small table and planted a kiss squarely upon his mouth before reaching in her bag for the gift she'd bought for him. Then, because it would take away from the pleasure he was getting out of her reaction to his gift, she left it there.

She really wasn't ready to give him the compass anyhow, she decided as she dipped into the steaming hot *pot-au-feu*, unexpectedly hungry all at once. Better to slip it into the pocket of his bathrobe or his shaving kit and let him come upon it by surprise. In her mind she composed a message to tuck in with it: *Darling—this is to make sure we will never be lost from each other. Julia*.

When they'd finished a tureen of the hearty soup and a crusty *baguette* with sweet butter, they sipped Beaujolais and lapsed into drowsy silence, indifferent to the bustle of passersby on the sidewalk around them. It was a kind of lethargy Julia knew well; it was due partly to the wine and partly to the warmth of the spring sun, but mostly to jet lag and contentment and lack of sleep.

Rousing herself with an effort, at last she said, "If we're going to do Paris night life this evening, I've got to get back to the hotel and take a nap."

Birch nodded. "I'm with you, Bride." With a cursory glance at their check he rose lazily to his feet and darted her a sly grin. "Which reminds me. Let's not forget to see the concierge this time about shutting off incoming calls. If I'd talked to him personally this morning instead of leaving it up to the switchboard, our...uh...pursuits might have gone uninterrupted. And I have no intention of being interrupted again...."

CHAPTER TWO

ENTERING THE RITZ, Julia recognized the dark-suited young man who came hurrying toward them as an assistant to the concierge.

"What do you suppose he wants?" she murmured to Birch.

"Monsieur Cheney," the young man addressed Birch as he drew up to them. "*Le concierge* requests you come to his office, *s'il vous plaît*."

Birch looked at him in surprise. "Gladly. I want to speak to him myself, about holding our incoming calls."

The young man's eyes held a look of puzzlement. "Indeed, Monsieur?" he said, continuing in a tone that seemed a tad accusing to Julia. "*Un homme* has called already many times from New York. *Monsieur* has been away all day. He is at this moment on the line."

Curbing his annoyance, Birch said evenly, "How about telling the gentleman we're not taking any calls until tomorrow, as I requested early this morning?"

"But, *Monsieur . . .*"

As if that settled the matter, Birch started to move off, leaving the young assistant gazing helplessly after him. Sensing the young man was new to the job, and intimidated, no doubt, by the concierge's standards of perfection, Julia laid a detaining hand on Birch's arm.

"Wait," she murmured.

Encouraged, the young man said apologetically, "He insists he calls on a matter of great urgency, *monsieur*."

At the familiar phrase, Julia and Birch looked at each other with sudden understanding. Who but their agent, Sid Unger, could find no matter too trivial to be referred to as one of "great urgency"?

"Damn!" muttered Birch.

"Sid knows it's our anniversary. He might at least let us have a full twenty-four hours without calling about some bloody assignment," Julia grumbled.

"I suppose I'd better see what he has on his mind," Birch said a bit grudgingly. "You go on to the room. I'll be up as soon as I'm through with Sid."

Turning to the young man, who was waiting uneasily, Birch had the grace to smile an apology, "I was wrong, my friend. I'll take the call," he said.

"Merci, monsieur," said the other with a slight bow of his head. "Come with me, please, to the telephone *du concierge*. He wishes to speak with you first."

REACHING THEIR TOP FLOOR bower, Julia folded the rose-printed spread back to the foot of the bed. In the dressing room she slipped off her clothes and moved on to one of the marble basins to wash her hands and face and pluck off a hook one of the thick apricot terry robes the Ritz provided for its guests. Wrapped in its plushy folds, she curled up on the bed's silken counterpane to wait for Birch and fell asleep wondering what was keeping him.

Some time later she was awakened by the sense of a presence beside the bed. Lifting one eyelid and then the other, she saw it was Birch. Her eyes traveled lazily up his long body, and when they reached his face, she was shocked at the sober, withdrawn expression she found there. Alarmed, she pulled herself to a sitting position.

"What is it, Birch? Did Sid—"

"It wasn't Unger. It was Evan Langley."

"Langley?" Julia repeated, trying to place the name.

"My father's accountant. You remember him. Dad's had a heart attack and is in the hospital," he said in a flat voice. "Langley says he's been trying to catch up with us for the past three days."

"Oh Birch, no!" she said softly, reaching out to take one of his hands and press his palm to her cheek in lieu of words. She could think of nothing more to say. The only feeling she could muster was a certain impersonal sadness. That the proud, overbearing man a Wall Street columnist had once aptly characterized as a "tough old blister" had been forced to submit to the humiliating mercies of hospital care roused in her a detached pity, even regret—but not the warmth of personal sorrow. Distanced thus herself, she had small comfort to offer his son.

"How bad is it?" she asked.

"'Serious but not precarious,' Langley says—whatever that means. It's hard to tell what message lay beneath the words," Birch told her grimly, sounding frustrated. "He seemed more concerned about the welfare of the company than the state of Dad's health."

"I don't see why your brother wasn't the one to call you, instead of this Langley," she said. "You might get a more satisfactory report if you talked to Matt."

A faint sigh escaped Birch's lips. "Matt's not around, and nobody seems to know where he is. He and Dad had another big blowup. Matt walked out, and said he wasn't coming back."

"Do you think he meant it this time?"

"Sure, he meant it, but you know Matt. He'll be back when he cools off."

"I don't know why. He could get a good job with another company."

"Not as long as he believes that once he lives down his playboy image he'll be in line to head the family firm," Birch said.

"I'd hardly call Matt a playboy," Julia said in a puzzled voice.

"Well, that's what Dad calls him. Matt went through a phase before you knew him that lasted just long enough to become solidly fixed in the concrete of Dad's mind," Birch told her grimly. "Now Matt works his tail off, and gets shrugged aside by Dad until his point of tolerance has been passed and he goes for a showdown he never wins."

"So it's showdown time. You can't really blame Matt," Julia said. "I suppose there's no chance you could reach him at his apartment."

"I've already tried. He's probably working off steam on a sailboat somewhere."

"I wonder if it's ever occurred to him that it probably doesn't help his image to take off for fun and games every time he loses a round with your father," Julia said and returned to the original point. "You plan to go to your father, of course."

"Langley wants me to drop everything and get there on the next plane out."

"Then your father's condition is critical?"

"No. He's out of danger, Langley says. It's Cheney, McCrae that's the problem. The stockholders are getting restless. They want Dad out as chairman of the board and are gearing up for a proxy fight."

"And you're supposed to take over while he's in the hospital and stroke them back in line?"

"That's about the size of it."

"Oh, Birch!" *He's using you again!* she thought indignantly. Aloud, she said, "Langley's your father's personal accountant, isn't he? What's he got to do with the firm?"

"He inherited a chunk of the stock from someone who bought it when the company went public, during the depression. Dad thinks he's some kind of a genius," Birch said glumly. "To the point that he lets Langley call himself a 'stock analyst' and give people advice on investments."

A sigh from Julia echoed Birch's frustration. "Why don't you sleep on it, darling," she said after a moment. "Except for a few hours before dawn this morning you haven't had any decent sleep for weeks. Wouldn't it be best to wait and decide what to do when your mind's fresh?"

"I can't, Julie. Dad's yelling for me to come, and you know Dad! The cardiologist seems to think that in his frenzy to get me home he's working himself up to another heart attack and won't calm down until I get there. The doctor says a second so close to the first could be a killer. I can't take the risk of delaying."

"Oh, Birch!"

He bent and sat down beside her, rubbing a hand across his face. Julia touched his cheek, patting it tenderly before she swung her feet off the bed and stood up.

"How soon can we get a flight to New York?" she asked briskly.

A choked sound came from his throat, and he reached for her blindly and pulled her to his side. "Julie, my angel," he said brokenly. "After all my father's put you through, how can you find it in you to urge me to go back? You know I could be going for nothing but to humor a difficult man!"

She smoothed her hands across his back and shoulders in gentle, soothing strokes, thinking of her own warm, funny, affectionate father, and wanting to make up to Birch for all the parental benisons his own father had withheld.

She picked up where he left off. "Who happens to be sick and your father. That's something you can't forget."

There was a long moment of silence. Then Birch said slowly, "I suppose."

There was a lonely sound in his voice that caught at Julia's throat. "What about plane reservations?" she asked.

"That's another thing. If I go tonight, it'll have to be without you," he said with a sigh. "The concierge called all the airlines while I was downstairs. All he could get was a single cancellation on a plane from Orly that gets me into Kennedy late tomorrow morning."

Oh God, Birch shouldn't have to go alone.

Aloud, she said, "It's all right, darling. I'll come as soon as I can get a seat."

"Better wait a few days until we see what lies ahead, honey," Birch said reluctantly after a minute's thought. "If you need to keep busy you could see Plongeon and interview some of the fashion people. After I've talked to the doctors and seen Dad, we'll know better how to plan."

In a team effort perfected through countless packings over the traveling years of their marriage, they began opening drawers and laying out Birch's clothes.

Taking her customary moment to glance through their daybook and make sure nothing important was being overlooked, Julia came upon the name of a longtime friend of Birch's, now a journalist with the Paris bureau of Global Press.

"What about Hugh Dryden? He's meeting us for dinner tomorrow night. Shall I cancel?" she called to Birch, who was putting together his toilet articles in the bathroom.

"Not unless you'd rather eat alone. I suspect Hugh'll be disappointed if you do. Why don't you go? It'll be good for you."

Their last act, before they boarded a cab to Orly Airport, where they would say goodbye, was to order champagne in the Ritz's Bar Espadon. In the haunt made famous by Hemingway, they drank a sad little toast to the fifth anniversary they'd traveled so far to celebrate and that had come to such an untimely end.

ACROSS THE ATLANTIC in their New York apartment late next morning, Birch gazed at the phone he'd just put down. The voice of Julia in Paris after she'd slept round the clock while he was winging his way to this part of the world, had sounded as fresh as springtime—especially after he'd shared a seat section with a woman and her ebullient two-year-old twins, who had spelled each other in gymnastics and were never both asleep at the same time.

And he had yet to see his father. He had come directly to the apartment from the airport to drop off his luggage and shower and shave before he went to the hospital, and to call Julia to say he'd arrived.

For a moment he was back in Paris. She was in his arms, the warm, silken-soft body and the sweet smell of her flesh kindling his arousal.... Reluctantly, he let the phantom Julia go, forcing himself back to the present.

Looking around the room, he decided he was infinitely glad he'd used the money from his mother's estate to buy the Central Park West apartment the first year of their marriage, even though it hadn't sat well with his father.

The apartment was their anchor—their home to come back to after their wanderings. The spacious unit covered half the fifteenth floor of one of the stateliest buildings on the west side of the park, and everything within range of his eyes now had been bought or collected by them together: Julia's antique snuffboxes in the curio case; the carved Jacobean chest that contained his sound equipment; the painting by an unknown artist that hung above it, bought from a bartender in Montmartre; the enamel triptych of the Nativity they'd found in an Italian flea market outside Pisa; and the small limewood goddess of mercy, Kuan Yin, given them by a friend in Taiwan.

Without Julia, however, the place held only reminders. He needed her to really live the memories. All at once he wanted to be on his way and get the meeting with his father over. By an act of will he overcame the temptation to crawl into the king-size bed he normally shared with Julia and forget everything. He showered and shaved and changed into fresh clothing, his energy store at an all-time low.

By the time he'd stopped at a neighborhood delicatessen for orange juice and bacon and eggs—to restore with calories what he lacked in sleep—it was nearly two o'clock. When he reached the hospital, he was shunted into an anteroom and told to wait until he had clearance from his father's cardiologist.

Waiting, he could feel tension building inside him. It was four years since his stormy parting from his father, and except for occasional distant conversations by phone when Birch was in New York and dutiful notes he'd posted when he was away, there had been no further contact between them, much less any effort on either's part to meet again face-to-face.

He felt an overwhelming compulsion to leave and come back after he'd had twelve hours sleep.

The clock on the wall said two-fifteen when the cardiologist at last walked in and introduced himself as Dr. Perry. Wasting no time on preliminaries, he said bluntly, "Mr. Cheney, you may see your father, but I must ask you to avoid any subject he might react to in a negative way."

The unexpectedness of the order left Birch speechless.

"He's doing very well at the moment, but you should understand, his condition is critical," the specialist continued. "Until his system has stabilized we can't risk having him upset. It could cost him his life."

But Langley had told him so positively that his father was out of danger! Birch was suddenly uneasy. Before he could gather himself to ask questions, the doctor was gone and an aide was there to escort him to his father's room.

Following her, Birch made a mental list of subjects to steer clear of that could upset his father: his own photographic work with Julia, the family business, his way of life, his brother Matt, *Julia* . . . above all, Julia.

That pretty much narrowed it down to the weather, he thought with a frustrated sigh.

HIS FATHER WAS PROPPED up in the narrow hospital bed when Birch entered the room behind the aide. Over her shoulder his eyes met the wintry eyes of his father.

Where was the enfeebled invalid he'd been preparing himself to face? Birch wondered. Except for an unnatural pallor and stubble on his face—Birch couldn't recall ever having seen him unshaved—his father appeared virtually unchanged by his heart attack.

There he lay, glowering like a chief executive officer about to put the screws to an underling. Filled with a vast relief, Birch crossed the room toward the bed. This was the father he knew.

"Well, Birch! You took your time getting here," Horace Cheney said in a formidable voice that belied the doctor's warning. Realizing he'd been looking for a warmer welcome from a father presumably mellowed by illness, Birch felt strangely let down and a little foolish.

"Sorry, Dad. Slow plane. No cancellations on the Concorde," he said dryly. "I took what I could get."

His father's eyes fixed accusingly on his son, a look Birch knew well. There was life in the old boy yet. The doctor underestimated Horace P. Cheney, he thought with a touch of grudging pride and a renewed conviction that Perry had overstated his father's case.

"I've been more than patient with you, Birch," his father said, allowing a well-timed pause before zeroing in. "It's time to put that picture-taking nonsense behind you and get back to Cheney, McCrae, where you belong."

In sudden counterpoint to his father's voice there flashed across Birch's mind an echo of the cardiologist's words: *can't risk having him upset . . . cost him his life.*

He cleared his throat and said evasively, "I told Langley I'd help out until you get on your feet, Dad. Between Matt and me—"

"Blast Matt!" his father mumbled irritably.

Inwardly Birch groaned, remembering too late that his brother was on the list of taboos. He started over. "Relax Dad. With Langley's help I'll hold things together until you're back. You have my promise."

"What the hell kind of promise is that?" said his father in a voice that sent a sudden chill along the back of his son's neck.

"Dad—"

"She seduced you away from the business you were born to—that woman!" his father interrupted. "You're back and I expect you to stay! Have you no pride? A kid with a Brownie camera can do what that woman has sexed you into doing for her."

Birch felt his scalp begin to prickle. For a moment he was beset by a fuzzy disbelief that his father had said what he'd just heard. In the next moment came a surge of rage. From the day he'd left the family business, never had he heard Julia's name cross his father's lips.

Without warning, four years of accumulated resentment churned in his head, wiping out all thought of the damage his words might do to his stricken father.

Disjointed sentences smothered in resentment flooded through his head: *Lay off Julia, goddammit! If I'd wanted . . . not even Julie could've lured me . . . couldn't wait to get out. No way anyone'll drag me back.* But in the suddenness of his outrage and the fuzziness of his sleep-deprived mind, he couldn't make order of his thoughts. The jumble of words backed up in his throat.

Then before he could come to a clear idea of what he wanted to say, the door opened, and his father's nurse came in. "He must rest now, Mr. Cheney. I'll have to ask you to leave."

From his restricted position his father glared at the young woman. "Stay, Birch!" he bellowed. "I'm not through with you yet."

"Your son can come back when you're rested," the nurse said, standing her ground.

Birch shook his head in dazed horror, the doctor's warning fixed again solidly in his mind. Certain the outburst from which the nurse had saved him might have destroyed his father, Birch listened dully as his dad, disregarding the nurse's orders, addressed him directly, his voice weaker now and slow. It troubled Birch to hear for the first time the sound of illness in his father's voice, as if he had stored up all his energy for the attack, and now it was spent.

"Let's don't...equivocate, Birch. I...want your solemn promise...you're coming back to the company. Today. To stay."

Though he'd seen it coming from the time he walked in, Birch felt sick; his whole being rebelled against making a promise he could never keep. He'd counted on postponing a showdown until his father was well enough to be dealt with honestly. Now he saw it was not to be.

The nurse interceded. "You must go, Mr. Cheney."

"Quiet, young woman," his father ordered hoarsely. "Let me...hear what he has to say."

The voices of the nurse, his father and the doctor came suddenly together, pulsating like strobe lights in Birch's head. All he wanted was not to have to think about this. Not to have to think about *anything* for a while. At the top of his mind the words that would bring escape waited only for him to voice them. But he couldn't say them now, he would have to straighten it all out when his father was well enough to be told the truth.

Since when was that the way Birch Cheney played the game? asked some voice within.

As if from a distance, he heard the failing voice of his father again. "Your promise, Birch. I'm waiting."

He wavered in limbo and knew he had no choice but to say whatever would calm his father and improve his prospects for recovery.

"You've got it," he said grimly, and wished at once that he'd bitten back the words. The look they brought to his father's face was one he'd seen there many times, more particularly whenever his father had succeeded in bending one of them—his brother, Matt, or himself—to his will. It was a look of satisfaction laced with disdain.

"Get on...to the office then...make yourself useful," his father muttered in dismissal, and turned his face away, leaving Birch to gaze down at his father's back unseeing, momentarily stunned by the weight of the words that had passed between them.

A few minutes later, on the sidewalk in front of the hospital, Birch wondered vaguely how near exhaustion a person had to be before he hallucinated.

It was as if the circuits of his mind, his senses, and his feelings had come unplugged. Over him hung the uneasy recollection that up there in the hospital room he'd managed to betray something of importance; yet it was as if it had happened to someone else—not himself.

He didn't want to think. If he thought, it would be about the promise.

His toe hooked into a sidewalk crack, and he stumbled. Why was he walking? he wondered and hailed a cab.

Five minutes after he entered his apartment and closed the heavy draperies, blocking out the midafternoon daylight and a fine view of the park, Birch was asleep.

LIKE A DIVER propelling himself to the water's surface, Birch pushed up through layers of consciousness a short time later to answer the phone. Some part of him knew it had rung many times. Only the assumption that it was Julia gave him the incentive to pick it up.

"Julie?" he said, trying to sound awake.

"She's left you, then? I don't know why I should be surprised."

It was the voice of his brother, Matthew.

"Bro!" Birch said. "Where are you, anyhow? Where the hell have you been? Have you talked to Langley?" But of course he'd talked to Langley, he thought leadenly, fighting his way through the veil of sleep that tried to smother him. How else would his brother know he was in New York?

"One thing at a time, Birch." Matt's voice sounded edgy. "I just got in. I've talked to Dad."

"How did he seem to you?"

"The doctors say his condition is critical, but he seems about normal, I'd say," his brother said caustically. "In the five minutes I was there he chewed me out, said what he had to say and turned his back on me. At which point I left."

Birch's head was beginning to clear. "Sounds familiar."

"That's not the way I heard it. The way I heard it, he and Langley welcomed you back like the prodigal son."

There was something unreal about the conversation. This angry young man was not the brother Birch knew. All of a sudden it seemed important to Birch to wrest himself from the dullness that was clouding his mind. He shook his head to clear it, forgot why it mattered and gave in to a yawn and then another, puzzling over the crack Matt had made about Julia and about the prodigal son.

By the bedside clock he saw it was still daytime. He'd slept less than two hours. Matt might have waited until tomorrow to call, he thought grumpily. It wasn't as if they hadn't seen each other only a few weeks earlier, when he and Julia were in New York. He yawned again.

"What's the matter?" asked Matt on the phone. "Did I wake you up from your nap?"

"No nap. Start of a marathon sleep I hope to get back to as soon as you let me put down the phone," Birch said between yawns. "We'll get together t'morrow, huh?"

There was no response from the other end. Birch came to his senses, suddenly uneasy.

"Bro?"

"Don't bother," his brother said stiffly, from wherever he was. "It's of no consequence. Our father informs me that from here on out I'll be taking my orders from you. Just reporting in."

There was a click in Birch's ear that told him he was holding a dead phone.

What the hell? And then the whole sorry confrontation with their father a few hours before came crowding back to Birch's mind in exquisite detail.

God! he muttered. Dad had told Matt—who believed Birch had thrown over his career with Julia and come back to run the family show. That was what the crap about Julia's leaving him and the return of "the prodigal son" had been about. Matt had taken what their father had told him to mean Birch was giving him the shaft.

Dammit, Matt should have known he wasn't about to give up the work he loved to go back to the stock market bull pen. Tomorrow when he was himself again he'd make sure Matt understood once and for all. Now he gave in to another horrendous yawn and let his mind shut down.

HIS HAND STILL on the receiver, Matt wished to hell he'd told Birch to knock off that old "bro" stuff. The nickname he and his brother had shared for so many years sounded patronizing all of a sudden. Birch might as well have called him *Li'l* Bro.

He remembered how he'd tagged after Birch like the tail of a kite from the time his legs were long enough to keep up, and how Birch had called him Li'l Bro and he'd called Birch Bro. Bro was the first word he learned, he'd been told. The day Birch had dropped the *Li'l* and started calling Matt plain Bro was one of the great days of his life, he thought sourly now. At the time, Birch had looked bigger to him than Joe Namath.

Looking back, Matt saw that early period in his life, which had ended when Birch went off to college and he to prep school, as a particularly sunny one. After that, he and Birch were never again so close, he thought as he slumped into a big brown corduroy chair facing one of the windowed walls in his downtown loft. Unseeingly he stared beyond the Art Deco spire of the Chrysler Building in the near distance. When he went to work for the firm right out of college, he'd understood that Birch was the chosen one, but he hadn't cared. Birch had taken the flak for everything. It was only when he began to find Birch's wry remarks about the business less and less amusing that he had realized the world of the stock exchange was where he truly belonged. That was when he'd started going overboard to prove himself to their father.

By the time Birch walked out, Matt had been ready to pack it in. But with Birch gone he'd been crazy enough to think their father would train him to step into the heir apparent's shoes. And now Birch was back to stay.

So where does that leave me? Matt thought bitterly.

He hadn't wanted anything on a silver platter. He'd wanted to earn a top position, but they'd never given him a chance, dammit. His dad had vetoed every good idea he'd come up with and then had turned around and put it into effect, only to give the credit to someone else. It was the same way with accounts; if he brought in a really big new client, the account would be turned over to someone else and he'd get the little stuff. After five years of playing company wimp, he hadn't moved one step up the corporate ladder, and with Birch back, he never would.

Levering himself out of the deep chair, he headed for the kitchen with its built-in bar and took down bottles of Bombay gin and imported vermouth, then mixed himself a martini.

"To hell with it," he said aloud. To hell with them. To hell with *Birch*! Cheney, McCrae wasn't the only brokerage firm on Wall Street. And there were still ski slopes, and sailing and a contingent of delightful women who didn't consider him a wimp—far from it....

DRIFTING TOWARD SLEEP again, Birch felt the emptiness of the apartment without Julia and longed for the sound of her voice. He roused himself, turned on the light and reached for the Rolodex on the nightstand, waiting a moment for his eyes to adjust before rolling the cards for the number of the Ritz Hotel.

As he was about to dial, his hand came to a full stop. What would Julia say when he told her he'd made a commitment today to his father he never intended to keep?

It would take a clear head to make her see it had been unavoidable—meaningless, in fact, since it was a promise he intended to withdraw as soon as his father was well enough to be confronted. With the uneasy fear that tonight he might botch any attempt to explain, he decided to forgo the comfort of her voice until tomorrow, and he reached across the big bed for her pillow. Pulling it to him, he breathed in her familiar, elusive scent. God, how he wished she were here....

He awoke next to find himself sprawled across the bed, the telephone pressed to his head. A strange voice was repeating his name impatiently in his ear. He had no recollection of hearing the phone ring or of picking it up.

"Mr. Cheney? Are you there?"

"This is Mr. Cheney," he said, wondering groggily if he was awake or if this was happening in a dream.

"This is Ms Kerner at Mount Sinai Hospital, Mr. Cheney. Dr. Perry has asked me to advise you that your father has had another attack."

"Oh, God!" Birch said under his breath, and aloud, "How serious is it?"

"I don't know, sir. That's all Dr. Perry said."

"But my father...he's not..." He couldn't bring himself to say the word, but the woman understood.

"Oh, no. He's alive, I'm sure. They're still working with him. Dr. Perry thinks you should come. He suggests you hurry."

For a moment Birch was too stunned to move. Under the woman's guarded words, the message was clear. Across town his father was dying. He felt a great emptiness inside, and sorrow that it hadn't been possible for him to be the man his father wanted him to be, and at the same time, the man he knew he had to be for his own sake. It saddened him that out of all the years, he could recall no single instance of tenderness from the unloving man who had sired him.

He heard the dial tone in his ear, saw the phone still in his hand and knew time was running out. His mind clearing, he was shaken by a sudden intense desire to speak to his father. Dropping the receiver, he sprang from his bed in a frenzy of movement and grabbed up the clothes he'd dumped on a chair when he went to bed, blind to their rumpled disorder. It was as if he were moving in a nightmare, yet he never doubted he was awake—awake enough to know there was something he'd left unsaid to his father. He wasn't sure what it was, except that it was important. He'd think of it once he was wide-awake.

Halfway out the door he hesitated and ran a hand over his stubbly beard, remembering he hadn't washed his face or shaved, at the same time remembering the sound of urgency in the voice of the nurse who had called. Leaving the door to close behind him, he hurried on to the elevator and was relieved when it opened promptly. Alone going down, he ran a hand through his hair in an effort to make it look combed, and walked past the sleeping doorman in his lobby cubicle into the darkness and the well-lighted street outside.

As he crossed Central Park West he scanned the street for an on-duty cab. When he saw one speeding toward him from downtown, he stepped out from the curb and raised his arm—and watched helplessly as it whizzed by. Swearing under his breath, he tried again with the same result, and then again, each time stepping a little farther into the street and waving a little more frantically. Frustration and fury grew with every cab that passed him by.

He began to walk, turning his head every few steps to watch for northbound taxis. In this ragged fashion he crossed Eighty-eighth and Eighty-ninth streets, and was halfway up the next block when he remembered his rumpled state and guessed why they wouldn't stop. He must look wild-eyed and suspiciously manic to the streetwise cabbies, he thought.

It was then he realized that the hospital was just across the park on Fifth Avenue, only a few blocks to the north. Satisfied he could get there faster on foot, he wasted no more time. Turning into the bridle path near Ninetieth Street in Central Park, he made his way to the jogging track that circled the reservoir, a course he knew well. He and Julia often jogged there when they were at home in New York.

Settling into a steady lope, he pushed ahead, his mind fumbling for the elusive something that had flicked across his consciousness after he was awakened by the hospital call—something he wanted to tell his father. It had come and gone as completely as if it had never been.

He wondered suddenly if anyone had called Matt, and realized the woman at the hospital had probably left all further notifying to him. Matt's name should have been on the notification card, dammit. Not his. It was typical of their father to name Birch as his next of kin and forget the son who was always there.

Suddenly Birch knew what it was he wanted to say to his father. He wanted his father to know that he'd hated the brokerage business for as long as he could remember, though if asked, he couldn't have said why. Now, unexpectedly, the answer came to him, clear as light. He'd always thought, in the very back of his mind, that the stock exchange had robbed him of a father. But he knew at once that, in fact, it wasn't the stock exchange that had made his father a stranger to his sons; the flaw was in the character of his father, not in the character of his business.

Their father hadn't even known his sons well enough to choose the right one to run his exalted brokerage firm when he was gone, Birch thought, feeling the bite of the irony. But even as the thought took shape, he knew now was not the time to give voice to it. He'd waited too long. Maybe there had never been a time.

Doggedly he pushed on, oblivious to whatever living creatures slept or stirred in the wooded terrain. He left the jogging trail where it curved south again, and plunged down a dark, pathless embankment toward the deeply shadowed ribbon of light that marked Fifth Avenue a short distance beyond.

His father was dying. He felt disoriented and alone.

And then, for the first time since his awakening, he remembered.

Oh God, the promise!

In a state of suspension, his mind barely registered the dark-clad figure that emerged from the shrubbery ahead—until it was upon him. At the same instant he was eerily aware of a moving presence in the darkness behind him, and he whirled to meet the force of the human body that lunged toward him from the rear.

He struck out with all the force of a fist empowered by a strong, muscular shoulder, but his punch was poorly aimed, and did no more than graze his attacker's shoulder as well as put Birch momentarily off balance. A blow form the back pounded into his rib cage and knocked the breath out of him. In the next instant a monstrous force jarred him, sending shock waves radiating throughout his body. He saw a blinding flash of light and his world coming to an end and then he was falling.

"Julie!" he cried as he went down.

CHAPTER THREE

IT HAD BEEN a long day. Julia's bones felt heavy, and her feet burned as she entered the Ritz at the Place Vendôme and walked through the fashion alleyway known as Temptation Walk. A minute after she'd kissed Birch goodbye the previous night she'd begun to miss him. This morning, to help her forget the hole his absence left in her life, she'd gone to work on the fashion article, spending most of the day with Claudine Bonet, one of the great couturiers. Following the designer from drawing board to cutting tables to sewing room, talking with a gaggle of models and with the couturier herself at odd moments when the great lady didn't have her mouth full of pins, had given her a wonderful behind-the-scenes perspective. She was quite satisfied with her day's labors.

At the same time, she'd been restless after taking leave of the designer. The thought of going back to the room at the Ritz—barren and bleak without Birch—had depressed her, and she'd walked aimlessly along the quais and boulevards until her feet at last rebelled and turned back, as if of their own volition, to the hotel. Having had her fill of high fashion, she hardly bothered to glance in the windows of the shops that gave the famous Ritz passageway its name.

"Madame Cheney, there is a message for you," the concierge greeted her with scarcely a trace of an accent, stepping forward to meet her when she entered the hotel. "Monsieur Cheney called you from New York while you were out. He left a number with me and requested that you call."

Julia's pulse quickened as it always did when she unexpectedly heard Birch's name. Thanking the concierge, she took from his hand the slip of heavy vellum paper bearing the number, and moved on to the elevator. The number was not familiar, which led her to conclude that he must have called from the hospital. It could mean anything, she told herself—that his father was better or worse, or simply that Birch wanted to hear her voice, as she yearned to hear his.

Back in her room, she dropped her handbag on the bed and kicked off her shoes. As she reached for the phone she slipped the wrapping off the small, heavy package in her hand for a glance at her single purchase of the day—a ten-inch-high, hand-sculptured copy of Michelangelo's *David*. It was carved in meticulous smooth, white stone and sat atop a black wooden pedestal. The meticulously detailed piece reminded her of Birch.

Impatient for the sound of his voice, she set the statue down on the bedside table, freeing her hands to place the call to the number in New York. The phone startled her by ringing under her hand.

"Madame Cheney?" It was the polished voice of the concierge again. "I have Monsieur Cheney on the line. One moment, *s'il vous plaît*. I will have our operator connect you."

"Birch, darling," she exclaimed softly, not waiting for Birch to speak after she heard the connection made. "How did you find your father?"

"Father is dead, Julia. He died early this morning," said the unexpected voice of Birch's brother at the other end of the line.

"Oh, Matt! I'm sorry," she said, groping for appropriate words. In the years she'd known him she'd found it next to impossible to carry on a serious conversation with this flip young man who was her brother-in-law. Now, however, his voice was grave, and strangely foreboding.

"That's not why I'm calling," the distant voice said brusquely. "It's Birch. You'd better come, Julia. He's hurt."

She listened without understanding. Of course he was hurt! True, the relationship between her husband and his father had been more like that between headmaster and recalcitrant pupil, yet she had no doubt the death had hurt Birch deeply. What she didn't understand was why he hadn't called her himself.

"I'll come as soon as I can get a plane, Matt. Let me talk to Birch now," she said, trying to hide her dismay. "I know he's upset, but—"

An ocean away, Matt broke in. "I haven't made myself clear, Julia. Sorry. Birch has been in an accident and is in the hospital, unconscious. Right now he's in intensive care. The doctors still don't know the full extent of his injuries."

For a moment she couldn't speak. Then in a stunned whisper, she pleaded, "Oh, my God. Not Birch! Please not Birch!" Rallying, she asked weakly, "What *happened*?" Not waiting for an answer, she demanded with new urgency, "How badly is he hurt?" Still not waiting, coming directly to the point, she exclaimed, "Tell me he's not going to die!"

"Look, Julia, he's in the hands of the best doctors in the city. He's going to be all right."

But she heard the false note in Matt's voice and knew her brother-in-law wasn't sure of his own words.

In a rush she said, "There's no time for talk. I must see about a plane."

"Call me back when you've made arrangements, and I'll be at the airport to meet you," he said as she was about to hang up.

"Thanks just the same, Matt. I'll take a cab in. I'd rather you stayed with Birch," she said and wondered in a detached sort of way how on the outside she could be so controlled when on the inside, she was screaming.

She heard the click of his receiver, and the phone slipped from her hand. She lay back on the rose-covered bedspread and wrapped her head in her arms, as if to ward off the blow that had already been struck. Her whole body began to shake.

Dear God! It was Birch Matt had been talking about. She had to get to him quickly. Once they were together, everything would be all right. With that thought a sudden flow of adrenaline shot through her. Springing to her feet from where she had thrown herself, her hand shot out for the fallen phone to enlist the concierge's help in arranging a flight home. In the act of punching the numbers she dropped the phone again. Seconds passed before she could control her shaking hands enough to press the right buttons.

The concierge assured her he would find an early-evening flight for her. Like a sleepwalker, mindless of all beyond the immediate arrangements that needed to be made—which somehow held the pain at bay—she rewrapped the figure of David and began methodically pulling things out of drawers.

In the small glove drawer in the chiffonier she came upon the antique compass she'd hidden there to give Birch at some appropriate time. She snatched it up and tucked it away in a hidden zippered pocket in a suitcase, knowing that if she let herself look at it, *think about it*, she would fall apart.

Not until her flight arrangements had been made, and she was packing her belongings with the help of a maid thoughtfully provided by the concierge, did she realize she hadn't waited to learn from Matt how Birch had been hurt.

IN THE VISITORS' WAITING ROOM facing Fifth Avenue on the ground floor of the hospital, Matt watched impatiently through the window for Julia, knowing she would be here momentarily to relieve him from his long vigil at Birch's bedside. At the same time, he dreaded the questions she would ask when she came.

When her cab finally arrived he felt paralyzed. He needed more time. He had just a few minutes more to decide what he would have to say and what he could leave unsaid. He saw her step from the cab, saw her chestnut hair blown back from her heart-shaped face by the breeze. For a moment he thought, as always upon seeing her after a long time, what a lucky man his brother was. With the thought now came a flash of Birch as he'd just left him. Suddenly he felt sick. Had Birch's luck run out?

Not until he saw the driver open the trunk and begin to unload her luggage onto the sidewalk did he realize she had a problem. What the hell was she going to do with all those suitcases in the hospital? he wondered. He could see by her face that the thought had hit her, too. Taking off in a long, purposeful stride, he left the visitors' room and headed down the narrow lobby, then out the door to intervene.

"Wait a minute, please," he heard her say to the driver, who was taking her last bag out of the trunk. "I'm afraid I'll have to ask you to take them to my apartment and leave them with the doorman. You may as well put them back in the trunk."

"Never mind, I'll take care of them," Matt called out.

"Matt!" she cried when she turned and saw him. "Is Birch . . . is he . . . ?" Her face had gone chalk-white.

"Better than when I talked to you last," he said. "He regained consciousness late yesterday and was moved out of intensive care to a private room this morning. His doctor says his condition's no longer critical."

"Oh, Matt! Thank God!"

She looked so fragile; the green eyes that looked up at him were full of hope and pain. He reached out his hand, unbidden to rest on her shoulder for a moment; then, quickly, he withdrew it. She smiled weakly.

"How did you know I was here?"

"Checked the arrival of your plane and came down to the lobby to watch for you," he said. "I've been here since they called me yesterday morning. I didn't want to leave until you got here."

She darted him a grateful smile. "I really appreciate that, Matt."

"I'll get rid of those bags for you on my way downtown," he said, feeling suddenly awkward and eager to get away. "I'm going home to catch a couple of hours' sleep and then on to my office, so your place is on my way. I have a key to your apartment. Wait here while I get the car."

He turned and walked hurriedly away. The hostility he'd felt toward Birch only hours before his brother had come so close to being killed had left him guilt-ridden. He had to get away. Moreover, there was much more to say to Julia—but he was unable to say it. He'd told her the good news, but when it came to telling her the bad, he was tongue-tied, terrified of breaking down. If he hadn't felt such bitterness a few hours earlier, maybe the heart wouldn't have gone out of him when he'd found out Birch was hurt. As it was, he couldn't talk about Birch's condition to anyone, let alone break the terrible truth to Julia, until he got himself in hand....

WATCHING HIM DRIVE OFF a short time later, Julia wished she hadn't asked Matt that one last question before he'd left: how, exactly, had Birch been hurt? She'd imagined a traffic accident, an act of God, even falling construction debris, but to be told he'd been assaulted by two fellow human beings filled her with an ugly rage like nothing she'd ever felt.

Two spaced-out junkies who wouldn't stop at killing to get crack money, Matt had said.

In sudden movement, she turned away from the street to the hospital, frightened by the powerful, savage force of hate that swept through her. She walked swiftly toward the entrance, driven by a new urgency to get to the bedside of the man she loved. But for the fast-moving undercover narcotics team who had arrested Birch's attackers and taken him to emergency, the one essential person in her life might now be dead.

Birch hated violence! He'd armed himself with a black belt in karate to handle violence in a nonlethal way. It seemed preposterous that two lawless thugs could have ambushed him in Central Park.

And what had he been doing in Central Park alone in the middle of the night, anyway? It was all too bizarre, she thought as she stepped into an open elevator in the hospital lobby. Like a piece in the *Daily News*. Something that happened to other people.

Only this time it had happened to Birch.

As the elevator bore her swiftly upward to the floor they'd moved Birch to, she realized she'd forgotten to ask her brother-in-law the room number. Stepping out, she looked around and made for a busy work station separated from the main corridor by a U-shaped counter. A stout, middle-aged woman wearing a white uniform and a pleated cap that looked like an inverted cupcake paper, was bent over a chart on a desk. A name tag pinned to her bosom identified has as Bertha Mullins, Supervisor.

"I beg your pardon," Julia said. "Could you tell me what room Birch Cheney is in, please? I'm Mrs. Cheney."

Seconds ticked by before the woman hoisted herself from her chair. In the labored, slow-footed gait that came from flat feet and being overweight, she moved to a phone on the rear wall where she dialed, consulted with someone briefly and returned to her station.

"Dr. Kritzer wants to see you before you go in to your husband, Mrs. Cheney," she said. "You can wait for him in the visitors' lounge at the end of the hall."

Julia felt as if a hand were closing on her throat. "How long will I have to wait?" she asked tightly.

"I wouldn't know."

Julia hesitated, hardly aware, in her disappointment, of the ebb and flow of hospital traffic around her. After a moment, she leaned over the counter, seeking the nurse's attention once more.

"I'm sorry, but could you please find out from the doctor how long it will be before he can see me?" she said. In spite of all she could do to steady it, her voice broke in midsentence. "You see, I've flown all night to be with my husband and it would—" She stopped short as the nurse's head came up from her work.

Fixing Julia with a glare, she said, "The doctor will see you when he can, Mrs. Cheney. He is a busy man, and your case is not urgent. Your husband is no longer on the critical list."

"I know, thank God," Julia said softly, "but I've come a long way to be with him, and I am very tired."

Clearly she was getting nowhere with the intractable head nurse, who turned away from her to answer a phone.

"Ms Mullins, I appreciate your position," Julia said in a level voice when the woman was off the phone, "but if you won't find out how long his doctor is going to keep me waiting to see my husband, I'm going to look into every room on the floor until I find him."

"And if you don't settle down and wait to see Dr. Kritzer as you've been told to," the nurse said in a voice that told Julia she brooked no nonsense, "I will call the guard and have you removed from the hospital." Raising her voice, she turned to a nurse working at a medications cart behind her. "Ingram, kindly show Mrs. Cheney to the visitors' lounge."

Wrapping her pride around her like a cloak, Julia squared her shoulders, and with a lift of her chin walked away from the counter, the young nurse at her side. Halfway down the corridor, Julia's escort spoke.

"Mullins give you a bad time?"

Surprised, Julia turned her head for a closer look at her companion, a cheery-faced little blond woman in her mid-thirties whose head reached the level of Julia's collarbone. The name tag pinned to her crisp uniform read *Heidi Ingram, R.N.*

She looked up at Julia with a sympathetic grin. "Mullins has family problems, and her feet hurt, and she's caught between us nurses on one side and the doctors on the other," Nurse Ingram explained. "It's no easy thing, being head nurse. Underneath, she's not such a bad egg."

"I suppose," Julia said without enthusiasm. Touched by the kindliness of the young woman, herself caught in the middle at the moment, she forced a smile and lifted her shoulders in a dismissive shrug.

"Here we are," her guide announced, stopping at the opening to motion Julia into the visitors' lounge, eyeing her anxiously as she turned to leave. "You *will* wait, won't you, Mrs. Cheney?"

"I'll wait," Julia said.

Too wired to settle down in one of the several seats in the empty waiting room, Julia riffled aimlessly through a stack of magazines on a side table for a minute and then moved on to a window, where she gazed broodingly across the tops of Central Park trees to the high-rise apartments on the other side of the park. An unexpected shiver whispered up her spine as she remembered what had happened to Birch in the darkness of the park two nights earlier.

A sense of desolation fell upon her—a feeling of despair that her perfect world had been desecrated and would never again be the same. With new understanding, she realized that until now she'd foolishly supposed the very oneness of her and Birch's love for each other had somehow brought with it immunity from harm.

Now she felt vulnerable. Her world was fraught with worries that hadn't occurred to her before; questions squeezed her heart like a cold hand. Had she sensed a certain evasiveness in Matt's hurry to get away this morning? Could it be he'd known more about Birch's condition and had been holding back? And why was this unknown Dr. Kritzer so determined to talk to her before he'd let her see Birch? Was it to prepare her for something so catastrophic that Matt had lacked the courage to tell her himself?

Panic rising in her, Julia thought of the time in Kenya, when she came down with a tropical fever the doctors had judged both lethal and highly contagious. Birch had defied all orders to keep away. Night and day, through all the mess and ugliness, he'd stayed by her bedside, until the doctors could assure him she was going to get well. She'd always believed in her secret heart that in some mystical way, simply by being there, Birch had saved her from the darkness she had sensed closing in upon her when she was so sick.

So why was she waiting for some strange doctor's permission to go to Birch now?

Abruptly she left the window and crossed the waiting room, wondering crazily what would happen if she started sneaking down the corridors and peeking behind doors. By the time she reached the door, she knew exactly how she was going to go about finding Birch.

Bribery.

She stepped into the main hallway, and noticed a uniformed nursing assistant with a water tray standing a short distance away, talking to a second assistant. Likely candidates? Julia asked herself, and as she drew near she sized them up, considering which might be the more readily approachable. Passing, she let her ears tune in to their conversation.

"Darn Mullins! She's ordered me to drop everything and go set up another IV," the one with the tray grumbled. "I'm already running behind. You don't suppose you could deliver this for me, could you, Halsey?"

"Okay. You can owe me one. Where does it go?"

"To the guy who got beat up in the park. Good-looking guy, name of Cheney."

Julia's pulse jumped. She heard the clink of ice in the pitcher as the tray changed hands, and then the sweetest music in all the world—the number of Birch's room. Her heart soaring, she engraved the number on her mind.

Relieved that she wasn't going to have to play on the baser instincts of one of them, as she'd intended, Julia waited and followed the woman called Halsey down the hall to the room she was to enter, then walked past it slowly, her ears attuned for the sound of the water bearer's departure. When it came, she marked time until Halsey was safely out of sight before turning to walk back to the door.

As she reached for the knob, a picture flashed across her mind of a bruised and bloodied assault victim she'd once seen on the news. She drew back her hand and steadied herself. Birch was alive. Everything else was insignificant.

After a minute she eased open the heavy door and slipped inside. At the sight of the still figure in the bed across the room she halted, struck suddenly with belated uneasiness as to the wisdom of her being there. Suppose it wasn't Birch. For a moment she was torn by doubt. The upper part of the body was slightly elevated, one shoulder and arm were bound in a kind of linen cat's cradle, and the head was swathed in bandages that made it look like a gauze balloon. But when she got past the wrappings and found the face, she knew for sure it was Birch. She caught her breath. A stitched red gash ran from below his right cheekbone to within an inch or two of his chin.

In the next instant she went giddy with relief as she saw with a spurt of joy that otherwise his face had not been harmed. Even the perfectly sculptured nose that could belong to none other than Birch Cheney—husband, lover, friend...her life—remained unscathed. *Thank God, the bastards spared his nose,* she thought deliriously, somewhere between a giggle and a sob.

Somehow the sight of Birch sleeping peacefully, his beautiful nose intact, reassured her more than words alone could have done. Her heart filled with thanksgiving. She longed to fly across the room and cradle the dear, battered head in her arms, but hesitated to disturb his sleep. So she stood there in a kind of limbo, knowing she should go back down the hallway and wait for the doctor. Then she saw Birch stir. She held her breath as his eyelids flickered and parted, then closed and opened again. She took a step to go to him.

His eyes were wide open now. He looked straight at her, and what she saw in those beautiful blue-gray eyes she knew so well cemented her to the spot. Clear and unblemished as ever, the eyes gazed not so much *at* her as through her, then moved on with no light of recognition, as if searching for something familiar to focus upon.

Words froze in her throat. For a moment she stood motionless, fighting the awful significance of the bewilderment she saw in her beloved's eyes—eyes that were not expressionless so much as devoid of content...as though the mind had failed to comprehend what the eyes had seen.

Momentarily paralyzed, she watched him move his fingers fretfully across the covers in much the same way as one would for a lost article in the dark. There was something so uncertain, so helpless in the movement that was so unlike the man she knew, he seemed for a moment a stranger.

Oh God! Birch, what have they done to you?

She turned suddenly as if to flee from the question's answer. Stumbling ahead of the closing door, she stared around her wildly, waiting only to escape the dreadful reality she'd run away from in the room the moment before. *Brain damaged!* The words screamed at her from someplace inside her head.

For a moment she felt a primitive urge to kill. When it passed she stumbled, limp-bodied, to the nearest wall and leaned against it. Sheltering her head with her arms, she gave in to great, convulsive sobs that bellowed up from within and racked her body. Aware of nothing but her own unbearable grief, she let it pour out, indifferent to the tears that streamed down her face and wet her sleeve.

The weight of a hand on her shoulder at last reminded her that she was in the corridor of a busy hospital. In a heroic effort to pull herself together, she swallowed the last remnant of a sob and turned away from the wall.

Through a mist of tears she saw a tall, barrel-chested, auburn-haired man with a large head and jutting chin, looking down at her with chilly, blue-gray eyes. A white coat marked him as a doctor; a Rolex wristwatch, as affluent. He had an unmistakable air of stubborn self-importance about him.

"Mrs. Cheney?"

Julia gazed at him helplessly. Not trusting herself to speak, she nodded in reply and groped in her handbag for a tissue, which she applied to her ravaged face.

"So you've seen your husband!" he said, his voice taking her to task.

Julia nodded again and fought to compose herself.

"I'm Dr. Kritzer. I am the internist in charge of your husband's care. I believe I left a specific order that you were not to see your husband until you had first seen me."

"Can't you...*do* something, doctor?" Julia cried hoarsely, far too distressed to take exception to the young doctor's patronizing tone and words. "He... Oh, God, he doesn't even know who I am."

The physician appeared surprised. "He didn't recognize your voice?"

"I didn't speak to him. What could I say? He didn't recognize me," Julia said, steadying her faltering voice. "He looked straight at me, as if he'd never seen me before. As if I wasn't there."

"You didn't speak to him. That explains it," Dr. Kritzer said impatiently, like one instructing a difficult child. "It's not that he didn't recognize you, Mrs. Cheney. If you had seen me first, as I requested, I might have spared you this misunderstanding."

"Misunderstanding?"

"Simply this. Since you did not speak to him, your husband most probably had no idea you were even there," the doctor said. "The problem is not one of recognition. The problem, Mrs. Cheney, is that your husband does not see."

Julia gazed at him a moment, too shocked to speak. She felt an instant of wild, crazy relief. They hadn't damaged his brain!

But in the next instant the full import of the doctor's words burst upon her. *The good news—no brain damage. The bad news, your husband's blind.*

There was an unequivocal tone to the man's voice that played on her nerves like a nail across a china plate. When words came to her she spoke in a tone of complete disbelief. "That's ridiculous. There's not a bruise on his face. They didn't touch his eyes. They look just as they've always looked. How can you say he's blind?"

"Do you prefer your layman's diagnosis of brain damage?"

For an instant Julia quelled an urge to hit him. Then she turned and bolted for the door to Birch's room. Pushing through it, she ran to the bed and fell to her knees beside it. "Birch, darling, my darling," she whispered hoarsely, "tell me you're all right."

From above her she heard a strangled cry and the sound of his body moving as he repositioned himself. When his hand came to rest on the crown of her head, she reached up and covered it with her own and felt the smooth gold contours of the ring she had placed on his finger five years earlier.

His voice, faint and strained, sounded above her, the words delivered haltingly. "Oh God..Julie...I...I've been...afraid."

Stricken, she raised her head to look at him. "Afraid, Birch?" she asked.

"Afraid...you'd never...get here."

A corner of his mouth lifted slightly and then drooped again, as if he lacked the will to hold it in place. It was the old, familiar, lopsided grin she loved so well, but the eyes that gave it meaning looked above and beyond her head.

"Why...are...we...in the dark, Julie?" he asked, the words labored. "Light...please...see...your face."

Julia caught her breath in shock. *He must know,* she thought. How could he *not* know?

Thinking back to what Matt had told her downstairs, it seemed reasonable that he might not. He'd gone directly into surgery when they brought him into emergency, and he'd been heavily sedated ever since. The slurred, broken pattern of his speech told her he was under sedation now.

Laying her head back on the bed beside him, she reached for his hand again, holding it to her cheek, hoping that with his mind dulled by medication he would forget about the light. She wanted to spare him the truth for as long as she possibly could.

His hand slipped away from her face after a minute to play idly with a strand of her hair. He said no more about the light, but this was small comfort to Julia. Sooner or later he had to find out. Her delaying action hadn't changed anything. It had merely bought him a little more time.

SILENCE AS THICK as the darkness that filled the room for Birch closed in around them. His mind drifted in and out of a lifting fog.

He'd heard the sharp intake of her breath some moments earlier, but when she had made no move to go for the light switch, he hadn't pursued it. For the moment it was enough to feel her head beneath his hand and know she was there. He fingered the smooth strands of her hair lovingly and tried to focus his mind on questions he needed to ask—questions that kept flickering through his brief spells of consciousness. He was in a hospital. He had been hurt. That much he knew. But how? Where? Why was he in the dark?

His thoughts blurred. Wearying, he gave up. The important thing was that Julia was here, so near he could reach out and bury his face in her hair. Forgetting his infirmities, he moved to pull her to him with his one free arm. With the action, he was seized by grinding pain that forced him back upon the pillow with a groan. His muscles tightened in spasms, and for a terrible moment it was as if all the agonies he'd ever suffered had come upon him in one screeching, all-encompassing nightmare of pain. He was barely aware of the murmurs of anguished sympathy from Julia beside his bed.

Then he heard her say, "I'm going to call the nurse," and the thought of the capsule the nurse would bring at once obsessed him, overriding everything but the pain; the capsule would float him into a phantom world where nothing hurt and nothing mattered.

Under the gentle stroking of Julia's hand, the torment began to subside, leaving him spent. He lay quietly, afraid the slightest movement would set the demons loose again. In a few minutes he heard the door open.

"Did you want something, Mr. Cheney?" a female voice asked. Drowsing off now, Birch was grateful when Julia spared him the effort of answering.

Through a haze, he heard her say, "Could you give him something for the pain, nurse?"

And he heard the nurse answer, "The last capsule he took hasn't had time to take effect. If he just lies still and gives it a chance to work..."

It didn't matter, Birch thought fuzzily. The throbbing torment that a few minutes earlier had seemed too much to bear was now fading to a tolerable ache.

"Could he have something stronger?" he heard Julia ask.

"The medication he's getting is quite strong. I'll have to see what his doctor says."

He felt far removed from what they were saying, as if they were speaking of someone else. Their voices seemed to fade and return. In a blurred sort of way, he understood it was the painkiller reasserting itself, and went with it willingly. Drifting away, he heard the sound of the closing door that signaled the nurse's departure. Hadn't he wanted to ask her something? No. Not the nurse. Julia. Something about... But he'd forgotten what it was.

Pleasantly aware that Julia was beside him, holding his hand again, he floated mindlessly on the edge of sleep until the sudden sense of falling shattered his lethargy. As abruptly as it started it was over, but his involuntary body movement triggered a new stab of pain that brought him awake with a gasp.

Placing his hand carefully back upon the covers, Julia cried out in a stricken wail, "Oh God, Birch, what have I done?"

He wanted to tell her it had nothing to do with her, but his head was groggy, his tongue thick. In a moment the pain eased off, but the shock of it had set the adrenaline flowing and cleared his head.

"Nothing. Not...you. Doesn't hurt...much.... Dope's start'n' t'work." He sensed it was not enough. Steeling himself against new pain, he reached up cautiously with his good hand toward where she stood.

"I need to touch...you, Jul'..."

The words came haltingly, but brought an immediate response. Her head came down to meet his hand, and he found her face; found, too, that her cheeks were wet with tears, tears he knew were for him. A lump of emotion filled his throat, and a new pain touched his heart.

"Not...to cry, Bride," he said tenderly. "We're... together...no time...for tears." Even to his own befuddled ears the playfulness he aimed for didn't come across. Bracing himself again, he pressed her head toward him, and she came, bringing the soft fullness of her lips down to cover his mouth.

Even as his own lips softened in response he felt her stiffen and pull away. Out of the darkness someplace beyond the bed a male voice spoke. It was a flat, nasal voice Birch knew as one of those that had come and gone in the endless night around him since the time he had first come to.

"Cheney, I am Dr. Kritzer. I'm your doctor, in case you don't know. The nurse tells me you've been asking for more medication. What you're getting is adequate. May I suggest the sort of conjugal gymnastics I have just now interrupted serve only to stir up pain."

Conjugal gymnastics, Birch repeated to himself, bemused, hearing no more of the doctor's statement. Then, a sudden awakening of his mind drove out all other thought but a single staggering question that raised goose bumps along the back of his neck.

Why were they carrying on this conversation in total darkness, as if it were a perfectly normal thing to do?

He was suddenly aware that since some measureless time ago when he'd fought through a sea of pain to consciousness, he'd seen no light. It had been as if he were closed up in a black velvet box surrounded by footsteps and voices that came and went.

If Kritzer had walked into a pitch-black room just now, Birch reasoned dully, he would have turned on the light; yet to Birch there *was* no light. Cold sweat suddenly beaded his brow. He tried to speak. His throat contracted and for a moment he could bring forth no more than the choked sound of his own frustration.

"Doctor!" he burst out at last. "Why...didn't you turn on the light just now?"

A soft, whimpering cry came from Julia. "No, Birch. Wait, darling. Not yet."

"Aha. The patient is beginning to come around," the doctor said with satisfaction, overriding Julia's protest. "Go on. Think about it, Cheney. Reason it through. You know why. Now you tell me."

For a long moment Birch refused to give voice to what he at last knew, as if to say the word would make it true. *Oh, God!* he cried out in the silence of his mind, but an inner strength told him it was no time to flinch.

"I know," he said quietly. "I am blind."

"Let's just say for the time being that you don't see," Dr. Kritzer demurred.

Julia was on her feet facing Dr. Kritzer, both hands clenched, her whole body afire with indignation. "You sadistic bastard!" she said scathingly. "Now that you've had your fun and gotten him to pronounce his own diagnosis, how about cutting out the word games and letting us know the truth."

CHAPTER FOUR

FROM HIS BED Birch protested quietly. "Don't...
Julie's......all...right."

"It's not all right," she said. "It's about time we got
a straight answer." Doggedly she turned back to the
physician. "You agree Birch doesn't see, Dr. Kritzer, yet
you seem to imply that this doesn't mean he is blind.
Will you kindly tell us just what—" she hesitated, got
her voice in control and went on "—that's supposed to
mean? All we're asking is the truth."

"Julie, no...it won't help...t'kill th'...mess'nger,"
Birch said in a tired voice. "No light. I...guess I already...knew. Capsules... Don't have to...know you're
blind when you're on...capsules."

As if he'd been waiting to hear Birch say the word
again, Kritzer now spoke. "That's where you're wrong,
Cheney. You are not blind," he said, his voice cool and
flat. Pointedly cutting out Julia, he directed his attention to Birch. "Your wife is an impetuous woman. Impetuous and impatient. Had she waited, as I left orders
for her to do, she would have known from the outset that
I find no evidence of injury in either eye. Both appear
healthy and sound."

From his bed Birch grunted sardonically. "Not a thing
wrong...except they don't...see."

"*Won't* see," Kritzer said sharply. "You remember
little or nothing of recent events. As your recovery pro-

gresses and you emerge from shock your memory will return. By the same token, so will your sight."

Julia's fists slowly unclenched. She realized she was trembling and knew it was in part from happiness and in part from the leftover force of her anger.

Kritzer was a self-important, arrogant, overbearing SOB, she thought resentfully. Under the circumstances she supposed she owed him an apology, but he could wait. After the hell he'd put her through today, any concession she made at the moment would be grudging at best.

Turning her eyes to Birch, she rejoiced at the first sign of a smile she'd seen since she'd entered the room. She saw him draw a deep breath. Wincing with pain, he let it out in a slow, shaky sigh. His deep-set eyes, clear and beautiful but without focus, reflected profound relief and unquestioning trust in the prognosis he'd just been handed.

A shadow of fear fell over Julia's own moment of celebration. More than she'd ever wanted to believe anything, she wanted to believe Kritzer was right. But the man was so full of himself. Suppose he was wrong.

The doctor turned to go, and she left Birch's bedside and followed him to the door. Stepping into the hall behind him, she let the door close quietly in their wake.

Kritzer looked back at her questioningly.

Without preliminaries, she asked, "Are you an ophthalmologist, Dr. Kritzer?"

The doctor turned his pale blue gaze upon her. "My specialty is internal medicine," he said coldly.

"Has an eye specialist seen Birch?"

"My dear Mrs. Cheney, if anything develops that I feel requires the attention of an ophthalmologist while your husband is in my care, I assure you that he will see one. It was clear when he regained consciousness that he couldn't see, and it took no more than a cursory examination to find there is nothing wrong with your husband's eyes. However, you are welcome to seek another opinion, of course."

There was something about the big, square-shouldered figure in the white clinic coat as he walked away, something about the leonine head, the imperious lift of his chin that defied one *not* to believe whatever he said.

I believe, she told herself and crossed her fingers.

She turned back into the room to find Birch saying her name, and realized with a shock that he had no way of knowing she had followed the doctor out.

"Julie," he said again in a panicky voice.

"I'm right here, love," she said soothingly and hurried across the room to his bedside. "I'm sorry. I should have told you I was going. There was something I wanted to ask the doctor before he got away."

After a moment he asked, "Like . . . what?"

She hesitated, afraid that if she told him, she would pass her uncertainties on to him.

"Nothing really. I just wondered if an ophthalmologist had seen you," she said, aiming for a tone of indifference.

He drew in his breath as if to sigh, but she saw him wince, brace himself against the pain and let the breath out very slowly as he lay still and waited for the pain to pass. She took his hand and bent to hold it against her face.

"Birch . . ." she said softly, wishing she hadn't told him; wishing she'd been quick enough to think of a plausible lie. But she knew she was very bad at lying, and it had always been a tacit point of honor between them to tell each other the truth.

"Let's . . . live with . . . Kritzer's diagnosis," he said at last, his voice so quiet she had to raise her head to hear it. "Don't rock . . . the boat."

There were new lines in his face that hadn't been there the week before. She felt helpless that she could think of no better comfort than to cover the hand she held with feathery kisses. Gradually his hand relaxed and freed itself from hers to feel for her face. Finding her chin, he gently pulled her toward him. Her lips found his and clung softly, sensually for a fraction of a moment. Fearful that if she stayed she would stir up the sleeping giant of his pain, she started to draw away. A soft, libidinal whisper stopped her.

"Care to join me . . . in . . . a . . . little . . . conj'g'l gymnastics, Bride?"

Her eyes turned to him in astonishment. At the sight of a Groucho Marx leer that belied the labored voice and the lines of pain on his face, she felt a ripple of delight cross her spirit. She saw a glimmer of wry playfulness in his eyes, and for a moment—until she realized they didn't quite beam in on her—she almost believed he could see. It was vintage Birch, she assured herself, bemused. Thank God his sense of the ridiculous hadn't been knocked out of him.

But before she could speak, her pleasure suffered a second blow. The valiant facade crumbled; the come-on look dissolved and she saw his eyes go dark. As if all at once they'd grown too heavy to support, his eyelids drooped, reminding her that the emotional trauma he suffered was surely as devastating to him as were the physical injuries and the pain.

"Julie," she heard him murmur. She saw what an effort words cost him. Knowing the jaunty front had been put on for her, for a moment she couldn't breathe. She leaned close so as not to miss what he said.

"So much f'r . . . con . . . con . . . jug'l—" There was a long pause. His eyes were closed. "Whatever."

When she could see his breathing was slow and steady, she leaned down, kissed his cheek softly and tiptoed from the room.

EATING A DELI SANDWICH at her kitchen table a short time later, Julia fell asleep over the *Times*, drowsed a few minutes and awakened even more logy than before. A shower and fresh clothing left her feeling a bit less grungy, but hardly refreshed. She added an extra dab of color to her cheeks and remembered it would not be seen by Birch. It really didn't matter whether she looked wan or wonderful. Suddenly she felt lost.

Back at the hospital she saw the nurse she'd spoken to about Birch's medication coming out of his room. A short, solidly built, middle-aged woman with warm dark eyes and black hair generously streaked with gray, she looked reassuringly like somebody's mother. Julia glanced at the tag on the uniform and greeted the woman by name. "Good afternoon, Mrs. Solari. Is my husband asleep?"

"Oh, you're Mrs. Cheney," the nurse said, in recognition. "I'm sorry to disappoint you, but you won't be able to see him this afternoon."

Determined not to let herself be turned away, Julia hastened to say, "I'll just sit quietly by his bed. I promise not to disturb him."

"You won't disturb him," Mrs. Solari assured her. "He's in surgery now, and from there'll he'll be going to the recovery room."

"Surgery?" Julia asked in sudden panic. "Not his eyes?"

"No, but don't worry about his eyes—you needn't," the nurse said soothingly. "The doctor says when the shock wears off he'll see as well as ever."

"But . . . surgery?"

"That's nothing to worry about, either. He'll be—" Mrs. Solari broke off in a sudden concern. "Mrs. Cheney, are you all right?"

The words reached Julia like an echo from far away, and she wondered dimly why her legs had turned to custard. The next thing she knew she was on a stool in a hospital supply room with her head between her knees. Mrs. Solari was standing over her, watching her with professional eyes.

"Wh-at happened?" Julia asked hoarsely.

"Keep your head down a minute longer. You passed out."

"I'm sorry," Julia said, uncomfortable that she had inadvertently created a scene. "I've never had jet lag affect me this way before."

"This isn't jet lag," the nurse said flatly. "You passed out. If you ask me, you're worn out from worry." The nurse sounded so much like her own mother with a Brooklyn accent that Julia looked up curiously. She tried to rise, but her knees buckled, and Mrs. Solari put a steadying arm around her shoulders. Unexpectedly, Julia began to cry.

"Oh God, I'm so ashamed," she said, accepting the handful of tissues the nurse thrust into her hand. "It's just that . . . everything seems to be dumping on us at once. Birch . . . was mugged . . . his father died . . . the ghastly . . . . flight home . . ." She blurted out the words between sobs she couldn't control. Why was she pour-

ing out her life history to this perfect stranger? she wondered, but she couldn't stop. "And Birch can't see...and
now you tell me they're taking him back to surgery...."

"Cry it out, honey. It's good for you," Mrs. Solari
murmured, patting Julia on the shoulder.

After a moment Julia swallowed and battened down
for the next unpleasantness she was sure lay ahead.
"This operation? Will he be in any...danger?"

"No more than with any general anesthetic. As op-
erations go it won't last long and shouldn't amount to
much."

"But what does he need surgery for?" Julia insisted.

Mrs. Solari hesitated. "I'm only supposed to discuss
patients with doctors, but I can't see what harm it'll do
to tell you," she said after a moment. "The orthopedic
surgeon isn't satisfied with the X-rays of one of the
bones and is going to reset it. That's all. He thinks it may
be what's causing some of your husband's pain."

Julia reached for one of the nurse's stubby, capable
hands and hugged it to her in a spontaneous expression
of thanksgiving and relief.

"You okay, Mrs. Cheney?"

Julia drew a deep breath and gave the other woman a
shaky grin. "I'm fine," she assured her. "Thanks for
putting me back together again."

"No problem," Mrs. Solari said, with a smile that
showed a gold crown on a molar. "Now, if you'll take
some advice from a woman who's got daughters older
than you, get yourself some rest. Your husband's going
to be all right, but if you ask me, you're on the verge of
collapse."

"Me? Not likely," Julia said defensively. "I told you,
it's nothing but jet lag. How long will all this take?"

"I couldn't say, but he's sure to be pretty much in another world until tomorrow. You might as well go home and get some sleep."

"With Birch in surgery? I wouldn't think of it!" Julia said, her voice shocked.

"Then what do you plan to do, Mrs. Cheney? For at least the next eighteen hours your husband's going to be so out of it, it won't matter to him whether you're here or not."

"Well, it matters to me!" Julia said stubbornly.

"So instead of getting the rest you need to welcome him back when he comes around, you plan to sit here and worry yourself sick? What do you want to do? Pass out on his bed when he comes in from surgery? Drown the poor man in your tears?"

"You sound just like my mother. But even my mother couldn't get me to leave until Birch is out of surgery and I know he's all right," Julia said flatly.

"Well, there's no law against it, so I guess you can do as you like," Mrs. Solari conceded. "Do yourself a favor, though. Once you're satisfied your husband's okay, go home and draw the blinds and sleep till tomorrow when he'll need you here."

EVEN AFTER Julia had been assured that Birch had come through the surgery in fine shape and that she would not be missed if she left and came back tomorrow, she was reluctant to leave. She had a moment of hope when his eyelids fluttered and opened heavily for a moment that he saw her, but they closed again with no sign of recognition. Not until she raised herself from her chair to kiss him and say his name did he show that he knew she was there.

"Bride," he murmured thickly, not opening his eyes. Lowering herself back on the chair, she took his free hand in hers and continued to hold it, though she knew from the way he breathed that he was asleep. Her own tiredness caught up with her after a moment, and she rested her head against his bed.

She awakened to find her shoulder muscles knotted and her arm asleep. Knowing Birch would be out of it for many of the coming hours, she decided to give in at last to her own growing need for some real rest. About to leave, she thought of the distress she'd heard in his voice when she'd returned after stepping out of the room this morning. She wanted suddenly to leave something of herself so he would know she had been there and was coming back.

She pulled the gold chain with the drop of amber he'd given her in Paris over her head, then wrapped the chain around his wrist, opened his hand and closed his fingers over the amber, sealing it with a kiss.

It was late afternoon when she got back to their apartment. In the bedroom she stopped for a long time, looking down at the king-size bed she and Birch had so often shared. On her side the bedding was smooth and undisturbed except for her pillow, which was squashed up next to Birch's on his side. There, the tangled, thrown-back covers testified that sometime during his first night back in New York Birch had slept there. It didn't make sense. That was the night he'd been mugged in Central Park.

She left the bedside, the nerves in her body taut. Restlessly she pulled back the heavy drapes that covered the windows and let in the late-afternoon light. She knew that before she could sleep she had to do something to unwind.

Dressed in running shoes and sweats a short time later, she walked to Central Park and the path that bordered the reservoir. There she started off at a slow, steady jog, gradually working up speed. She was on her second lap and running fast when it occurred to her that she must be no more than a few yards from where Birch had been struck down. Overwhelmed suddenly by the enormity of all that had happened in the past twenty-four hours, she came to a stop and stood motionless, breathing hard. Then, as if Birch's junkies were at her heels, she took off running again, forcing herself to concentrate on her own moving parts and erase the dark pictures that filled her mind.

Lost to all feeling she ran on and on, keeping no track of laps, until the sun blazed red behind the Jersey horizon, and she let her mind return to the day. Sweat had soaked through to her outer clothing, and her muscles cried out for her to give them a break.

Slowing to a walk, she left the reservoir and headed out of the park. Back in the apartment she unpacked Birch's bags and her own, which still stood in the entry hall where Matt and Birch had left them. After she'd showered it took all of her will to keep from going straight to bed "on an empty stomach," as her mother would have said. In deference to Mom and Mrs. Solari, she rustled up a box of stale crackers and a can of mushroom soup, which she heated in the microwave oven.

She drank the soup from a coffee mug and called the hospital, to be told that Birch was sleeping comfortably and wouldn't be fully awake before morning.

A few minutes later, about to crawl into the oversize bed on the side where she normally slept, she stopped and reversed herself to curl upon the unmade side, between the rumpled sheets where Birch had lain two nights before. Only then did she at last give in to fatigue.

SLIPPING INTO BIRCH'S ROOM at the hospital the next morning, Julia tiptoed silently to his bedside. He lay sleeping quietly, the amber bauble she'd left for him cradled loosely in his hand. At the sight of the gold chain twined lovingly through his fingers like rosary beads, her own love became a deep, helpless ache that filled her breast.

He was not blind, she told herself. She had to believe that Kritzer was right.

She willed his eyes to open, willed them to see. He'd see when the shock wore off, Kritzer had said. If he were an ophthalmologist, maybe she'd find it easier to believe, she thought. As an internist, he wouldn't necessarily have to know everything there was to know about the eyes.

A small, worried sigh escaped her lips. Birch stirred and lay still as if listening. Slowly he turned his head until he was facing her directly, his eyes open. She caught her breath. They looked like any perfectly normal pair of eyes in the first moments of awakening.

"Julie?" Her heart leaped—*did he see her?*—and fell as she realized the light sound that had slipped from her a moment earlier had interrupted his sleep. His next words answered her question. "Is it you?"

"Well, it's not Tinker Bell," she managed to say with a clumsy lightness that belied her state of mind. "If it were, we wouldn't be wasting our time here. We'd be in Paris at the Ritz, in that bed the size of a ballroom...."

"Making love," Birch finished for her with a weak grin as he groped for her hand and carried it awkwardly to his face. He held her palm hard against his lips. After a while he said, "I remember...."

Julia leaned forward to catch his fading voice. He was starting to remember. Her pulse surged with excitement. The mind first. Then the eyes.

"What do you remember, Birch?" she prompted softly. But the moment was gone. His lids drooped shut, and he was again asleep. Disappointed, she withdrew.

And so went the day. In the aftermath of the night's anesthetic he slept and wakened and slept again. In a lounge chair by the window Julia took what comfort she could from the fact that sometime since she had last seen him, the bandages around his head had been removed. The dark, sandy hair had been hacked off ruthlessly and a broad runway shaved across one side of his skull. The ugly sight of a patchwork of neatly stitched bruised and scabbing flesh turned her stomach.

At her seat by the window she read the same paragraph over and over in the paperback she'd bought in the bookshop, her mind forever wandering to the sleeping man across the room. Whenever she saw his eyelids flutter and lift she hastened to his side, only to be crushed by a wave of disappointment when she found no change in his sight. At a strange loss of words in the face of his blindness, she was reduced to murmuring worn platitudes of cheer until the shadow of a wry grin on his face told her she hadn't succeeded in keeping the sound of her own disbelief from her voice.

"Patience, glad lady. Not to worry," he said.

But he sounded tired, and she realized that her false optimism was only wearing him out. She retreated into a watchful silence and was heartened to notice signs of general improvement that she'd overlooked until now.

For one thing, the only reminders of the grinding pain that had tormented his every move the day before were an occasional wince and a sudden intake of breath. And each time he came out of one of his postoperative cat-naps his mind was more alert, his speech more coherent and clear.

When the night nurse came in late that evening with his bedtime medication, Birch declined it.

"It could save you a bad night, Mr. Cheney. You had surgery just yesterday," she nurse said.

"Thanks to that surgery, the pain's not that bad any-more. I'd rather hurt a little and know I'm alive than keep on drifting in and out of narcotic dreams," he said.

"It's up to you, sir," the nurse told him. "If you find yourself awake and hurting, don't be afraid to turn on your light."

WHEN JULIA STEPPED into Birch's room the next morning, she found him standing alone at the window holding on to the armchair she'd sat in the day before. His head was turned toward the scene outside.

He can see!

The thought took shape and swelled, filling her mind like an anthem of joy. She stood motionless as the import of the sight that met her eyes took hold. Kritzer had been right. Birch could see.

She gazed in wonderment at the man in the ridicu-lous hospital robe that bared the long, hairy contours of his legs and strained against the broad masculine back, sure that he was the most beautiful man in the world. The ladders of stitching, the yellowing bruises, the dark scabs covering angry red gashes on his head and upper body would heal. What mattered was he could see.

With a sense of deliverance, she started forward, and stopped as suddenly. In her singleness of mind she'd failed to notice the nurse who now stepped into her line of vision to take Birch's arm as he turned from the window. There was a sudden knotting in Julia's stomach as his unfocused gaze passed over her. The great weight she'd so blithely set aside a moment earlier settled back darkly upon her spirit.

She saw the nurse guide Birch back to the bed, and, as if from a great distance, heard her say, "You've done very well for your first time up, Mr. Cheney. Let's not overdo it."

Through a haze, Julia heard him ask, "Didn't I hear someone come in just now?"

And the nurse replied, "Yes. You have a visitor."

Julia had been standing cemented to the spot with no will to move or speak. Now she rallied herself and moved forward. Unready to risk words, she came to Birch's free side and lifted her face to kiss the stitched cut on his cheek.

"Julie!" Birch's voice reflected pleasure. "Go easy on my new dueling scar, lady. It has to get used to being kissed."

"Don't worry. It will. It looks dashing even now. No warm-blooded female can resist," she said. Still raw with disappointment she thought, *How can he be so bloody cheerful?* But her voice gave no hint of the hidden ache within.

She wore her smile like a mask as Birch introduced her to the nurse and allowed himself to be directed back to bed. When the nurse was gone Julia forsook the place by the window for a straight chair at the side of his bed where she could reach out and touch him. Encouraged by his improvement, she hoped they might talk.

But a strong self-consciousness fell between them. Birch soon closed his eyes and lay in a detached silence she took for sleep. Julia rested her head against the mattress and tried to convince herself that all she had to do was hang in there until Birch would see again.

"Help me, Julia."

His words, coming suddenly out of a vacuum, were taut with anguish, and brought Julia's head up in alarm. She'd heard no echo of the flip cheeriness that had grated on her senses just a little earlier. Now, he sounded like a stricken man. Knowing instinctively that he'd been falsely cheerful to shore up her own flagging spirit, she felt humbled. She reached out and took his hand. Softly she asked, "What is it, darling?"

Birch groaned. "Oh God, if I could only remember," he said. She waited. Then, slowly, he continued.

"It's coming back to me, Julie, but it's full of holes. There was the call in Paris from Langley about Dad.... Then I remember getting back to New York and going to the hospital to see him...and then everything gets muddled. I remember running, and there's a vague feeling that somehow I got Matt sore. Has he said anything to you?"

Julia shook her head, and then, with a renewed sense of shock as she remembered he couldn't see her, she said aloud, "No, but if you did I suspect he's forgotten it. He's been here every day to see you. Why don't you ask him?"

His forehead furrowed with thought, he withdrew into an uneasy silence. After a while he said in a puzzled voice, "Someone said I was mugged. Where did it happen, for God's sake?"

"Below the bank of the reservoir on the east side of the park," Julia told him, "though it beats me what you were doing in Central Park in the middle of the night."

Running...running...running. He had to get to the hospital before...

As if to protect himself from an oncoming blow, Birch brought his arm up and covered his eyes as it came flooding back to him: the late-night call from the hospital...his father...no taxi...

"My father...?" he asked hoarsely.

A part of his mind heard the reluctance and compassion in Julia's voice as she answered, and understood that his father was dead, while another part picked up loose ends and knit them into the fabric of those missing hours. The business. Matt. The promise. A promise made under duress. A promise he'd expected to retract when his father was well enough for a confrontation....

"Get Matt, Julie," he said in a choked voice. "I've got to talk to him."

"I will, darling, but he could be coming in any time. He's been sticking his head in two or three times a day. You've been asleep."

Unexpectedly, for the first time since she'd become the focal point in his life, he did not feel like talking to Julia. He couldn't tell her about the deathbed promise that put him in bondage to his father. Not that she wouldn't understand why he'd had to make the promise, he thought, or that she'd disbelieve he'd made it expecting to confront his father with a retraction later. What she wouldn't understand was that death had altered the option. As he saw it, he had to either abandon the life they'd built together and go back to the family firm—as his father died believing he would—or do something he'd vowed years ago he would never do: go back on his promised word.

If he kept the promise, it meant giving up everything he and Julia had built together. Yet if he broke it, could he live with himself?

And what about Matt? From the looks of things, Matt intended to stick to the family firm no matter what. He obviously had a feeling for it that Birch himself had never shared or known. What would it mean to Matt if Birch came back to head the firm when by rights the spot should belong to him?

For a despondent moment it seemed almost better to Birch to keep on being blind. As long as he couldn't see, the board would look to Matt for company leadership, and Julie would never know that Birch had sold out.

But blind? Never again to see her sweet, impish, witty-wise face; never again to feel warmth spread through to the core of his body at the passion he saw in those surf-green eyes? And never again to peer through a camera lens and compose a picture from a fragment of life?

What if his sight was gone for good!

God, could that self-assured bastard Kritzer be wrong? Panic overtook him, and it was a minute before he could get a grip on himself. He let the arm that covered his eyes fall away. Almost experimentally, he opened his eyes and met with the same darkness he saw when they were closed. He groped for Julia's hand.

"Well," he said, "they've peeled off the bandages and my memory's gone back to work. According to Kritzer I should be about ready to see." Meaning it as a statement of cheer for Julia, he was troubled to hear the echo of his own anxiety in his words. He felt Julia stir and let go of his hand. He sensed she was on her feet and moving away.

"I'll be right back," she said in a steely tone he'd never heard before.

OUTSIDE THE ROOM Julia set out looking for Mrs. Solari, the nurse who'd mothered her that first day. She tracked her to where she was on duty on another part of the floor.

"Forgive me for imposing upon you again, but I've got to talk to Dr. Kritzer about Birch," Julia said when she'd thanked the nurse again for her previous kindnesses. "I don't know how to find him, and I need your help."

"I can get a message to the doctor if he's in the hospital. Wait here. I'll check for you."

"He's not here, but he's supposed to be at his office," Mrs. Solari told her when she returned. "Here's the number, a few blocks down on Park Avenue. Good luck."

Thanking her again, Julia went on her way. She stepped out of the elevator on the ground floor, and through a window, caught sight of a familiar figure coming up the sidewalk toward the hospital. Recognizing the gait and the craggy, ugly-handsome face of Matt—so like Birch's, yet not really like it at all—she hurried to meet him at the door.

"Matt! You couldn't have come at a better time," she greeted him. "Birch is asking for you. You can keep him company while I run an errand. It will give you two brothers a chance to visit alone."

DIDN'T SHE KNOW you were never alone with Birch? Matt thought as she left him, a slight smile tilting a corner of his mouth. Julia and Birch were so much a part of each other that he always felt the presence of both, even when he was with only one of them.

Still, this would be the first time since Birch had regained consciousness that they would be together by themselves. This was the time he'd been waiting for. He had a driving need to say something to Birch—and what he had to say was for his brother's ears alone.

He found him sitting, but slumped down on his pillow, his eyes closed, the strong face reflecting an inner sadness. Except for a scattering of small bandages, the dressings that covered the healing wounds had been removed, leaving them exposed. Disconcerted by the raw look of the stitches and bruises, Matt took a moment to get used to Birch's appearance before trusting himself to speak.

"Is that you, Julie?" Birch asked, opening his eyes and holding his hand out in Matt's direction.

"Sorry, old man. It's me. Your brother." Matt strode across the room to grasp the extended hand.

"Matt! God, I'm glad you're here," Birch said. "I hear from Julia that you've been coming around, but I've been more or less out of it until today. I really need to talk to you."

"You do? I thought I was the one who needed to talk."

Birch went on as if Matt had not spoken. "It's about what Dad told you . . . that I'd promised—"

"Forget it, Birch," Matt broke in. He couldn't bear the misery he heard in his brother's voice. "That's what I want to talk to you about. I'll be sorry as long as I live for the way I talked to you on the phone the night it all happened—the way I felt! That wasn't your brother Matt, Birch. That was a soreheaded son of a bitch who hadn't taken time to noodle things out."

Once started, Matt couldn't stop. Birch let him talk.

"Dad had just told me, and I saw red. All I could think was that you didn't hate the brokerage business as much as you liked to pretend, and that you'd come back to take over. And Dad wouldn't be there to growl down your neck. So where did that leave me?"

"It really matters to you, then," Birch said in a strained voice. "How can I convince you you're wrong about my motives?"

"You don't have to. I knew it all along, but I had to cool off before I could see that the promise crap was only wishful thinking on Dad's part. God, I can't tell you how sorry I am about that lousy telephone call."

There was a long moment of silence after Matt finished. Then slowly, quietly, as if each word were a granite block, Birch began to pour out to his brother in painful detail the events and circumstances leading up to the fateful promise.

"And so you are wrong, Matt, old brother. There was a promise. A deathbed promise I never really looked on as a promise until it was too late," Birch said, soul weariness in his voice. "And now I'm stuck with it."

"Stuck with it? What the hell do you mean, 'stuck with it,' Birch? You're not going to give up your photography to come back to work you hate?"

"It's a matter of honor, Matt. I can't be released from a promise just because the person I made it to died right after it was made."

"No one is bound by a promise made under duress. The law says that," Matt said hotly. "Dad was up to his old tricks. He used the threat of dying to get you to do what he could never have gotten you to do otherwise."

"The fact remains, it was a promise."

Matt could hear the deep weariness in his brother's voice but he couldn't let go.

"Dying was the farthest thing from his mind," he said dryly. "He expected to beat death just like he beat everything else that got in his way. Just like he beat you by squeezing a promise out of you he thought you couldn't break."

"And he was right. Damn it, Matt, can't you understand, it's a matter of honor?"

The stubborn voice had taken on a labored sound that reminded Matt of his brother's condition and warned him it was time to knock it off. The wind went out of his sails.

"It's all right, Birch," he said quietly. "If that's the way you feel about it. Only it looks to me like you're making all of us pay a hell of a price for your honor."

There was another long moment of silence and then Birch said thickly, "What the hell, 's a moot point. The firm's yours. Go for it. I . . . gotta get my head straightened out so I can see again. We'll figure out what to do then."

To HER SURPRISE, upon reaching Kritzer's office after a short walk, Julia had no trouble getting to see him. He was between patients and directed his receptionist to admit her to his private sanctum almost at once. Julia went straight to the point.

"Dr. Kritzer, my husband has regained his memory and, as you know, will be ready to go home in a few days. As you also know, he is still blind," she said bluntly.

"Ah yes, indeed, Mrs. Cheney, I'm inclined to think we may have something more complicated here than simple shock," the doctor said. "I may as well tell you that I, myself, suspect your husband may be suffering from amaurosis, in which case he may not regain his sight for some time after he returns home."

"That may very well be, Dr. Kritzer, but I've had my fill of guesswork. I want a qualified specialist to see Birch with no further delay."

"That's up to you, Mrs. Cheney," Kritzer said coldly. "Now if you'll excuse me, I will see what can be arranged."

WITH HER JAUNDICED PERCEPTION of Dr. Kritzer, Julia was hardly prepared to find Kritzer at Birch's bedside the following morning, and with him, a second white-coated man whom he introduced as Dr. Inzelman, a "psychiatrist of considerable renown."

Psychiatrist! Had she heard wrong?

"Excuse me, Dr. Kritzer," she broke in when she had a firm grip on her composure, but he, in turn, interrupted her.

"Just a minute, Mrs. Cheney," he said coolly. "You will be gratified to know that after spending the greater part of the morning testing and interviewing your husband, Dr. Inzelman has confirmed my opinion that Mr. Cheney is suffering from amaurosis, a syndrome with which he had considerable experience in the field hospitals of Vietnam."

Vietnam?

"What exactly do you mean by amaurosis, Dr. Inzelman?" Julia asked.

"Amaurosis is the medical term used when blindness becomes a subconscious means of escaping some threatening factor in a patient's life that the patient feels locked into, Mrs. Cheney," Inzelman said. "Amaurosis is fairly common in battle zones where the patient has

been subjected to severe emotional and physical stress
for a period of time preceding injury. We must assume
the violent attack upon Mr. Cheney acted in much the
same way, incurring serious injuries and no doubt disturbing an already traumatized psyche that, in turn,
provided him with hysterical blindness as an escape
hatch from insoluble problems his conscious mind may
not even have acknowledged.''

Why was he telling them all this? thought Julia, refusing to be impressed by the doctor's convoluted language. There were no insoluble problems in Birch's life.
If there were, they would be hers, too. Their marriage
was their life. Never, as long as they breathed, would
either of them be found looking for an escape hatch.

''Nonsense!'' she said sharply. ''All that may apply to
someone else, but it doesn't apply to Birch. With all due
respect to you, doctor, I think you're wrong. Before we
go any farther along this line I want the opinion of an
ophthalmologist. And you needn't trouble yourself
about it, Dr. Kritzer. I'll arrange for one to see him myself.''

There was an instant of strained silence, and then
Birch spoke in a flat, quiet voice that was like an icy
hand upon Julia's heart.

''I'm afraid I don't share your opinion, Julia. I'm not
dissatisfied. Dr. Inzelman's diagnosis may well be right.''

CHAPTER FIVE

STANDING AT THE WINDOW of the apartment's study, facing Central Park, Julia looked out upon trees that had been in full flower when she brought Birch home from the hospital eight weeks earlier. Now the blossoms were gone, and the trees looked freshly washed in their new summer green.

Otherwise, everything was about the same, she thought drearily, her mind wandering ahead to summer's end when the leaves would lie in a multicolored carpet on the ground. Would Birch be able to see them?

Not if she couldn't talk him into having an ophthalmologist look at his eyes.

The dispassionate voice of Dr. Inzelman intruded upon her mind, as cool and impersonal as a mechanic telling the car owner why his engine wouldn't start. *Hysterical blindness. Traumatized psyche. Amaurosis.*

"I don't believe it," she muttered aloud, knowing she'd said the same thing as regularly as a mantra every day since Inzelman had pronounced his diagnosis.

But Birch believed it, and because of the implied promise that hysterical blindness would go away, she'd almost let herself become a believer, too. After all, the only grounds she had for her disbelief was an irrational mistrust of the doctors Kritzer and Inzelman, and an instinctive certainty that the word *hysterical* was completely out of character for Birch.

And there it stood, even after she told Birch what she'd heard from Mrs. Solari—that Inzelman and Kritzer were partners in a highly profitable association of midtown medical specialists—which had set her wondering whether Kritzer had brought Inzelman into the case on the basis of merit or of money.

"So they're getting rich," Birch had said indifferently. "That doesn't mean Inzelman doesn't know his stuff. If it'll make you feel better, I've seen the last of him. I don't want any psychiatrist poking around in my psyche until I've done some soul-searching myself. If I ever decide I need a psychiatrist, it won't be Inzelman."

And she'd said, "What you need is an ophthalmologist, not a psychiatrist."

And he'd said, "For the present I don't need either one."

In spite of a nagging fear that there could be danger in delay, Julia knew she'd have to wait until Birch was ready to see an ophthalmologist himself—and that wouldn't be until he decided to quit believing in Inzelman's diagnosis.

The ringing of the telephone broke into her thoughts, and she crossed the room to the desk in the far corner to answer it.

It was their agent, Sid Unger, calling to inquire about Birch's progress and to report on some work he'd been handling for them. That taken care of, Sid said, "By the way, Julia, the new magazine *Metropulse*, which is taking Manhattan by storm, contacted me to see if you'll do a series of articles for them on New York, showing the city as a cluster of small ethnic towns. I said I'd get back to them. What do you think?"

"Oh, Sid, why ask? You know we can't," Julia said almost crossly, keeping her voice low. Instinct told her that the conversation would be a hurtful reminder to Birch of their damaged career. "No telling when Birch is going to be able to work again."

"No problem. The magazine pays well for quality articles, but it's printed on newsprint, so they aren't really interested in Birch's high-quality photography. The idea is for you to prowl the city for subjects, and they'll send along some staff flunky with a camera to snap any pictures you think you want."

"Sounds interesting, Sidney, but I can't," she said without hesitation. "I have to be here. I wouldn't think of deserting Birch even if he could get along without me—which he can't."

There was a moment of silence at the other end. Then Sid said nervously, "This outfit pays good money, Julia."

"The answer is still no, Sid. And in case you're worrying about us money-wise, don't. Thank goodness money isn't a problem."

Thanks to my late father-in-law, she reminded herself as she returned the phone to its cradle, sorry she couldn't put more heart into her gratitude. Horace Cheney had failed his sons on a regular basis in his lifetime, but he'd left them very well off when he died.

The whisper of soles moving cautiously over the carpeted floor, the sound of a hand brushing lightly along a wall, told her Birch was making his way down the hall from their bedroom. Turning, she saw him pause at the entry to the study as if to get his bearings before forsaking the support of the wall. Instinctively she hurried to him, taking his arm to guide him before remembering, too late, that her help would not be well received.

"I wish you wouldn't swoop down on me like that," he said, his voice prickly, pulling away from her. "I can make it all right by myself."

"I know you can. I've seen you do it." She was determined not to let the sting of his words betray her into an angry retort. Striving to keep it light, she said, "But I like being arm in arm with my husband. Is there anything wrong with that?"

For a moment Birch stood fixed, his face tormented with regret. "Sorry I barked at you," he said gruffly. "It's just that having you lead me around . . . Oh hell! It makes me feel . . . God, I'd never have believed I could feel this way."

"What way, Birch?" she asked quietly.

He hesitated. "*Emasculated*, dammit!"

At the blurted word a flash of anger flared through Julia. "Well, don't let it!" she snapped, but as quickly as it came the anger was gone, and she was a partner in his hurt. *Oh, my dear,* she silently mourned. Aloud, she said, "You know there's no way I would emasculate you, Birch. *You must understand!* Everything I do is to remind you that we're in this together, just like we've always been in whatever we've done."

"Well, we're not," Birch said with disdain. "However much you may *think* you want to share my affliction, you don't. You can't. It's mine." He took a tentative step forward, hesitated, then moved stubbornly on.

Sick in spirit, Julia watched him make his lonely way across the room, feeling from chair to table to sofa until he reached a favorite club chair in the corner. Positioning himself, he eased into its softly worn leather and settled back in the seat with his old grace, looking for all the world as if in the next moment he would reach over to the bookshelf beside him for a book.

She could see the contours of his firm, muscled chest and shoulders beneath his yellow polo shirt. Well-cut tan cotton twill pants accented the long, hard lines of his thighs and legs, legs that were now spread out in a relaxed position. He was the sexiest man she'd ever seen, she thought with a sudden intake of breath. For a moment it was as if the nightmare of the past two months was over. Deep inside she felt the sweet, sensual ache of desire.

Unbuttoning her blouse as she went, she moved quietly across the deep pile of the carpet to the big chair where he sat, dropping the blouse on her way. Seating herself precariously between his legs on the chair's edge, she pushed her way back on the seat until her buttocks pressed against his loins. She brought his hands from the chair arms around to her chest, and placed one of his hands on each bare breast.

She felt the thrust of his sudden awakening, and for a long, pulsing moment, lost track of everything but the burst of ecstasy that rose and fell and burst again deep inside her.

In a choking whisper Birch said, "Julie...oh, my God. Julie. Julie. Sweet bride."

She had come to him so softly he hadn't known she was there until he'd heard the glide of her derriere across the leather and in the same instant felt its soft, firm contours against his groin. Her breasts sat like two small, silk-skinned melons in his hands. With a sense of wonder he felt the awakening within him of sensual energy for the first time—except in frequent wildly erotic, sweat-drenched dreams—since their last day together in Paris.

The darkness that had shadowed his passion since he'd come back home was still around him, but his swift arousal dulled its significance.

He wanted to tell her...oh, God!...what? How much he loved her? That without her, life would be death? Murmuring wordless endearments into her ear, he reached to weave his fingers through her glorious hair, seeing it in his mind in mystic abundance, framing her face like a nut-brown halo. He let his hand travel lovingly over her features, remembering them with the pads of his finger: the high, intelligent forehead, the long-fringed eyelids, the flaring nostrils, the high cheekbones and the heart-shaped jawline that came to a point at her clefted chin. He swallowed to relieve the lump of emotion that rose in his throat and touched her lips, first with his hands, then, turning her toward him, with his mouth.

"Julie," he said softly. And on the swell of a new wave of life, he caught her around the waist with one hand and with the other, found the zipper of her pants. Together they peeled off the last of her clothing, but she slipped away, and he lost her. Then he heard her laugh— deep, throaty, provocative laugh—and knew she was waiting for him on the floor. In a splendid surge of passion—seldom thought of in the days of darkness since Paris—he knew the moment had come.

The pervasive dark forgotten, he slipped his feet out of his loafers, rose unsteadily and quickly removed his clothes.

Above the sound of his wildly beating pulse he heard the voice of Julia, thick as honey, sultry with desire, urging him softly, "Hurry, Birch. I'm right here at your feet, love."

In his haste he became disoriented and cursed the dark. Her voice seemed not to come from where he had imagined she was. Groping, he moved toward the siren sound—two steps—and tripped over her body to fall spread-eagle across the floor, cracking his head on the corner of the dictionary stand as he came down.

Julia scrambled up and crawled to him on her knees across the carpet. "Oh, my God, Birch! You're bleeding," she cried, grabbing up her shirt from where she'd dropped it just a little earlier, and using it to wipe away the blood.

He was still for a moment, and then he grabbed the shirt from her hand and pushed her away. "Cut it out, Julia," he said, his voice harsh with suppressed rage. He began awkwardly to right himself. "Do you have to make a federal case out of everything? It's nothing."

And it was nothing, she saw: a small bump and a nick that had already quit bleeding.

He was on his feet now in precarious imbalance, and she jumped up to steady him only to realize as she touched him that doing it was a mistake.

"Damn it, Julia, *leave me alone!*"

Stung, Julia drew back in time to see his fury slip away as quickly as it had come. He stood solidly now, but his body sagged in defeat.

"I'm sorry," he said simply.

"It's all right," she said, not daring to touch him now, even when she saw him move his head in an uncertain arc in what she recognized as an effort to orient himself.

"What time is it?" he asked finally.

Automatically, Julia glanced at the watch on her wrist, the only thing she now wore, though it seemed a strange question when they were standing naked in the middle of the study. The sight of the watch dial brought everything back into focus.

"Oh, my goodness! Matt!" she exclaimed, as she remembered Birch's brother would be arriving in a few minutes to take him to the rehabilitation center he'd been going to regularly for the past few weeks. "He'll be here in a few minutes."

Hurrying, she put her clothes back on, except for her bloodstained shirt, and gathered Birch's clothing together. Looking back, she saw him take a tentative step in the wrong direction.

"Over here, sweetie," she said, directing him back toward the leather club chair with her voice. She arranged his clothes on the chair seat. "You can get dressed while I run in and find another top to wear."

She was pushing, she knew—and she knew how Birch hated it. But she also knew his brother's reputation for being punctual, and the thought of either delaying her brother-in-law on the other side of their locked door or having him catch them in dishabille filled her with unreasoning panic.

Returning from their bedroom, she found Birch still only half-dressed and palming the chair in search of his shirt, which had fallen to the floor. At the same time came the buzz of the house phone. It had to be the doorman downstairs calling to announce Matt's arrival, but Julia ignored it and rushed over to Birch. Bending down, she picked up his polo shirt, and over protests and flaying arms, managed to pull it on over his head.

"There!" she said, and, leaving him to finish putting on the shirt himself, scurried to answer the house phone. A moment later she was beside Birch again, hurrying him into his socks and shoes.

Not until he was fully dressed did she acknowledge the tight set of his face with a sigh. "I'm sorry, darling," she said. "I know how you hate being maneuvered, but there just wasn't time for your pride."

The resentment she read in the blind eyes hurt. Sometimes, like now, when his eyes showed so clearly what he felt, it was hard to remember he was blind, she thought, resentment rising within her, in turn. She tried hard enough to give top priority to his tender pride, dammit. He might at least try to understand there were times when other things had to come first.

The silence of the charged atmosphere between them was broken by the sound of the door chimes. With a feeling of relief, Julia went to open the door for her brother-in-law, aware that behind her Birch was rising from his chair.

"Hey, aren't you supposed to have a cane or something?" Matt asked at the sight of Birch groping his way across the room toward the sound of their voices. The bluntness of the question made Julia flinch.

"It's around here somewhere," Birch said, his attention focused on navigating himself to the doorway that opened into the study, where they'd come to a stop.

"I put it in the foyer closet, Matt. He doesn't have to use it here on his own ground," Julia said, suddenly defensive.

Julia was surprised and a little annoyed that Matt made no move to help his brother across the room, even when she darted to push aside a small table dead on Birch's course. In the foyer she retrieved from the closet the light white aluminum cane she had yet to see Birch use and handed it to Matt, who passed it to Birch, who seemed an almost reluctant receiver.

She watched them out the door and was surprised to see Birch reach for his brother's arm, clearly intending to let Matt guide him to the elevator only a few steps away. After the surprise came shock and anger; her brother-in-law firmly detached the hand that had taken his arm.

"Let go of my arm, Birch," she heard Matt say in a firm voice, completely devoid of pity. "What do you think that cane's for, for God's sake?"

You insensitive clod! thought Julia furiously. *How can you forget he's blind?* She should never have agreed to let him take Birch to the rehab center today.

She wanted to call them back, to find a plausible reason for suddenly deciding to go with them—or better yet, to send Matt away and chauffeur Birch herself as she normally did.

Standing uncertainly in the open doorway of their apartment, she heard Birch say uncertainly. "You expect *me* to lead the way?"

And anger rose in her again at Matt's reply: "You got it, brother."

To her surprise, she saw a vestige of the old lopsided, sardonic grin take shape on Birch's face.

"What are we waiting for, then?" she heard him say. And then the elevator door opened, and to her astonishment, he moved the cane in an arc until he found the opening and tapped his way inside alone, Matt following. A moment later the elevator door shut them from her sight.

Julia closed the apartment door and pressed her face against its frame, swept with an unexpected sense of relief. For the first time in the eight weeks since she'd brought Birch home from the hospital, she was alone—

not at his side measuring everything she was about to do or say by the effect it might have on Birch.

Alone. Responsible for no one for the next few hours but Julia, she thought, luxuriating in her sudden release.

But her euphoria had scarcely blossomed before it withered in guilt. Guilt first because she'd let Matt persuade her to abandon Birch—she'd never let that happen again—followed by a more profound guilt at the realization she was actually looking forward to the hours ahead without her husband.

IN THE ELEVATOR Birch's mind stayed back with Julia, locked with regret and dismay into the scene they had just enacted. The echo of his own words—*Leave me alone!*—filled him with shame. They were unforgivable words his greathearted Julie had forgiven almost as soon as he'd said them. But could she ever *forget*?

Oh God, what's happening to us? he thought.

The clatter of the elevator door broke into his thoughts, and he realized they had come to a stop.

"You know how to use that cane?" Matt asked.

"Roughly. I haven't had a lot of practice," Birch admitted.

"Well, come on then. It's time you got some. Get that thing going and follow me to the car."

Through the open car window a few minutes later a breeze brought the new summer heat whispering across Birch's face, but in the shock of sound that assaulted his ears he barely noticed it. Before he lost his sight he'd taken the roar and jangle of the streets for granted. Now, unable to pin down the source of the sounds to know whether they were coming directly at him or standing still or going away and how fast or slow, he found himself tightening inwardly against the confusion that closed in around him. The din seemed ten times louder than it once had, and unexpectedly menacing.

Like a turtle retreating into its shell, he hunched his shoulders and tucked his head closer to his collarbone, until he remembered that today his driver was Matt. He felt none of the compulsion to put up a good front for his brother that he did in the presence of Julia. He hadn't felt the need for pretense with Matt since that long-ago summer day when, side by side, he and his brother had clung to the hull of their swamped sailboat in Long Island Sound, waiting to be rescued, sure they were going to die.

"How about closing the windows and turning on the air-conditioning, Matt?" he said now.

"Too hot?" There was a note of surprise in his brother's voice. The whisper of air on Birch's face died away as the window whirred up, muting the onslaught of sounds from outside.

"It's not the heat. It's the racket," he said. "It's funny, I used to think all the pulsing sounds of the city were exhilarating, but now that I'm blind they scare the livin' bejabers out of me. I feel like they're all coming to get me—the jackhammers, the pile drivers, the sirens." He gave a self-deprecating laugh and then remembered it was his brother to whom he was confessing his foible—his brother, who would think none the less of him for it.

Why was it so easy to speak of his weaknesses to his brother? he wondered, and decided it was because no matter how Matt reacted—with sympathy, empathy, pity, even—it didn't alter their relationship as brothers. The bond between them would, in some way, even be strengthened.

But the very thought of pity from Julia caused something inside him to shrivel, something that felt like his soul and reminded him—as if he needed a reminder—that he was no longer the man she'd married, no more her partner, her confidant. He was someone else. *A blind man!* He couldn't even be her lover without making a bloody fool of himself, he thought with bitterness, and vowed that next time he'd put a rein on his libido until they were safely in bed.

His brother's voice broke in upon his thoughts. "You're not seeing Inzelman?"

"What's to see him about?" Birch said indifferently. "He gave me his diagnosis. I have no reason to doubt that he knows what he's talking about."

"Well?" his brother asked. Getting no reply, he amended amiably, "Forget I asked. It's between you and him."

"I haven't talked to Inzelman since I left the hospital. Look, Matt, I don't need a psychiatrist to tell me what's messed up my head," Birch said.

"You're not still hung up on that promise you made Dad, are you?" asked Matt sharply.

The question reminded Birch that this was the first time he and his brother had talked together—alone—since that day at the hospital, after he'd learned what his eye problem was.

Birch felt a warm affection for this brother whose arguments that day had saved him from his own specious conviction that their father's death bound him to the promise he'd made him only hours before. He could still hear himself trying to explain to Matt how he'd gotten suckered into the promise, though his explanatory powers had been decidedly limited by the cloudy haze brought on by the painkillers and anesthetics.

Matt's words that day had been like a rubber blade to
a fogged window, he thought now. After Matt left he'd
asked himself if he was willing to sacrifice himself and
his brother and risk losing Julia, all to keep an uncon-
scionable promise wrung from him under duress. In the
light of what Matt had said, he'd seen with sudden clar-
ity that the problem had nothing to do with honor.

"The answer to your question is no, Matt, but I guess
the blindness must still have something to do with the
way I've felt about promises . . . and Dad," he said now.
"That withering crack of yours about messing up all our
lives to coddle my precious honor made me stop and
look at what I'd promised. For the first time with a clear
head."

"You know what would have happened if he'd lived,
Birch? He wouldn't have released you," Matt said. "He
would have tried to shame you into keeping the damned
promise. If you'd broken your word, you would have
heard about it from our father as long as he lived. From
our father, who never kept a promise in his life!"

"Where do you think I got the hang-up about keeping my word, Matt? From the promises that were made
and broken when we were growing up! Like the camera
workshop he promised me with Ansel Adams at Yo-
semite in return for getting a business degree."

"Yeah," said Matt sourly. "I was supposed to have a
trip to Spain if I spent my college vacations as company
gofer. I should have made him put it in writing."

He broke off with a muttered expletive and applied the
brakes. The car jerked to a sudden stop. Birch slammed
forward, the restraining seat belt pressing against him,
and back hard against the seat. Sealed in the ignorance
of his sightless cocoon, he braced himself against . . . he
wasn't sure what.

In a matter of seconds the car was back on course, and in the driver's seat Matt muttered angrily. "Crazy bike messenger...trying to get killed."

Birch's alarm and confusion quickly subsided. When his heartbeat had slowed to normal, he tried to pick up what he'd been about to say as if there had been no interruption. "Remember, Matt, how he bought the place at the beach and dumped us there every summer, always promising to come back on weekends and never doing it?"

"Do I? Those were the best times of my young life," Matt said, his voice warm with nostalgia.

"Mine, too, but did you ever stop to think how lousy it was for Mom? I used to catch her crying sometimes, there in that big house in the salt grass so far away from everything. She never saw anyone but Cora Meigs," Birch said broodingly. "She was lucky Cora was a good friend and a widow and willing to sign on as housekeeper, especially when we were at the beach. If she'd depended on Dad, Mom would have been completely alone out there except for us—two beach-bum kids she only saw when we got hungry."

He lapsed into silence, reluctant to say to his brother what he'd kept buried in silence through the years. "For a long time, I blamed him for Mom's death," he said at last without emotion. "Maybe I still do."

"How so?" Matt asked in a puzzled voice.

"Well, I guess the bottom line for me is this—if he'd bought her a car like he promised, she wouldn't have been riding into Seahampton to get groceries that day in a car with a woman who ran a red light," Birch said. "I promised myself then that I'd never make a promise I wouldn't keep. That's where the honor came in."

For a minute neither of them spoke. Then Matt, his voice gravelly with emotion, said, "I don't mind saying I'm proud to be your brother." He cleared his throat, and as if nothing had come before, added self-consciously, "Well, old Bro, it sounds like you know where you're coming from. What's holding things up?"

Birch felt a familiar chill of fear. He wished Matt had left the question unasked. But he addressed it angrily, head-on. "You mean, why am I still blind? It looks like I may have oversimplified," he said, trying to keep the fear out of his voice.

Silence. Then Matt asked unexpectedly, "You still haven't told Julia? About the promise?"

"Oh God, no!"

"You ought to tell her, Birch. It might have something to do with getting your sight back."

"Dammit, Matt, no one knows better than Julia how I've always felt about keeping my word," Birch said explosively. "At first I thought she would understand why I made the promise. Now I'm not so sure. After all, it was a betrayal of her and our life together. I'm not sure she'll be able to be objective about it."

Birch felt the car slowing to a stop.

"Here we are," Matt said a moment later. "Right in front of the rehab center, across the sidewalk to your right." They agreed on a time for Matt to pick Birch up later in the day and Birch unbuckled his seat belt. About to get out he felt Matt's hand on his arm.

"Wait, Birch. There's something I want to say. A while ago you told me you'd oversimplified. Well, I think you're right," Matt said. "For God's sake, stop trying to be your own shrink."

"It doesn't seem to be working out," Birch admitted. "But Julia distrusts Inzelman, and I'm inclined to think the guy may be more interested in his fees than his patients.''

''I happen to know a psychiatrist who might interest you. I'll tell you about him on the way home.''

Opening the car door, Birch got out and stood uncertainly on the sidewalk. This was the point where Julia regularly abandoned their double-parked car and stayed with him until she'd turned him over to someone from the center.

''You go in by yourself, don't you?'' Matt asked.

Birch quelled the panic that rose inside him and made tentative arcs with his cane in an effort to orient himself. The thought of crossing the sidewalk to the door on his own for the first time scared him crazy, but to confess that Julia didn't let him do much of anything for himself seemed somehow disloyal to her, not to say embarrassing to him.

His ears caught the familiar, purposeful tap of a cane nearby. It was as good a time as any to start getting his act together, he thought grimly.

''Go in by myself? Of course,'' he lied. ''What do you think I am? Blind?''

With what he hoped was a jaunty wave he took off, sweeping his cane in front of him and following the sound of the other tapping cane with trepidation until he knew for sure that his leader's destination and his own were the same.

From where he sat in the car, Matt followed his brother's uneven progress across the sidewalk with his eyes, his feelings knotting in this throat. There was a kind of nobility about Birch that put an ordinary fellow like himself to shame. It haunted him that the new understanding and closeness they'd arrived at during the past two months had been reached as a result of Birch's blindness.

"Bro," he said softly. He brushed a hand across his eyes to get rid of a sudden moisture.

FOR A LONG MINUTE after the elevator door closed on the two men, Julia stood with her head pressed against the door frame and listened to a whisper of her recent arousal echo through her. It was like having her lips moistened with a sponge when her whole body was parched from thirst.

From the day she'd brought Birch home, she'd wanted to make love with him. Knowing how preoccupied he was with the trauma that had befallen him, she had held back, waiting for a sign from him. It seemed ironic that, when she had finally set aside everything but her need for Birch and gone for what might have been a seduction tour de force, it had turned into a slapstick comedy.

Still, for a minute it had been as lovely and light-hearted and wildly exciting as ever. Except in other days Birch's tumble would have struck them as hilarious and added fuel to their lovemaking instead of dousing the fire. But then, in those days Birch would never have tumbled in the first place.

"Stop it!" she commanded herself aloud.

If she was going to spend this day brooding about problems, their sex life was number two on the list. Number one was how to get Birch to another doctor and find out if his blindness was really only a passing phenomenon. If it was hysteria, it was her opinion that he shouldn't be trying to worry it out for himself. If it wasn't—if there was a physical cause for his blindness—well, either he could be cured or he couldn't, and if he could, this delay might do him real harm. On the other hand, if there was no cure and he had to go on being blind, wouldn't they both be better off knowing what they had to deal with? At least then they could get on with their lives. Once they were able to do that, their sex life would take care of itself. It always had.

Pausing to straighten a towel here, a bedspread there, she wandered aimlessly through the apartment, deciding, finally, to go out onto the terrace that elbowed around the sunny corner facing the park. There, Julia took a moment to spray the planter boxes, where newly planted petunias and impatiens were just coming into bloom.

Her gardening finished, she looked around and realized with dismay that for the first time since she could remember, she had time on her hands, and she found herself at a loss for something to do.

For once she almost wished the widowed Cora Meigs, who'd come out of retirement to offer her help after Birch was hurt, had left some of the household chores undone when she'd taken the day off—or changed her mind and stayed at the apartment. The aging housekeeper was a wise and cheerful person, easy to talk to. Julia longed for a little wisdom and cheer.

Having Cora to take care of the house had freed Julia to spend all her time with Birch and steer him clear of as many frustrations and hazards as she could. She liked to think that, in her own way, she made him feel less blind.

Now, with Birch away, she felt purposeless. He was what she *did*. Why, she hadn't even seen a movie since... She brought the thought process to a screeching halt before it could lead her onto ground she was trying not to think about today.

A matinee would be nice, though. Something new and sexy, or old and romantic. Or just funny. How long had it been since she'd enjoyed the sublime pleasure of a real belly laugh? Could she even recognize funny anymore?

In the end she put on her sweats and running shoes and headed for the reservoir, there to discover that two months without exercise had left her noticeably out of shape. She circled the reservoir in a warm-up run, then gradually settled into a steady pace that she stuck to stubbornly, though it was far beyond the pace experts recommended starting at.

She arrived back at the apartment much later, her skin and clothing soaked, her muscles twitching in protest. Inside, she heard the phone ringing and she hurried to unlock the door in sudden fear that Matt had let something happen to Birch.

"Hello?" she said into the receiver, her voice tight with alarm and still breathy from her run.

"Julia? It doesn't sound like you," said the voice on the other end. "It's Hugh Dryden."

"Hugh!" she cried out in delight. "We haven't heard from you since the night you invited Birch and me to dinner in Paris and I showed up alone. Where are you? Here in New York?"

"In D.C. on a story," the journalist told her. "I just heard Birch was beaten up in Central Park, and I'm in a state of shock. He's not really...?" He broke off. Julia knew the feeling. He couldn't say the word.

"Blind," she supplied tonelessly. "Not forever, we've been led to hope. Otherwise, he's more or less recovered."

"If I take the late-afternoon shuttle out of here I can be in Manhattan for dinner. Would Birch feel up to going out? Some quiet place, just the three of us? I'm on a tight schedule, but I'm not about to go back to Paris without seeing for myself that the guy's doing all right.''

Julia felt a sudden rush of hope. Hugh was just what Birch needed to bring him out of the cave of darkness she was beginning to fear was swallowing him up. These days he received visitors reluctantly, declined dinner invitations and vetoed her every suggestion that they have people in. She couldn't get him out of the apartment except to go to the rehab center.

But Hugh was different. This could be the turning point, she told herself. Birch didn't have to see to match wits with his old friend from prep school. They'd shared gleefully with each other from the time they were kids.

"Oh, Hugh, that would be marvelous. Just seeing—'' she broke off and amended "—just jousting verbally with you over dinner will make a new man of him.''

When she finished making arrangements for the evening and hung up, the house phone buzzed.

"Mrs. Cheney, your husband will be getting off the elevator in a minute,'' the doorman said. "He asked me to tell you he forgot his key and wants you to unlock the door for him.''

Julia caught her breath in astonishment. She couldn't believe even Matt would do something as irresponsible as dropping his blind brother off downstairs, leaving him to get up to the apartment on his own.

"Tell him to stay right there,'' she said through tight lips. "I'll be right down.''

"You'll miss him, ma'am. He's already on his way up.''

Seething with anger at her brother-in-law, Julia was waiting at the elevator when the door opened.

"Thank God you got here," she exclaimed, reaching to take the cane from his hand as Birch moved to step out. "That blasted Matt! This is the last time I let you go off with him."

"Please let go of my cane, Julia," Birch said evenly.

Still grasping the cane, Julia said, "But you're home, sweetie. You don't need the cane here with me."

"I said, let go of the cane, please." He said it calmly, quietly, but she heard a sound in his voice that brought her hand back to her side. Something was different. She wasn't sure what. She knew only that she'd hit a nerve. Suddenly uncertain of her role, she went on ahead and waited for him at the open door. She saw him touch the cane to the wall and hesitate.

"Julia?" he said.

She knew then that he wanted her voice.

"I'll wait for you here in the doorway," she said, and saw him move in the direction of the sound, brushing the wall with his cane. Now that she understood, she kept talking, leading him with her voice into the study and to his chair, at the same time thinking impatiently how much easier it would have been for them both if he had just let her take his arm.

She was puzzled at the look of satisfaction she saw on his face; she felt pleased for him, in a way, but at the same time, somehow shut out. Watching him closely, she had no question that his mood had mellowed in the few minutes since he'd stepped off the elevator. It seemed as good a time as any to tell him about the plans she'd made for the evening.

"Good news, darling," she said. "Hugh called this afternoon. He's in Washington, D.C."

"Hugh? Hugh Dryden?"

"None other. And guess what? He's flying in on the late-afternoon shuttle to take us to dinner. One of those quiet, posh little places Hugh's expense account can afford."

She didn't have to wait for words to know his reaction. The negative, accusing look on Birch's face told her everything there was to know.

CHAPTER SIX

"I'M NOT GOING, Julia!"

He couldn't mean it, she thought. A second look at his face left no doubt in her mind that he did.

Trying to stay calm, she said, "I can't think of a single good reason why not, Birch."

"Well, for starters, when I cut my own meat for the first time it's sure as hell not going to be in public, and not with Hugh Dryden looking on. You might have asked me before you said yes."

"That's two reasons, neither one of them very good. And I couldn't. You weren't around," she said mildly, hoping to deflect his annoyance and hide her unexpected resentment. They'd been holed up in the apartment for so long, the place was beginning to feel like a cage. "Don't I always cut your meat? I can do it just as well at the table as in the kitchen. I really don't mind."

"Well, that's great, because I do."

His heavy sarcasm brought her up short. She was shaken to see that her words had hurt him when she'd meant them only to reassure. She hurried across the room and dropped to the floor beside his chair. Seizing one of his hands in both of hers she pressed it to her face, stroking the back of it with her lips.

Through the lump that filled her throat she said unevenly, "No one will notice, dear. Having someone cut your meat is no big deal."

He answered with a derisive snort. "It's a big deal when you're lucky if you can find it on your plate after it's cut—lucky to find the plate."

"Birch! No!" she protested, feeling his hurt as if it were her own. "Don't be so hard on yourself, love. You do splendidly. After all, it'll only be you and me...and Hugh."

"*You* and Hugh, Julia. I'm staying home."

She'd been so sure he'd welcome an evening with Hugh. Unexpectedly, she felt as if she'd lost her way. "But Birch, you can't," she pleaded in a last desperate attempt to change his mind. "Hugh's your best friend. He's been your friend longer than anybody."

"Right on both counts," Birch said a bit glumly. "When we were kids, if we weren't trying to out-hotdog each other on a surfboard or ski slope we were trying to cream one another on a tennis court. Same thing with girls and academics and anything else you might name. Sorry, Julie. You're going to have to count me out. I'll do my socializing with Hugh Dryden when I can relate to him again as a peer."

She wanted to tell him that neither Hugh Dryden nor any other man would ever be his peer. Blind, deaf, with both hands tied behind his back, Birch Cheney would still be the best. But he'd look on such an endorsement as fulsome. She'd already said enough to upset him without making him uncomfortable as well.

Still holding his hand she rubbed the back of it across her cheek, tempted for a moment to rise from where she curled beside his chair and do a replay of the morning's fiasco. Only this time do it right.

But a certain taut-muscled resistance she felt in the hand she held warned her that the moment was not propitious. Curbing her budding desire with a sigh, she let go of his hand and rose to her feet.

"I'd better try to get Hugh at the Mayflower Hotel before he leaves Washington, and tell him not to come," she said.

"Why? You made the date. There's no reason for *you* not to go."

"And leave you here by yourself? I wouldn't think of it. Cora won't be in until late."

"Cut it out, Julia!"

The expression of outrage, the flush of anger she saw on his face unnerved her. She realized, without knowing why, that her words had caused it. What had she said wrong *this* time, she wondered crossly, feeling her own color rise. What was the matter with Birch, anyway? Wasn't she letting him have his way? They were staying home. What more did he want?

"I don't need Cora! I'm blind, not incompetent. Quit baby-sitting me, for God's sake!" he roared. He drew a deep breath. After a moment he went on quietly, "I'm sorry, Julie. God! I'm really sorry, but this has got to stop. You're dead set on turning me into an invalid, dammit, and I won't have it."

Julia struggled for control of herself. "I am not! I just don't like for you to be alone. That's not turning you into an invalid," she said defensively. "You used to like to have me around."

"That's not the point. Just what do you think is going to happen to me if I'm left here alone for a few hours without somebody watching me?"

"Stop it, Birch. This isn't some kind of a guessing game," Julia said quickly, but even as she said it she couldn't think of a single real hazard that might befall him here at home. It was just a feeling she'd had ever since he was blinded. Overnight this man she loved—this man who on the day of their marriage had become the other half of her strength—had become painfully vulnerable.

But he would only close his mind to that explanation, just as he'd scorn the other reason that had haunted her with guilt from the moment she learned he'd been struck down in the park; yet in the bottom of her heart, she would always know that if she had followed Birch on the first plane out of Paris that night twelve weeks ago, he wouldn't now be blind. She'd have been with him when the call had come informing him that his father was dying. She would have asked the doorman to have a cab waiting when Birch went down. She would have saved him from taking off across the park on foot in the middle of the night.

Birch was waiting. "Answer me, Julia. I want to know what you think can happen to me while you're away?" he persisted.

Trapped, she said weakly, "Well...you could trip and fall or bump into an open door or... Oh Birch, honey, it's just that I love you so much...." She hesitated and then made her escape by taking the offensive. "And as long as you keep trying to be your own psychiatrist and refuse to see an ophthalmologist—"

"Please, Julia. Let's not get into *that* again," Birch interrupted her wearily.

"Dammit, Birch, you won't even try..." She broke off and hurried out of the room, afraid of what they might say to each other if she stayed. Unfortunately, it was not the first time in recent weeks that they'd backed down from a potentially horrendous quarrel.

Something awful was happening to them, and she didn't know how to stop it, or even what it was. There was the blindness, of course. But that was only the beginning. There were other things—Birch's blasted male pride, for one. And he never used to be touchy. It was getting so that she had to think twice every time before she opened her mouth.

But she knew she wasn't being fair. If anyone had a right to be touchy it was Birch, considering the monumental problems he had to deal with from moment to moment. She might have been a little more sensitive and avoided setting up dinner until she'd sounded Birch out.

In their bedroom she picked up the phone and put in a call for Hugh in Washington. She was disconcerted to learn that Mr. Dryden had just stopped by the desk and left word that he would not be available to return calls until the following morning.

She sat on the edge of the bed and tried to think how to handle the situation. Hugh would be here in a couple of hours to take them to dinner. For a moment she entertained a flicker of hope that Birch would change his mind once he knew Hugh was already on his way.

Still in her running clothes she went back to the study. "Darn it, I missed him, Birch. He's already on his way," she said when Birch, still in his chair, turned his head toward the sound of her footsteps. "Please, honey, won't you reconsider? He's really coming to see *you*."

"Nothing doing, Julia. I told you I'm staying home."

She stood uncertainly for a moment, trying to think of an alternative. If Cora weren't off, they could have dinner here, and that would take care of the problem, but Julia had no illusions about her own abilities as a cook. Their mobile life meant most of their meals were eaten in restaurants. Except for an occasional omelet or a simple pasta dish, she'd never done much cooking even here in the apartment. They either ate out or had food sent in. And now, of course, there was Cora.

Food sent in. Why hadn't she thought of that before? Her mind riffled through her rather extensive list of restaurants and caterers in Manhattan who delivered anything from chop suey to haute cuisine.

"*Voilà!* I have the solution!" she exclaimed in her most positive voice, though she guessed, even as she said it that she could be off base. "We'll eat here. I'll order some of that wonderful—"

"*Please*, Julia!" Birch said angrily, and there was something in his voice that made her sorry she'd pressured him for no better reason than to save face. It wasn't as if Birch were acting on some perverse whim. He really hated having Hugh Dryden feel sorry for him, she realized too late.

Seen in that context his reluctance seemed suddenly reasonable and completely human and even more endearing, somehow. Still, it posed a problem. They couldn't both let Hugh down. She didn't want to go without Birch, and she didn't want to leave him alone. Yet how could she *not* go?

"It's all right, darling," she said and hesitated, not wanting to badger him. "There's one thing, though. Hugh *is* flying down here to see you. Do you really want to shut him out completely or, when he comes for me, would you like me to invite him in for a drink?"

His answer was slow in coming, but it was reasonably gracious when it came. "That'll be all right. Invite him in."

"You're a sweetheart," she said. Relieved, she leaned over and gave him a kiss on one cheek. "I've got to scoot now and get out of these sweaty clothes and take a shower."

When she reached their bedroom she paused in thought. After a moment, she picked up the phone and dialed Cora's number.

"Are you doing anything special this evening, Cora?" Julia asked hesitantly when the housekeeper answered, keeping her voice low though she'd closed the bedroom door behind her and knew the room was too far away from the study for Birch to hear.

"Just watching TV. What's on your mind, my dear?"

"Well, something's come up and I have to go out. It's probably just silly of me, but I don't like to leave Birch here by himself. Could you—"

Before she could finish, Cora interrupted her. "I can be there before seven. Will you want dinner before you go out?"

"Not for me," Julia said and went on to give Cora a candid account of how the evening had evolved, avoiding any reference to her disagreement with Birch.

"I'll order dinner in for you and Birch, but don't let me forget to give you money to pay the delivery person. Birch does fine with coins, but a one dollar bill feels pretty much the same as a twenty," Julia said. "If you could just see to it that everything gets on the table so he can manage..."

"Why should you have food brought in? I don't mind fixing something for Birch. I'll eat with him, in fact."

"Oh, that would be so nice," Julia said. "I can't thank you enough, Cora." About to hang up, she remembered one more favor she had to ask and added uncomfortably, "Oh, and Cora, would you mind letting Birch think you decided to come back early? You know—that you didn't come because I called and asked you? He gets furious when he thinks I'm having you 'baby-sit' him, as he calls it...."

DRESSED IN HER BEST for the first time since Paris—a silk suit in a shade called nymphwood-green that Bonet had let her have at cost—Julia greeted Hugh Dryden warmly when he arrived at their door. She genuinely like this old friend of Birch's. Seeing him again, she was glad she'd taken the trouble to dress up for the occasion. She sometimes forgot Hugh was a bit of a dandy.

"Julia! It's great to see you. You look absolutely smashing," he said, bending to kiss her cheek.

"I was about to say the same to you," Julia said, laughing. "Looking the way you do, you're wasting your talents writing for Global Press. Ever think of modeling menswear for *Esquire*? You could make a bundle."

Hugh let out a whoop of laughter. "In that case, I'll look into it."

"Birch is waiting for you in the study," Julia said. She hesitated a moment, then continued, lowering her voice. "He's…a bit of a recluse these days, Hugh. I hope you won't mind taking me out alone again. It seems it's getting to be a habit."

"You mean Birch isn't going?"

"I'm really sorry, Hugh, but I just haven't been able to get him to leave the apartment since he came back from the hospital, except to go to the rehab center."

"I'd like nothing better than to have you to myself," Dryden said with his familiar gallantry. "But don't worry about it. I'll talk him into coming along."

"It might be better if you didn't, Hugh. I'm afraid his mind's made up," Julia said uneasily, not sure how Birch would take more arm-twisting, even from an old friend.

Lightly touching his shoulder, she gestured down the hallway to the study. "He's waiting for you. Come in and say hello," she said. "We can all have a drink together and you and Birch can talk about old times before we go.''

They found Birch sitting in the leather chair he'd been in when Julia left him to shower and dress. She saw at once that he had not been idle during her absence. He had rolled the portable bar cart from its storage cabinet across the room and wheeled it over within easy reach of his chair. The path taken was evident by the furniture left askew.

He'd also poured a drink for himself. *Scotch and soda with plenty of ice,* she thought automatically, knowing his taste. He'd placed the glass with nothing left in it but a few shards of ice within easy reach on a small table at his side. Noting the full ice bucket on the cart, she realized that it could only have been filled by Birch from the ice maker in the kitchen three rooms and a hall and countless obstacles away—hardly an easy task for a man who couldn't see.

He could have saved himself a lot of trouble by asking her to bring out the cart and the ice before she left him to take a shower, she thought impatiently. On the other hand, she probably should have thought of it herself. In any case, the room was a shambles now. Nothing was broken, thank God. She remembered certain small treasures that hadn't survived Birch's first days at home, before she'd moved breakables out of harm's way.

As they entered the study she saw Birch turn his head in the direction of their voices. Handsome and self-assured in his impeccably cut, dark gray suit, Hugh Dryden walked across the room. Behind him Julia straightened lampshades and pushed chairs back in place.

"My God, Birch, you're looking good. It's great to see you, old man," Hugh said heartily, grasping the hand Birch extended from where he sat.

"I'm sorry I can't say the same to you, Dryden," Birch said with a laugh as dry as ashes.

Hugh looked a bit taken aback. Julia guessed Birch had thrown him off balance and on purpose, if the hint of smugness she saw on Birch's face was any clue.

"Birch!" she said sharply. And to Hugh in apology, "Don't mind his little joke, Hugh. What are you drinking?"

"Scotch and water, if you don't mind, Julia."

There was a heavy moment of quiet. Hugh seemed at a loss for something to say. Quickly, Julia dropped ice in a glass and sloshed in whiskey and water. She was surprised when Birch silently held up his nearly empty glass to be replenished. A white ring marked the leather-topped mahogany table where he'd had the glass, and she was momentarily exasperated that he could fetch a bucket of ice from the kitchen but couldn't get a coaster from the bar cart for the glass. She slipped the glass into a moisture-proof jacket and handed it back to him full, then poured a glass of white wine for herself. Turning to the two men, she touched glasses with them.

"Cheers!" she said, struggling for a semblance of a cheery tone.

Recovered, Hugh said to Birch, "Julia tells me you're thinking about standing us up for dinner tonight, and I say you can't do that. I didn't fly here for a no show."

"I suppose she told you I've developed an aversion to public dining salons?"

"She implied as much, but I don't buy it, Cheney."

"Implied? Well, let me tell you what she left out," Birch said in a sardonic voice. Julia realized there was a slight, hardly noticeable slur to his words. If she hadn't known how little taste Birch had for hard liquor she would almost have thought he'd had more than the one drink.

He went on. "I doubt if she told you how I knock over wineglasses and throw food around and lose tableware and napkins on the floor. The truth is, Dryden, if I was foolhardy enough to go with you, by the time we finished dinner your sartorial elegance would be polka-dotted with veal Marsala and pâté de foie gras."

"Birch! That's not true!" Julia cried. She had to stop him. But how?

"And that, old friend, in a nutshell, is why I do not choose to dine with you tonight," he said, the thickness in his speech now quite evident.

"Don't listen to him, Hugh," Julia broke in. "He's just trying to be—"

"Ju...liah!" Birch interrupted with elaborate diction, and when he continued, there was a note of wicked mischief in his voice that did nothing to still her qualms.

"On second thought I *will* go with you, Hugh, old pal. On one condition, I'll go," he said. "Tha's if you put on a blindfold while we're eating. Julia c'n referee 'n count the spills 'n when we're all through dinner she can pin a medal on the one with the fewest spills. Jus' like old times. See which one of us 's top dog."

Through it all Julia sat listening in horror—helpless, hopeless horror, wishing she had it in her to throw a tantrum or fake a faint. Anything to bring this nightmare to an end.

It was a Birch she didn't know. It was as if he resented his old friend because Hugh could see. She understood then the full dimensions of Birch's suffering. For a moment everything stood still.

Birch, whose hearing had become extremely acute as if to make up for lost sight, broke the silence. "I hear someone at the front door, Julia," he said. "Could you see...?"

Though she'd missed the sound and had for the moment forgotten about Cora Meigs, Julia knew immediately that the housekeeper had arrived and let herself in with her own key.

"Excuse me," she said, and like a freed bird, escaped and flew to intercept Cora in the front hall.

"Am I ever glad to see you," she said, keeping her voice low. "I'm in a quandary. I don't want to leave. Birch has been...drinking."

"*Drinking*, for goodness' sakes!" the housekeeper repeated with disbelief.

"Quite a lot," Julia said reluctantly. "His friend Hugh Dryden's here, and Birch expects me to go out to dinner with him...."

"Has he been drinking with Hugh?"

"No. Oh, that's right—you know Hugh," Julia said. "He just got here. Birch has been drinking alone. I can't understand it. As long as I've known Birch I've never seen him drink more than small amounts."

Cora chuckled indulgently. "Well, *I* have," she said. "Only that time his friend Hugh was as drunk as he was. They were all of seventeen, and thought they were surely going to die. Birch swore he'd never do it again, and I'd be willing to bet he never did. Until now, it would seem."

"I can't go off and leave you—"

"Sure you can. Mind if I run in and say hello to Hugh before you leave?"

"By all means, but I feel awful about—"

"About what? Leaving Birch with me or me with Birch? Don't be. In either case both of us will be all right. Relax, dear. Run along with Hugh and have a nice dinner.''

Not much caring at this point if Birch caught on that she'd sent for Cora to stay with him, Julia went back to the study, the housekeeper beside her.

It was plain to her that whatever had been said between the two men in her absence had done little beyond causing the urbane Hugh Dryden to look even more discomfited.

"It's Cora, Birch. She came back early tonight," Julia said as she entered the room.

"Don't get up, Birch," Cora said as Birch started to rise unsteadily to his feet. Slowly he let himself back down in his chair. Hugh came across the room and put his arms around the housekeeper in a bear hug that lifted the chunky little woman off her feet.

"Hugh, you scamp. Put me down so I can look at you," she ordered sternly, laughing at the same time. "I haven't seen hide nor hair of you since your bylines started showing up in all the papers. I liked you better when you shaved. Without the mustache and that silly beard you'd look just like Peter Jennings on ABC."

"Hey, don't knock my hirsute adornments. They're the work of one of the most famous tonsorial artists in Paris, and they don't come cheap. If you could convince me I'd look like Jennings I'd get rid of them both."

"Whatever," Cora said with a sniff. "Is your wife with you, or are you alone?"

Julia saw Hugh stiffen, once more uncomfortable. *Poor man,* she thought. *He's really getting the treatment tonight.* She should have told Cora about the divorce when it had occurred, but she hadn't thought of it.

They'd married in London and the marriage had ended before she and Birch had had a chance to meet the bride.

"Alone," he said shortly. With a glance at his watch he turned to Julia. "If you're ready, maybe we'd better be on our way. If we don't get caught in traffic we should get to the restaurant about the time our name is called."

Left out of the conversation, Birch sat slumped in his chair, his eyes half-closed. Approaching him from across the room, Julia dropped to her knees beside him, turned his face and pressed her lips to his in a gentle goodbye.

"I'm sorry," she said softly in his ear, meaning it; she was sorrier for *everything* than she'd ever been in her life. "I love you. Be nice to Hugh when you say goodbye. Please, darling, if not for him, for you. For me."

Birch rose unsteadily again and held out his hand for Hugh to take. "So long, Dryden. Till we meet again in...better times," he said, his voice suddenly hoarse with emotion. "Thanks for... Oh, what the hell? Be very good to Julie. She's my other half."

HE LISTENED DULLY to their voices as they moved away, on down the hallway and out the front door. When the sounds were gone, he felt for the chair with the back of his legs. In line with it, he sat down again, slumping deep into the seat.

He sat very still, waiting for his head to stop going around inside. His mind was fuzzy, but not so fuzzy that he didn't despise himself. It was a feeling he'd never before experienced.

He heard footsteps slipping softly along the hallway carpet and closed his eyes, pretending to be asleep, not ready to talk to Cora—old friend, surrogate mother— just yet. He'd been furious for a moment when he'd realized Julia had overridden his wishes and called her back to stay with him. Assessing his immediate condition realistically, he forgave Julia, deciding it was just as well Cora was here. It was tricky enough to circumnavigate the furniture, but he'd managed to screw up the room entirely trying to show Julia he could get the damn bar cart where he wanted it and fix himself a drink without her help.

His head gradually began to clear. One piece at a time he put together his own indictment: he'd shown her, all right. And made a royal horse's ass of himself. Two double Scotches and he couldn't wait to cut Dryden down to size!

Why should he mind that Julia was going to dinner alone with Dryden? he wondered. He hadn't minded in Paris. He'd never thought of himself as a jealous type.

Of *course* he didn't mind. Not as long as he upset the bastard's apple cart first and made sure Julia wouldn't forget over dinner which one of them was king....

As miserable as he'd ever been in his life, Birch dropped his face in his hands. For the love of God, what was happening to him? He'd never been able to drink and he knew it, so what had made him belt down two double Scotches with no more than a couple of breaths between them?

The answer was there almost before the question was formed: he couldn't stand the thought of Hugh Dryden's pity. Or was it that he couldn't stand the thought of sending Julia off alone with Hugh? In any case, he'd gone for the normal adult antidote, he thought with bitterness. He'd had a drink...a double. And then another double. And then he'd embarrassed Julia, alienated his old friend and humiliated himself.

"How about a cup of coffee, Birch? Black and strong, the way you like it?"

From her voice he located Cora Meigs across the room, standing in the study doorway, and roused himself. Sitting up straight, he turned his head to her. "Sounds fine. That is, if you go back and get another cup for yourself and join me."

"I intend to," the housekeeper said. "I brought my cup along."

He heard the sound of a tray being slid onto the table next to him, and in his mind's eye, saw the old family Sheffield tray and graceful silver coffeepot. The brew's rich aroma drifted soothingly into his nostrils, and he breathed in deeply. He held up his hand and in a moment felt the handle of a cup near his fingers. He closed them, and by the feel of it, he knew it wasn't a cup, but an ancient porcelain mug, at the bottom of which a frog squatted. The mug had been given to him by Cora when he was very young. Knowing the frog waited to grin up at him when he reached the bottom had broken him of dawdling over his milk.

He lifted the mug carefully to his lips. When he was satisfied he'd gotten it there without spilling anything, he took a cautious sip of the hot liquid and let it roll back over his tongue.

"Did I ever tell you you make the best coffee in the world, Cora?" he asked.

"Oh, pooh, it's just the cup. You'd always drink anything out of that mug."

"Where the devil did you find it? I haven't thought about that frog for years."

"One of the things I kept. Brought it when I came back. It was always a good distraction."

"You think I need a distraction?"

"A distraction from running away. That's what all that Scotch drinking was, wasn't it, Birch?"

He sipped his coffee in brooding silence. At last he said, "I suppose."

"On your twelfth birthday you ran away because you hated the way things were going at home. And when you got back, it was all waiting there for you, just the way you left it," Cora reminded him slowly. "I thought you'd figured out then there are some things you can't run away from."

Silence settled between them again.

Then Birch said, "I won't say I'm crazy about the way life's going right now, but if you're worried I'm going to try to drown it in a bottle, don't bother. I never will."

"Birch, lad, I never for a minute thought you would," said the housekeeper, getting to her feet. "Just the same, you're going to feel terrible in the morning if you don't eat something. I'll go put some food on the table for us. I'll call you from the kitchen when it's ready."

There was a dull ache at his temple and a bitter taste in his mouth, though his mind was reasonably clear. He didn't feel drunk, just sluggish. He also didn't feel like eating, but he knew Cora was right. Waking up tomorrow would be hell if he didn't.

Something inside told him it was going to be hell regardless. Most days seemed so now....

God, how he hated being blind. It hadn't been so bad at first. He'd been so absolutely certain he would get back his sight simply by coming to terms with the promise he'd made his father. Now the sureness was gone. He'd begun to wonder if what Dr. Inzelman spoke of as "psychic trauma" went deeper in him than the promise. Perhaps there was something his conscious mind didn't know about, over which he had no control.

It was driving him crazy. All of it. All of *them*. All those well-meaning friends and acquaintances flying in like bluebirds of happiness with casseroles and cognac and tape recordings of bland, upbeat books. And, *oh God*, Julia. His dearly beloved Julia. The thought of what he was doing to her made him sick—a different sick than the way he was sick with love for her; a sickness of longing that swelled in him and collapsed at the slightest reminder that he was blind.

But she hovered over him! Dammit! If only she wouldn't hover and be so bent on getting him away from the apartment into unfamiliar places where he didn't know his way around. And she kept wanting to have people in to see him. Couldn't she understand he needed to be left alone?

Sometimes it seemed as if the only people he felt comfortable with were the other blind people at the rehab center. They didn't treat him as if he'd lost all ability to function or, worse, as if he'd suddenly become stupid or sprouted a second head.

Oh God, oh God! Would he ever see again? Sometimes he wondered.

A cloud of despondency settled over him, and for a moment he gave in to it. Then with a deep sigh, he levered his way out of his chair and fumbled through the maze of furniture until he at last found the phone. Careful not to press the wrong buttons, he touched the numbers that would summon his brother.

"Matt," he said when the familiar voice answered, "that psychiatrist friend of yours . . . how about getting an appointment for me? As soon as you can."

CHAPTER SEVEN

THE NEXT MORNING Julia overslept and awoke with her hand outstretched to touch Birch. She was surprised at first when she didn't find him, then her mind unfolded in layers, remembering first that she was alone and then that she was not in her own bed nor in her own room. And the reality that hit her each time she'd awakened since that traumatic morning at the hospital struck her full force again: *Birch was blind*.

As she had each time previously, she rejected the notion initially. It was a nightmare, she told herself. It wasn't true. Then, fully awake, she acknowledged the truth with a shudder and hurried on to other things. To dwell on Birch's blindness was to paralyze herself.

He'd been sound asleep when she walked into the bedroom after Hugh had brought her home. Pajamaless, he'd been lying spread-eagle on his back, cattycorner across the big bed they normally shared. Gazing on the sleeping man—so terribly damaged yet so handsome, so beautifully male—the killing anger she'd first felt against his attackers blazed again and vanished in sudden longing to strip off her clothing and lay her naked body on top of his. Halfway down the row of tiny buttons in her suit jacket, she'd remembered the condition he was in when she last saw him. She'd hesitated, unsure what his reaction would be if she went through with it, and suddenly she hadn't felt strong enough to risk rejection.

She'd finished undressing in the dressing room, slipped on her nightgown and gone to sleep in the bedroom across the hall. Waiting now for the push she needed to get her up, she let her thoughts drift to the evening before.

It wasn't one she'd care for a repeat of, even though Hugh had passed off Birch's alcoholic performance with good humor and had been decent enough to express grudging and affectionate admiration for his old friend.

"Considering what's happened to him, you've got to admire a guy who can still put the ball in the other guy's court," he'd said wryly. "No one can ever accuse Birch Cheney of lacking esprit."

Actually, Hugh had been so bent on convincing her that Birch's behavior hadn't put any strain on their friendship, he'd made the first part of the evening almost fun. He'd started off by regaling her with tales of his and Birch's harum-scarum escapades as boys together, and had gone on to entertain her with anecdotes of the famous and powerful, gleaned in his journalistic career. Hugh, like Birch, knew how to make her laugh, and she hadn't done much laughing for a long time.

It wasn't until dessert that things had got heavy, when Hugh started questioning her about the attack in the park and what it had done to Birch. Looking back, she realized uncomfortably what a surfeit of anxiety and frustration she'd dumped on the poor man last night. It was as if someone had pulled the cork and everything that had been bottled up inside her for weeks had come pouring out.

Into Hugh's listening ear she'd spilled all the worries that had gone too long unheard. She'd imposed on their long friendship to unload everything, from her misgivings about Birch's doctors and Inzelman's glib diagnosis of amaurosis to her fear that her failure to get Birch to an ophthalmologist could jeopardize a chance of his regaining his sight.

And as if that weren't enough, she'd told Hugh about Birch's new vulnerability, and how when she brought him home from the hospital she'd made up her mind to save him from the humiliations of his helplessness as much as she could. She'd even mentioned how good she'd gotten at anticipating his needs before they occurred!

She'd told that to Hugh Dryden, of all people! In the light of day, she was mortified to think she'd betrayed Birch to his friend, and for no good reason. It certainly hadn't earned her any pat on the back from Hugh, she thought wryly, remembering his parting words.

"Give him a little room, sweetheart," he'd said. "Birch has always had a great instinct for survival. Let him work it out on his own. Trust him to yell for help if he needs it. And for God's sake, don't fuss over him."

But what did Hugh Dryden know? she thought a little crossly. Just because he and Birch had made like Tom Sawyer and Huck Finn when they were kids, Hugh thought he was an authority on Birch Cheney.

Smiling faintly, her thoughts went back to Birch across the hall in their big bed. She wondered if he was awake.

With the picture of his naked body fanned across their bed at the top of her mind again, she felt a rekindling of sensual heat. On impulse, she threw her peignoir over her nightgown and padded across the hall. Quietly she opened their bedroom door, and to her surprise, found the covers thrown back and Birch gone.

"Birch?" she called out, thinking he must be in the adjoining dressing room or bath. When he didn't answer she hurried inside and, not finding him, left the bedroom and started through the apartment, calling his name.

"He's all right, my dear," Cora said, coming to Julia from the kitchen. "He's taking a little walk before breakfast, while it's still reasonably cool."

"Walk?" Julia repeated in alarm. "By himself?"

"Well . . . yes. He had his cane."

"Why did you let him go, Cora? My God, don't you realize he could be killed? You should have called me. I would have gone with him."

"I don't think that's what he had in mind, Julia. He's going to have to learn to get around by himself sometime, and now seems as good a time as any. There aren't a lot of pedestrians on the streets this time of day," Cora said reassuringly. "It's not like it's Times Square."

"I've got to go find him."

"My dear Julia, if I were you—" but Julia was gone.

Half-frantic with anxiety, she was running back to her dressing room where she pulled a bra and underpants out from a drawer, tossed them on the tiled counter and hurriedly washed her teeth and face. In her haste, as she reached for her underwear she bumped a tray of perfume bottles with her hand, tipping several over and knocking the stopper off one.

"Damn!" she muttered as she righted the open bottle and saw it was one called Antonia's Flowers, a unique blend Birch had first gotten for her at a small shop in East Hampton—one she wore so often it was almost her trademark. She mopped up the spill with a towel and snatched up her pants and bra from where the scent puddled. Over them she put on jeans and a plaid shirt, and then she slipped a pair of tennis shoes on her bare feet.

Cora was waiting for her when she came out. "Would you mind if an old lady who cares about the two of you asks what you are planning to do?"

"Find Birch! I can't have him out there alone."

"I'm not sure about that, Julia, but supposing you're right. How's he going to like it when you grab his arm and lead him back home like a naughty child?"

On her way to the door, Julia stopped in her tracks and stared back at the housekeeper. She shook her head as if to clear it. "Oh, Cora! What am I going to do?"

"If it'll make you feel better, go down and look for him," Mrs. Meigs said. "I doubt if he'll go any place but around the block a few times, this first time out. He should be easy enough to spot."

"But he'll be furious when he finds out I've followed him."

"He would be, if he could see you."

Julia sighed unhappily. "You're right, of course. We always promised we'd never do things like that to each other, but I can't see any other way."

OUTSIDE, in front of the apartment building, Julia paused nervously and looked in both directions. Seeing no sign of Birch, she hesitated a moment longer, trying to decide which way to go. If Mrs. Meigs was right, it really didn't matter; she'd find him as long as he hadn't ventured outside the boundaries of the block. If he had . . . she couldn't bear to think about it.

Starting off at a fast clip that matched the anxious beat of her heart, she turned the corner and had a clear view up to Columbus Avenue. There were few people out and no sign of Birch. Jogging now, she continued on, her apprehension growing with every step.

Turning onto Columbus she ran into a heavier flow of foot traffic and slowed again to a fast walk as she zigzagged in and out among pedestrians.

Two young women, each with stroller and child, had stopped in the middle of the sidewalk to chat, oblivious to the barrier they were creating. Julia fit herself into one of the lines of disgruntled people breaking around them and forged on. In the clear again, she looked up to the corner, and her pulse leaped in relief as her eyes found Birch.

He was standing on the sidewalk not far from the curb, his body facing downtown, his head turned to the right as if to observe the oncoming traffic. The breeze had tossed his thick, dark sandy hair into pleasing disarray, giving him a carefree look belied by the slender white cane in his hand. He stood very still, almost as if he were listening.

What was he doing there? she wondered, and came to a stop to watch. Why hadn't he turned left when he'd reached the end of the last building, and walked on back to Central Park West where he belonged? For a moment she thought he had gotten turned around. She was about to go to him until she realized he was showing no signs of confusion. He held himself straight, his shoulders back and his head up with a new kind of alertness.

In the next second the light changed, and people began to cross the street. Julia let out an audible gasp as she saw Birch step off the curb and sweep the ground ahead of him with his cane. Her heart beating erratically from a new location in the hollow of her throat, she took off after him—furious at herself for not stopping him before he got onto the street, furious at him for being there.

Keeping apace with the other pedestrians in the crosswalk, Birch was already nearly across by the time she drew close enough to reach for his arm. The housekeeper's words came back to her just in time.

How *would* he like it if she were to lead him home like a naughty child? Did she really care to risk finding out? She let her hand drop without touching him and followed him with her eyes.

She saw the tip of his cane touch the curb and held back, watching as he hesitated momentarily before taking a cautious step up to the sidewalk and moving on with care. She pictured the old Birch, a camera or two slung casually over one shoulder most of the time, sallying forth wherever he went with easy confidence.

Anger swelled in her. Anger at the cruel injustice. Anger at the shattering realization, growing stronger with each passing day, that there wasn't a thing she could do about it—not a single damn thing. For a moment she closed her eyes, unable to bear the sight of the once self-confident man she adored feeling his way uncertainly along the street.

Following a few steps behind him, she took small comfort in the fact that other pedestrians on the busy walkway made way for him, reminding her that the city was full of normal, decent people. The reminder did nothing to erase the reality of the mean ones and the crazies and the indifferently careless, who made the streets unsafe for people like Birch.

Up ahead he approached another cross street, clearly intending to go on to the other side. She stood back and watched tensely as the light turned green. She saw him step down from the curb and then, with something like his old agile grace, unexpectedly step back.

Only then did she hear the clatter of small wheels and see the approaching danger. She suppressed the yell of alarm that rose in her throat when a teenager on a skateboard thundered out of nowhere and skimmed around the curb corner perilously close to Birch. Mentally she added teenagers on skateboards to a growing list of reasons Birch shouldn't be out alone.

He hesitated before moving on, and she saw a pleasant-faced young woman, herself only a few years out of her teens, step up to him. Moving as near as she could without crowding them, Julia heard the young woman offer to help him across the street, saw his jaw tighten, his cheeks flush. Then his face relaxed in the wonderful, friendly smile that had won people in every part of the world for as long as she had known him.

"That's a gracious offer and hard to refuse, but I'm trying to learn how to do this myself," she heard Birch say. "Thanks for your concern."

"Have you been at it long?" the woman asked.

"First time out alone," Birch told her, starting to move forward again.

The young woman walked slowly a few steps away from his side. "No kidding? I saw you get out of the way of the guy on the skateboard. You're doing a great job." She stopped talking to look at him closely as they moved on.

"You've got that cane, so I guess you're blind, but you'd sure never know it to look at you," Julia heard her say after a minute and was astonished to see Birch grin wryly.

"Thanks again. I assure you I'm not faking it," he said. He had turned his face toward the young woman's voice, and Julia could see the scar from the slash on his cheek. It had healed into a long, intriguing dimple that gave a Pan-like look to that side of his face, especially when he grinned—something he hadn't done often enough lately for her to have noticed it before.

The young woman slowed her steps and stayed with him as he crossed the street, uttering pleasantries as they moved along but offering no more help, even when he paused uncertainly for an instant at the curb.

Julia followed a few steps behind, listening curiously, not missing a word.

"This is where I leave you," the young woman said when they reached the other side of the street. "Good-bye now. Keep up the good work. You're pretty incredible."

"Thanks. I could say the same to you," Birch said, smiling again with a look of genuine pleasure Julia hadn't seen since—she couldn't remember when.

He moved on ahead, but the young woman stood for a moment looking after him before she turned and caught the light to cross Columbus Avenue and disappear into one of the small shops on the other side. Instinctively, Julia knew that in that last moment as she'd watched him go, Birch's erstwhile companion had not been looking with pity upon a blind man. She'd been looking with respect on as attractive a man as she'd ever seen, knowing she was unlikely to see him again.

One thing was sure: whatever uncertainties blindness had burdened him with, Birch was still the same virile, vitally attractive man he'd always been, Julia thought as she followed him on his way, amused to add to her list of reasons he shouldn't be out on the streets alone, young impressionable women with pleasing voices.

At the end of another block, when she'd begun to wonder if he would lead her all the way to Columbus Circle, Birch turned himself around and stood for a minute as if to take stock of his situation and get his bearings. From only a few feet away, he looked directly at Julia and she had the eerie sensation, as she had a few times previously, that she'd suddenly become invisible. Facing north now on Columbus, he set off along the route they'd come, in what proved to be their return trip. As he came toward her, Julia stepped out of the way of the sweeping cane and fell in behind him again.

Though he moved with more confidence now and no hazards arose along the way, Julia felt a moment of great relief when they came to the end of the long block between Columbus and Central Park West and turned south again on their home street. Without hesitation, Birch walked to the entrance of their apartment building and went directly in.

Behind him but still outside, Julia was mystified. How could he be so sure he was entering the right building, she wondered; then, in a fatuous double take, thought, *Darling Birch, how clever you are!* as she realized he must have counted his steps to the corner and counted again on his return to bring him back to where he had started from.

Entering the building, Julia saw he was waiting at the elevator. About to retreat, she saw that he'd turned his head at the sound of the front door opening and was aware of a new presence inside.

She motioned frantically to Gallagher, the doorman, before he could greet her and give her away. With her finger to her lips and a definitive shake of her head, she managed to convey to the bewildered doorman that she didn't wish to be identified. She stopped a short distance from the elevator and waited in silence, half-convinced that Birch had taken the sound of her coming for the sound of someone going out. When the elevator door sprang open, Birch stepped inside and turned so he was facing the lobby.

"Get in, Julie," he said. "You may as well ride up with me."

She was too shocked to speak. When she'd recovered enough so she could, she decided not to. If she kept still he might eventually conclude the opening door had let someone out, not in. Why had he thought it was she?

"Come on, love. It's not like you to be coy. You've been following me since I turned around. God knows for how long before that."

With a resigned sigh, Julia gave in. "Darn you, Birch Cheney. How did you know it was me?" She stepped into the elevator beside him. Counting, he moved his forefinger up the control panel and pressed the number 5 button. The elevator started to rise.

"That's a nice perfume, Julie," he said, "but it's too damned expensive for a woman to take a bath in."

Julia groaned. "You smelled me, dammit. That's how!" Recovering, she said, "If you think I smell expensive, wait till you walk into the bathroom. I spilled Antonia's Flowers all over the place." Inspired, she added, "It was so strong it gave me a headache. That's where I've been. To get aspirin. Out to get aspirin. We're all out."

She ran out of words, and then in the next instant she couldn't believe what she was hearing from Birch. For the first time in nearly three months he was laughing—a great belly laugh that started as a kind of snickering sound in his throat and expanded from a dry chuckle into a rumbling bellow of mirth. In the confined space of the elevator he groped and found her. Letting his cane fall to the floor, he pulled her into his arms and burrowed his face into her luxurious hair.

"Oh Bride, Bride," he said, a little laughter still left in his voice. "Now I know why you're the most honest person I've ever known. It's because you're the world's most inept liar."

"Moi?" she asked innocently into his collarbone, almost giddy with relief that he wasn't coldly furious with her, as she'd expected him to be.

"Yes, you. I'm not sure how long you were on my tail, but almost from the first, I suspect," he said. "I caught your scent when I turned around to come back, and it's been with me ever since."

"You aren't mad at me?" she asked in a small voice.

He didn't answer at once. Oblivious of the fact that the elevator had come to a stop on their floor, and that they stood framed by its open door, he pulled her more closely into his arms—so close it was hard for her to breathe. He held her next to him for a long, still minute, then gradually let her go, drew a deep breath and let it out in a resigned sigh.

"When I first realized you were there—yes. I'll be honest. I was mad," he said seriously. "But then as I went along, knowing you were trailing along behind me like some guardian angel, it came to me that being angry with you was just adding another dimension to my personal hell."

"You're not going to be angry with me anymore?" she asked dubiously.

"We-e-ll . . . God knows, I'll try not to be," he said after a moment's thought. "Look, Julie, I love you with all my heart, but if you don't stop smothering me—"

"*Smothering!* But that's not what I'm—" she blurted out defensively, then stopped. She went on, her voice hardly more than a whisper. "I'll try not to, Birch. I really don't want to smother you."

She meant it, but even as she said the words she was wondering how she could get around them. Birch had no concept of how helpless and vulnerable he was, nor should she inform him. Knowing would destroy his intrepid spirit. Calling her "smothering" had saved him from the humiliation of facing the full extent of his handicap, she thought sorrowfully.

Still in his arms, she wriggled her own arms free and wrapped them around his neck, her hands pressing his face down to hers. Moistening her lips, she rubbed them gently back and forth over his until he opened his mouth and took hers in a fervent kiss.

After a long moment they pulled away from each other, and she saw for the first time that she was looking out upon their own private foyer. At the same time a light on the elevator call panel summoned their trysting place to another floor. Julia let her arms fall from around Birch's neck and pressed the hold button to keep the door from closing with them still inside.

"Darn!" she said. "Someone wants the elevator just as I was beginning to like it here."

About to guide him out, their recent words came back to her just in time. She bent and retrieved his cane, slipping it into his hand as unobtrusively as possible, and stepped out into the hall ahead of him, reaching back to release the elevator.

Wrapped in the warm cocoon of the moment before, her head full of visions of a long, lovely morning interlude in their king-size bed, she wasn't prepared to be pulled back to the moment by Birch's asking for the time.

Glancing at her watch, she said, "It's a few minutes after nine, but does it really matter, darling? Couldn't you skip the rehab center today?"

"No," he said without elaboration. With his free hand he reached into his pocket and brought out the key to their door. Julia sprang forward automatically to take it from him and as quickly drew back. The morning had lost its glow. Disgruntled, she watched him struggle first with one of the double locks and then the other. When both gave in he pushed the door open and stood aside for her to enter.

"Matt said he'd pick me up, so you won't have to take me," he said. "I'd better go tell Cora she can fix breakfast."

But he didn't go. Letting the cane fall again, he reached out his arms and she walked into them, to be enfolded with her ear next to his pounding heart. Her own heart raced suddenly to match it.

"Too bad we got off to such a late start," he said softly into her hair. "But it's a start, dear bride, it's a start. We'll have all day to look forward to tonight. Let's try not to forget where we left off this morning."

HER WHOLE BEING warmed by a new feeling of hope, Julia dreamed through the morning and planned the evening to come, with the intention this time of leaving nothing to chance. She began by calling the Vivian Beaumont Theater at Lincoln Center and arranging for two tickets to be held for that evening's performance of the long-running musical playing there. Then she went to Cora, who was running the vacuum in one of the far rooms of the apartment.

"I was wondering if you'd seen the musical at the Beaumont, Cora?" Julia asked, when the vacuum had been silenced, knowing quite well that she hadn't.

"No, but I'd like to. They say Bill McCutcheon's a riot. I remember him from way back."

"Good, because I've come by two tickets for tonight that I can't use, and I thought you might like to take the night off and see the show with your sister or someone. After all, I do owe you one for last night."

"You don't owe me anything, Julia, but it would be nice. My sister and I haven't done things together so much since I came here."

"Then the answer is yes?"

"What about you folks?"

Julia gave the older woman a conspiratorial grin. "We have our plans."

Cora blinked. She said nothing for a moment, then asked curiously, "He wasn't mad? You were together when you came back, so I guessed he caught you."

"He caught me, all right," Julia admitted sheepishly, "and yes, he was mad but he got over it and now...well, everything's wonderful. Better than any time since..."

She left it hanging. She still had trouble saying the word aloud.

Cora gave her a sympathetic smile. "In that case I'll be glad to take the tickets off your hands, my dear. I may even stay overnight with my sister and come in early tomorrow, if you think the two of you can make it all right without me."

"I think we'll do just fine."

The phone called Julia to another part of the apartment, and as she went to answer it she heard the vacuum cleaner start up again.

An unfamiliar male voice at the other end of the line greeted Julia when she picked up the phone. She had to ask him to repeat his name.

"Oh, Mr. Langley, of course," she said on the second try, recognizing the name of the family accountant, if not his voice. "I'm sorry Birch isn't here. I assume he's the person you want to speak to. I'll be glad to take a message."

"What time are you expecting him home?" His was a cold, nasal voice that made no effort to encourage amenities and left Julia feeling less than friendly.

For a moment she debated what to say, then settled for the truth. "Around five. I can have him call you, if you like."

"Tell him I'll be there to see him at five-thirty."

If he came, they'd never get rid of him, Julia thought despairingly. The mood would be spoiled; their beautiful evening together would die an early death. The man must have learned his manners from Birch's father, she decided, not caring that the thought was mean spirited.

Aloud she said into the phone, "I'm afraid you'll have to come another day, Mr. Langley. Birch and I have made plans for the evening."

"This has to do with the family business. It's important and won't wait. I'll be there."

"But Birch has been out of the family business for years," she protested. "I don't want to seem rude, Mr. Langley, but as you know this has not been an easy time for him. I have to ask you to please refrain from bothering him with whatever is on your mind. I suggest you talk to his brother. He's been in charge since their father died."

She heard an angry snort at the other end of the line.

"That's what I'm coming to talk to Birch about. Tell him five thirty." The line went dead.

MATT'S CAR had been delayed in traffic and Birch was late getting home, but when he finally arrived, he was in a more expansive mood than Julia had seen him in during all the weeks he'd been blind. For a moment, as he greeted her in the entrance hall with a kiss that was almost exuberant, she thought about telling the doorman to send Langley packing. But how could she, without Birch's knowing? He was blind, but he wasn't deaf; and when he heard, he'd want a full explanation. She might as well tell him now.

His response was immediate and filled with dismay. "Why didn't you turn him over to Matt?"

"I tried, but he said Matt's what he wants to see you about."

"Oh hell, it's the same old story," Birch said with a disgusted sigh. "Matt's got the makings of a damned good executive, and it's what he wants, but my dad and Langley have called him an irresponsible playboy so long they've got him believing it himself. Now he's in a position of responsibility, and he doesn't have any confidence in himself or his own judgment."

The phone buzzed.

"You want me to tell Gallagher not to let Langley come up?" Julia asked.

Birch grunted. "No. I'll see what he has to say."

A few minutes later when the door chime announced the man's arrival, Julia went to let him in. Upon seeing the middle-aged, balding man in the pin-striped suit, she at once remembered him, or at least remembered the heavy-lidded, calculating pale blue eyes in an otherwise forgettable face.

At the door of the study, she paused to let Birch know they were there. "Mr. Langley is here to see you," she said. Alerted, Birch rose from his favorite chair. It pleased Julia to see it was in one smooth movement and with something like his old fluid grace.

"Hello, Evan," Birch said, "Julia tells me you want to talk to me. Please find yourself a chair."

Feeling her presence unnecessary, Julia made a quick exit into their shared office, which opened off the study. She seated herself at her desk and picked up a file filled with notes and memoranda—ideas for a travelers' handbook she'd been thinking of doing before their world had come to an end. She hadn't had the spirit to look at them since.

As she leafed through the collection of papers now, the sound of the men's voices in the next room faded from her mind, and thoughts on the book took over. In the interests of portability there would have been few if any photos in it, so they'd always considered it "her" book. But it wasn't really hers, she realized. It was a collaboration. Birch had suggested it to begin with, and some of the best ideas were his.

Through all the agonizing she'd done since Birch had been hurt, she hadn't let herself think about what they would do with themselves if Birch never regained his sight. A blind photographer? And what would happen to their partnership—their marriage—if she hired a camera man and went on without him?

Now, unexpectedly, she saw the handbook in an altogether new light. They wouldn't be the first husband-and-wife team to make a career of a travelers' handbook kept current by frequent updating. With hundreds of thousands of new travelers hitting the market each year, there was always room for one more good travel book. They could still do the traveling part of it together. They might even do a spin-off on traveling for people with disabilities.

She was startled out of her fantasy by Birch's voice, calling her from the next room.

She found him sitting solidly in his chair, but Langley was standing. The animosity that hung on the air was almost palpable.

"Yes, Birch?"

"Would you mind showing Mr. Langley to the door, Julia?"

"This way, Mr. Langley," she said, and with a fervent hope that the visit hadn't put a hex on the rest of the evening, she hustled the man out of Birch's presence.

"You didn't waste any time getting rid of our visitor," she said on her return to the study. "Mind if I ask how you pulled it off?"

Birch grunted. "I told him to go to hell."

Julia raised her eyebrows. "My, my. That's hardly your style," she teased. "You usually accomplish your purpose with more ... *je ne sais quoi.*"

Birch grinned. A good sign, Julia thought.

"I didn't exactly put it in those words, but he got the message," Birch said. "Can you believe it, the bastard came to get me to vote my company stock against Matt."

"I'm not sure I understand."

"Well Matt's really only the interim CEO right now. He's only filling in until a stockholders' meeting is called to vote on someone to replace Dad," Birch said. "I believe I told you Langley had inherited some of the stock and thinks he runs the place. Well, it now appears he's managed to scoop up some more shares and is trying to get himself voted in as CEO in Matt's place."

"But you and Matt hold the controlling shares, don't you?"

"Only as long as no one gets control of enough proxies to override our combined voting shares. That's what Langley's visit was all about. He's got the mistaken idea that as long as the company keeps paying dividends, I don't really give a damn what happens in management, especially since...the lights went out," Birch explained. "So he comes here with the old pitch about playboy Matt, and has the unmitigated gall to tell me I've no choice but to vote for him, Langley, because if Matt ever gets in charge, the company's headed for the tube."

"Not a nice man!" said Julia. "But as long as you and Matt stick together, he can't do anything, can he?"

"Only if he can convince enough shareholders that what he says is true and get their proxies. It's a chestnut I can't pull out of the fire for Matt this time," Birch said with a sigh. "He's going to have to figure out how to go after those proxies for himself."

Watching him as he talked, Julia was almost glad Langley had taken it upon himself to barge in on them just now. It had made Birch forget for a while that he was blind. For the first time since what they'd come to refer to as "the accident," Birch was thinking with feeling about something outside himself. But had the negative reactions erased all the progress they'd made in the elevator together this morning?

She saw him shift his body in his chair. As if the movement freed him from the problem holding him there, he held out his hand and motioned her his way.

"Come here to me, Bride," he said, smiling. "I seem to remember you and I have some unfinished business to attend to ourselves...."

CHAPTER EIGHT

FOR WEEKS, Julia had dreamed of times past when they'd explored the infinite varieties of making love. Now, her body was moist with the warm, sensual fluid of desire, but she came to Birch's chair almost hesitantly.

Easy does it, whispered something within. Yesterday they'd plunged headlong into lovemaking as if time were running out, and look what had happened. Tonight was for building—little by little, touch upon touch, caress upon caress.

At his chair she took the hand he held up to her and pressed her lips into his palm for a long moment before slipping into his lap and cradling his arm around her so that her breast lay in the hand she'd just kissed. She heard the sharp intake of his breath and lifted her face until their mouths came together and their tongues began a slow, provocative dance that left her breathless and dizzy. When at last she pulled away, his eyes were closed and his breath was coming quickly. She wanted to kiss his eyelids, but she restrained herself, fearing that he might attach some negative significance to the act. In the curve of his lap she felt the rise of his desire. This was her lover, she thought, her rapture touched with sadness. For there was a difference now—a difference that sometimes made him a stranger she didn't understand.

His hand moved to push aside the soft cotton dress she'd chosen to wear because it was cool and loose and gave him easy access to her nearly naked body beneath. She felt suddenly shy, more shy than she'd felt as a bride. Afraid, too; afraid she would do or say the wrong thing and destroy the magic.

Easy does it. It was happening too fast. They were rushing into another yesterday.

Reluctantly detaching herself, her voice throaty with love, she said, "Whoa, lover, methinks we'd better slow down. We're running away with ourselves."

For a moment he tried to hold her, to stifle the rise of resentment at the momentary feeling of rejection her words brought. Then his mind broke through his cloud of sensual euphoria and recalled the debacle of the morning before. He loosened his hold on her and let her slip away from him to perch on the arm of his chair. She took his hand again and held it securely in hers.

Struggling to cool his smoldering passion, he breathed in deeply and waited to speak until his thinking cleared. Then he understood the wisdom of what she'd said and done. "You may be right," he said, with no enthusiasm. "Could I interest you in adjourning to our bedroom?"

"Not only can you interest me—I insist," Julia said, rising to her feet from the chair arm. "But later. First we dine. Cora Meigs spent half the day creating a divine salmon and cucumber mousse and, as the real estate people say, 'much, much more' for our pleasure."

"How about doing dinner later?"

"Not a chance," Julia said. "There's a strong possibility eating won't even be on our agenda later."

"So?"

"After all the trouble Cora went to, we couldn't take a chance on her coming back early in the morning and finding everything still in the fridge, untouched."

Smiling slightly, Birch asked, "Then I take it we're all by ourselves till morning? What happened to Cora?"

"I happened to come by two tickets to the musical at the Beaumont, and Cora didn't mind taking them off my hands," Julia said innocently.

"You are a sly one, Bride," Birch said, his face breaking into a grin.

"It's so balmy out, I thought it might be nice to eat on the terrace and smell the honeysuckle. It's just beginning to bloom."

Birch was already on his feet, his cane in hand.

"I'd offer to help you carry things out, but you know how I am. All thumbs," he said lightly, with a self-deprecating laugh. Recognizing the valiant stab at humor for what it was, Julia stared at him, bemused. It was black humor, and not one of the year's ten best one-liners; but it was a joke, nevertheless. In it she caught a glimpse of the old Birch and felt a sudden new rush of hope.

"It's amazing what lengths some people will go to to get out of domestic chores," she said in the same vein. She could barely get the words past the lump that filled her throat, and when they were out, she was terrified that she'd gone too far, until Birch answered with a chuckle.

"Well, go on then, and take care of your 'woman's work,'" he said, moving unhesitatingly into the hallway ahead of her. "I'll wait for you on the terrace."

"Wait a minute, Birch—" Just short of saying, Let me help you, she stopped. He wouldn't take kindly to her offer of assistance. But though the terrace was enclosed by a three-foot brick wall topped with wooden boxes overflowing with plants, the very thought of Birch out there by himself set off all her inner alarms.

"Yes?" Birch asked amiably, his cane poised to move on when he'd heard what she had to say.

She couldn't risk shattering his beneficent mood. "Never mind," she said. "I'll be out in a minute with our food."

Then, as she watched him move on down the hallway leading out to the deck, she couldn't stop herself from calling after him. "Sweetie, don't forget when you get out there that the wall's not all that high. It's a long way down to the street." The words were no more than out before she wanted to call them back.

"Dammit, Julia," she heard him say, and was not surprised to hear a sudden edge in his voice. She retreated softly to the kitchen. There she hurried to load a wheeled serving cart with linen, silverware, dishes and food. Adding a bottle of white wine in an ice bucket she trundled the cart out to the deck.

She found him standing close to the wall, facing the french doors that opened onto the terrace from the living room, his head turned at an angle, as if he were listening to the symphony of street sounds far below. Leaving the cart beside the table, Julia moved quietly across the tiled deck and slipped her arms around his waist, sure he had heard her coming, and that he was still cross over her ill-considered warning.

When he didn't immediately respond she stood away and ran her forefinger gently down the length of the mark left by the assailant's knife on his left cheek. "You've no idea how distinguished it makes you look," she said.

"Things to be grateful for," Birch said tonelessly. There was a moment of silence that he ended with a groan. Catching her hand, he pulled her to him and enfolded her in his arms.

"I'm sorry, Julie. God, I'm turning into a real sorehead." His voice was filled with remorse. "I know you don't mean to sound patronizing, but when your voice takes on that nurturing tone and you start counseling me as if I were a six-year-old and none too bright, it cuts me down. I find myself acting like I'm six."

What could she say? He didn't want to hear the truth—that she did it for love of him. What he wanted was to hear her say she'd never do it again. But her words didn't wait for permission. When her anxiety for him took over, the words just came rolling out.

"Don't worry about it, Birch. I'm sorry, too," she said quietly. "Neither of us seems to be able to quit doing what we do." She sighed and eased herself out of his arms.

An uneasy quiet settled over them as she readied the table for them to eat. She lifted the wine from the bucket and then retrieved the cork puller she'd set on the cart, too. Suddenly she wished she'd brought a corkscrew, even though she might have ended up mutilating the cork and getting bits of debris in the wine. She'd never gotten the hang of the two-pronged puller Birch favored for opening wine. He maneuvered it so deftly, working the prongs in on either side of the cork to exactly the right depth, and with a twist and a quick pull it was out. Of course, he wouldn't be able to maneuver it so deftly now...or would he?

Debating whether to go back for the corkscrew or do what she could with the two-pronged tool, she suddenly decided to ask Birch to open the bottle for her. It would show him she had confidence in him. Maybe he'd forget what he'd considered her put-down a few minutes before.

"Could I get you to open the wine for us, darling?" she asked. "I always end up pushing the cork down into the bottle or breaking it into little bits."

He looked at her in surprise and she could see the request pleased him, but he hesitated a moment before he answered. "I don't mind giving it a try."

She watched him finger his way around the bottle opening until he was satisfied with the juxtaposition between tool and bottleneck. With a slight rocking motion he pushed the prongs down inside the neck and pulled.

There was a faint popping sound as the cork came out and Birch's eyebrows rose in surprise. In the next instant his mouth curved into a slow, wondering smile. "How's that for revenge?" he murmured.

Julia gave him a startled look and then chortled with relief. She'd asked him to do it on impulse. The second after she'd asked, she had thought, "Suppose he fails?"

The palms of her hands were moist with the sweat of her fears. She rubbed them down the sides of her cotton gown and said with a touch of her old sassiness, "Glad you haven't lost your touch, great man, or we'd have to give up drinking wine. Show me a device that uncorks a bottle, and I'll show you a device that has my number."

Sitting at the table now, Birch reached and found her, wrapped an arm around her and pulled her down to him for a kiss, letting her up again with a pat to her fanny.

"If you're determined that we should eat, let's get on with it, my sweet. Need I remind you, man cannot live by bread alone."

The silliness set the tone for dinner. Cora had made sure there was nothing to cut and little to spill except the wine. Birch, heady from the triumph of the cork, made a show of disappointment that the menu didn't include artichokes or lobster or the like—foodstuffs more of a challenge to his developing skills than salmon mousse.

Then, just as Julia had begun to worry how they were to reach the security of their bed without breaking the spell, Birch pushed back his chair and rose, reaching to touch her shoulder. "I've cleaned my plate. Now, can we go to bed?"

Julia jumped to her feet and into his arms, still not sure how they were to get there.

Birch quickly put her mind at rest. "Keep your arm around me, and we'll go together," he said simply. Thigh to hip, arm in arm they made their way to their bedroom, he holding her closely, she steering their course.

When Birch's leg brushed against the bed, he came to a stop and let his arm fall away from her. His hand found her forehead and his fingers moved to trace the contours of her eyelids, her nose, her lips and the delicate cleft of her chin. Touch and memory shaped her face in his mind. Her neck felt as smooth and silken as the skin of a ripe pear. He pressed his lips into the hollow of her throat. She smelled of Antonia's Flowers.

Fingering the low-cut neckline of her dress he explored the soft fabric that fell away from its binding in small countless folds. Moving on a fraction, he found that under the cloth her breasts lay bare.

The tumescent nipples pressed into the palm of his hand, and he uttered a sound of pleased discovery. He took first one, then the other in his mouth, bathing them with his tongue until she cried out with rapture and pressed her hands upon his head to hold him there. He slipped away to cup a breast in his hand and touched the circle of moisture left by his mouth. He had trouble catching his breath.

As long as he had this with Julia, he thought, he could learn to live with the rest. While they'd been away from each other all day, he'd fantasized the postponed tryst so often his need for her throbbed in him now like a second pulse.

As if she had read his thoughts, Julia said softly, her voice husky with desire, "If you want to curtail the preliminaries, I won't mind. The dress comes off over the shoulders."

Birch slipped the garment down over her arms to fall in a circle around her feet and came back to roll off the lacy bikini pants he'd touched as he dropped the dress. When she was naked, he scooped her up in his arms. He heard her sandals hit the floor as she kicked them off her bare feet. He laid her carefully across the bed. Peeling the polo shirt off over his head, he finished his own quick undressing and lay down beside her, seeking her bare breasts. Finding them with his mouth, he dallied and then moved down to explore her navel with his tongue and bury his face in the soft, wiry triangle of curls that pointed the way to where he longed to be.

He raised himself over her, and the night hummed with the music of their wordless endearments as her fingers curled lovingly around his erection, and she spread her thighs. Her hand guided him to the hidden chamber he longed to enter, and the wonder of what was happening carried him over a threshold beyond the reach of reason. A sudden thoughtless hunger to gaze on the beauty hidden by the dark impelled him to reach for the light.

Julia's voice, thick with passion, murmured lazily, "What is it, love?"

At her words, the dream ended. He plummeted back to his world of unrelenting darkness. The torment of his blindness poured over him anew like a deluge of cold rain. He felt sure then that he would never see again; felt sure, too, that the full joy of making love with this woman he adored above all would nevermore be his.

"Birch, darling. Oh my darling, what's the matter?" he heard Julia cry out, as if from a distance.

I'm blind, he said in his mind but had no voice to say the words. Oh, God! I'm really blind. Knowing he had taken her to the top of the mountain and was leaving her to find her way down as best she could, he groaned. It seemed the subtlest cruelty of all. He couldn't help her. He needed help himself. He was lost.

His body leaden, he moved away from her, turning his back to her and burying his head in the curve of one arm.

Julia lay stricken, frantically searching her mind for a clue as to what had gone wrong. Had she been too eager, come on too strong? Their lovemaking had always been straightforward, from the heart. They'd let their passions lead them where they would. But before Birch had lost his sight, that had been true of all aspects of their life together. A growing fear that she must now always be on guard—even when she poured out her love—gave her a stark feeling of loss.

She moved nearer to him and softly stroked his bare shoulders and back, desire still throbbing within her. "Birch, what happened?"

His only response was a stiffening of the shoulder muscles under her hand.

"Please, darling. You've got to tell me," she pleaded, unable to keep the sound of despair from her voice. "How am I to know what I did to cause it, unless you tell me what it is?"

Though a part of him felt dead, Birch knew he had to speak to Julia. His voice muffled by his own misery, he said, "It's me, Julie. Not anything you've done."

Struggling, too, for control, Julia didn't respond at once with words, but leaned forward and kissed the back of his neck, then left a sprinkling of kisses on her way around to tease the lobe of his ear with her tongue.

"It's all right, dearest," she said when she could trust herself to speak. "I've read that this happens to every man sometimes. Roll over and let me hold you, love. We'll forget."

"Don't, Julia. Please. I'm not 'every man,'" Birch said wretchedly. "I'm the guy who got mugged in the park and came out with various and sundry traumas, of which this appears to be one."

"That's not true, Birch," she said. "Just give it a chance, darling." She moved her hand around his waist to gently caress his belly. He pushed her hand away.

For a moment she was too hurt to speak. Then she said in a small, miserable voice, "I love you, Birch."

And Birch groaned.

"Oh God, Julie," he said at last, "there's no way you can understand. After two failures I think I've got the message. You know I love you, with all my heart, but I'm not in a hurry to risk a third failure that would put us through this kind of hell again."

If he had struck her, Julia couldn't have felt more destroyed. For a long time, she lay still beside him, frustrated in body and mind, her whole spirit rebelling against what he had just said. Finally she got up and

made her way to the bathroom in the dark, forgetting in
her stress that she could have switched on the light by her
bed without fear of disturbing Birch. In any case, there
was a tenseness about his still body that told her he was
no nearer sleep than she. He'd known she was leaving
and he had let her go, she thought, her hurt now cou-
pled with resentment.

To ease the aching pulse within, she stood under a cold
shower until she was covered with goose bumps. When
she'd toweled herself dry, she brushed her teeth and
slipped a soft cotton nightgown over her head.

No way you can understand, he'd said. What did he
mean? No way she could understand what had stopped
their lovemaking so abruptly?

Or had he meant there was no way she could understand what it felt like to be blind?

In the drawer before her, a black elasticized headband she wore when she ran caught her eye. Picking up
the band, she impulsively slipped it on, pulling it down
over her forehead until it covered her eyes so tightly it
shut out even the faintest glimmer of light. After a moment she began to move uncertainly, feeling her way out
of the master suite into the hallway, the main artery of
the apartment.

Following its walls with her hand, she had no trouble
reaching the living room, where she moved by memory
from one piece of furniture to the next until she reached
the center. There she stood for a moment, then slowly
began to turn. Gaining speed she went around and
around until she began to feel dizzy. Completely disoriented by the time she came to a stop, she waited for her
head to clear.

Groping for landmarks to tell her what direction she was going in, she started off cautiously, a single short step at a time, her hands out to feel the way ahead.

When she'd traveled what seemed the full distance across the living room without touching anything, she began to have a disconcerting feeling she was in a place she'd never been before. Surely her own living room didn't have so much empty space, she thought, and a step later she fell headlong over some small, low object, bumping her head on a table corner on the way down.

She scrambled to sit up and yanked the band off her eyes. By the pale light from the window, she saw beside her the small needlepoint footstool her mother had embroidered for her, the obvious cause of her downfall. Sitting on the floor, she buried her head in her arms and wept for herself and for Birch.

He was right. She could play her child's game of being blind and get a sense of its awfulness, but it didn't help her to understand what being blind did to someone who couldn't pull off the headband when the game got too much to bear, what it could do to her when that someone was her beloved Birch.

When she'd cried out all her tears she pushed herself up on her feet and walked a few steps to the powder room off the hall, hurriedly grabbing a handful of tissues from the counter and blowing her nose, even before she turned on the light. When the light was on, she saw that a lump had popped out on her forehead where she'd hit the table, and her eyes were puffy and red.

"If you aren't a sorry sight," she said aloud. In all the five years of their marriage up to the first moment after she saw Birch at the hospital, she hadn't shed a tear, and tended to be disdainful of easy criers. Now, in an exercise in futility, she'd poured out a bucketful. She was none too pleased with herself.

In their bedroom again, she stood for a moment looking down at Birch's still figure by the light through the open door from the bathroom. He lay turned away from her, as she'd left him. She was sure he was not asleep, and considered slipping into bed next to him and curling her body around him. The strong, beautifully sinewed body seemed paradoxically vulnerable. She longed to take him in her arms and make him forget.

But she'd already done that. She wasn't ready to set herself up and risk being shot down again.

For the second night in a row Julia settled herself in bed in the room across the hall, the second night in all the years of their marriage that they'd slept under the same roof in different beds.

Sometime in the last hours before dawn, after she'd made a tangle of her sheets, thumped her pillow until it threatened to leak feathers and called into service every time-honored trick to vanquish insomnia, she counted her last sheep and fell asleep.''

ALONE IN THEIR BED, Birch served out his time—a prisoner in a night of despair. He heard Julia leave and come back and heard her leave again, but he didn't stir from where he'd first turned away from her. Half-sick with fear that the battering that triggered his blindness had made him impotent, too, he lay wrapped in a near-paralyzing misery. So entangled was he in his own torment, he failed to take note of the dull thud that fell distantly on his ears from another part of the apartment.

Thank God, the appointment Matt had made for him with the psychiatrist was first thing in the morning. He'd been at a low ebb and a little drunk when he'd called Matt last night. Off and on all day he'd been on the verge of canceling. He still thought he didn't need a psychiatrist to tell him his hang-up had something to do with the promise and his relationship with his father. Given the time and the patience, he could work through it alone without exposing his psyche to some head doctor who could only tell him what was there to be found out for himself.

But that had been today, before his new nightmare—hinting at some dark, hidden emotional secret so deep-seated he hadn't even suspected it was there—had raised its ugly head. If he was impotent, he knew damn well he needed professional help.

Under the shadow of the new fear, Birch's mind moved as if by magnet to the unthinkable thought: what if, after all, he was doomed to live out his life in darkness? That thought was joined by another unthinkable one: what if he could never again fulfill the love he shared with Julia? He'd been deprived first of his sight, then his career—the soul-satisfying work of making pictures—and now the joy of their love's fulfillment. What was there left him in life to be savored?

Why me? Why the hell me?

A terrible, consuming rage seized him and overcame rational thought, until at last he raised his fist and drove it into the mattress with all the explosive force of his bottled emotions. Quieted by the single act of violence, he listened to another small, inner voice that said, *Why the hell not me?*

Rolling over on his back, he opened his blind eyes and saw in the darkness the darkness of his future. He vowed then to put himself in the hands of the rehab center and learn to function within the limitations of his blindness as efficiently as he could, and after that to find something productive and rewarding to do with himself that didn't depend on his ability to see.

Of one thing he was certain: blind or not, he had to learn to control his own life again if his and Julia's relationship was to come back to normal—even survive.

With the thought of Julia, the new fear washed through him again like a wave of nausea. He closed his mind against its sickness and thought instead of Matt's friend, Dr. Luke Shields, the psychiatrist to whom he was preparing to bare his soul in a few hours.

How *many* hours? he wondered, impatience burning inside him like an ulcer. The fact that he couldn't tell night from day without locating a phone and dialing POPCORN was suddenly galling. He lay perfectly still and listened for distant street sounds that would herald the morning, but the apartment was too far up from the ground and too well insulated to allow him a clue. Eventually he dozed, and awakened later to the same driving impatience for morning and his appointment with Dr. Shields.

He felt as if he'd been in bed forever. It had to be morning. Rolling across the bed, he fumbled and found the phone. On his first attempt to find out the time he got a surly wrong number. Breaking the connection, he swore and tried again.

"Good morning. At the tone Eastern Standard Time will be three forty-seven and fifteen seconds," the recorded voice announced. Birch put down the phone with a groan of disappointment. It was still a long time until daylight.

He slept again, dreamed of Julia and awakened pulsing with desire. With his hand, he reached to her side of the bed. Not finding her, he remembered the bedroom across the hall. Hopeful, suddenly, he left their bed. He stood for a minute, recalling the path he had to take. Feeling his way, he started off, thinking through each move before he made it, out the door and into the broad hallway until his hand touched the opposite wall. He fumbled for the door and, finding it, stilled. Only then did he realize that in the effort to get there, he had lost the urgency of his desire.

Leaning his forehead against the doorframe, he pictured Julia in bed on the other side of the door and felt a new ripple of arousal that faded away as it became the focus for his hope.

He stood there for minutes in a kind of limbo, longing to go to her, if only to hold her in his arms and tell her he loved her. But suppose he found again that tenderness was all he was able to give her? Tenderness alone would never repair the damage his ardor had already dealt her tonight.

His beloved, passionate Julie! How could he carry her again and again to sensual highs without being sure he could take her all the way? The risk of destroying the one perfect thing in his life—her love—by endlessly disappointing her was a gamble he dared not risk.

Turning away from the wall with a sigh, he felt his way back across the hall and into his bed, but not to sleep. There was no rest there for him tonight. When restlessness finally became unbearable, he left the bed and made his way into the dressing room and bathroom, where he labored through the difficult steps of getting himself ready for the day.

Not until he was shaved and showered and was applying a towel to his dripping body did he think about what he was to wear. For the first time since he'd come home from the hospital his day's apparel was not wait-

ing for him on a rack within easy reach of the shower,
laid out by Julia. Nonplussed, he reviewed the room in
his mind before feeling his way hesitantly to the walk-in
closet with its wall of drawers. Pulling out a drawer, his
hands dipped into filmy pieces of silk and lace that could
only belong to Julia. Finding his own territory, he felt
through more drawers until he'd collected socks and
jockey shorts and one of the easy-to-get-into cotton knit
polo shirts he'd taken to wearing. After he'd put on these
items, he reached into the closet and pulled a pair of
pants off a hanger at random.

When Cora Meigs arrived somewhat later, he was
standing at the window in the study deep in thought,
staring out as if he could see. At the sound of her key in
the door he put the tool of his blindness, the wandlike
cane, into action and went to meet her.

"What time is it, Cora?" he asked at once after they'd
said good-morning.

"Seven thirty-five," the housekeeper told him. "Are
you going for a walk again?"

"Not this morning," Birch told her. "I've got an appointment downtown at eight-thirty."

"Looks like I'd better drop my overnight case in my
bedroom and hustle up some breakfast for you in a
hurry. Is Matt picking you up?"

"No. I'm taking a cab," Birch said.

There was a long moment of silence in which he imagined the look of astonishment Cora Meigs was directing at him. He braced himself for her demur, which
never came.

"Oh...well..." she said, and he heard her move away
from him, presumably to her room.

He followed the by-now familiar line of the hallway
into the kitchen, and felt his way along the counters to

the phone. Picking it up, he carefully tapped out Matt's number.

"Sorry to wake you, Matt," he said when his brother's sleepy voice answered. "I just wanted you to know you don't have to take me to Shields's office this morning. Go back to bed and sleep for another hour."

"Julia's taking you?" Matt asked, his voice surprised.

"Julia's asleep. I decided it was about time I started riding taxis," Birch said.

There was silence at the other end of the line. Then Matt asked, "Have you told Julia?"

"That I'm going to a psychiatrist or that I'm taking a taxi?"

"Now that you mention it, either. Both."

"No."

There was another pause. "But you are going to tell her, aren't you?"

"Yes, about the taxi."

"What about the psychiatrist?"

"Yes. But in good time, Matt," Birch said, a little testily now. "First I want to get an idea of how things are going to work out."

FOR A MOMENT after Matt set the phone back in its cradle at the other end, he felt a disappointment so strong it was almost anger. Dammit, he'd been counting on Birch to tell him what to do. Now he wasn't even going to see Birch before he confronted Langley this morning.

There was no question in his mind that what Langley was up to could not only bring down Langley but cast doubt on Cheney, McCrae's long-standing reputation for integrity. But suppose he was wrong?

If he was right, somebody had to hurry up and blow the whistle on the guy or it would be too late. Instinct also told him that if he blew it before he had Langley cold, he'd be putting Langley in the catbird seat.

He'd wanted to wait for Birch to get squared away with his own problems before he yelled for help, but since he had found out the night before that Langley was out gathering proxies, he'd known time was running out. Someone had to do something in a hurry or the Cheneys would no longer be in charge at Cheney, McCrae, and everything would be out of control.

God! If only he'd started out proving himself from the day he'd walked into the firm, maybe now he'd be ready. He should have shown initiative instead of slinking around in Birch's shadow as long as Birch was there. Maybe if he had, they would have listened to him when Birch quit the firm and he tried to convince them he was capable of handling some responsibility himself.

God! He'd gotten so he took himself at *their* value. They'd managed to destroy his faith in his own judgment when a real crisis arose. He was the little brother, the playboy, the klutz! The one from whom no one had ever expected much.

And maybe they were right. He couldn't handle what was going on down there at the firm alone. Suppose what he was thinking of doing was all wrong? By the time the press and the courts got through with the company there would be nothing left. On the other hand, suppose he was right, and waited until he'd ironed out all his own uncertainties. The lull could give Langley a chance to squeeze the last Cheney out of the firm and take the company to hell before anyone caught up with the bastard.

The most important decisions in his life, Matt had made with Birch's support. This was by far the most important he'd ever had to face, and he was damned if he was going to go it alone.

He reached for the phone, dialed Birch's number and was greeted by Cora, who, after a few moments of affectionate pleasantries, turned the phone over to Birch.

"Forget about the taxi, Birch. I'll pick you up and take you to Luke's office," Matt said quickly. "There's something I've got to talk to you about."

For a moment Birch said nothing. Then he asked, "Something about Cheney, McCrae?"

"And about Langley," Matt said, wondering how Birch had guessed that much of what was on his mind. "A hell of a big problem has arisen, and I'm not sure just how it should be handled."

"Listen to me, Matt." Birch's voice came to him firmly over the phone. "It's time we got something straight. Where the company's concerned your judgment's far better than mine. The fate of the firm's in your hands, and in my opinion that's where it belongs."

Matt's throat felt suddenly tight. "Thanks, Bro. I . . . wish I had your confidence in my abilities. Since I don't, I really need to talk this thing over with you. How about postponing your maiden voyage in a taxicab until tomorrow and go with me?"

"Not a chance, Matt. You may not know it, but today's a banner day for us, brother. Today's the day you and I take charge of our own lives," Birch said, and Matt was warmed by the camaraderie he heard in the other's voice. "For me, it means taking a cab downtown by myself without a keeper. For you . . . well, you'll know when the times comes, Matt. Trust yourself. Do what you have to do.''

The phone went dead. Matt stared at it in his hand numbly. *Oh God*. He'd been cut loose from his moorings.

After a moment he put the phone back in place and straightened his shoulders. He suddenly felt that for the first time in his adult life he was about to do something right.

CHAPTER NINE

IT WAS ALMOST TEN before Julia awakened the following morning after her stormy night. The moment she opened her eyes and saw she was not in her own room, the recollection of the night's debacle burst upon her. She scrambled out of bed and hastened to get it made and herself back in her own room before Cora arrived and discovered where she'd actually spent the night.

Not that Cora would ask questions. Actually, Julia wasn't sure *why* she didn't want the older woman to know the evening had gone awry, other than a reluctance to see the disappointment it would bring to Cora's face.

The battery in the room's clock had died, so it was not until she crossed the hall and was in the master bedroom that she discovered she was already too late. The bed had been made, and the room put to order. On her bedside table the pretty little antique cloisonné clock given her by Birch told her how much too late she was.

About to put on a robe and join Cora in the kitchen, where she had no doubt she'd find Birch, she changed her mind. She wasn't ready for the kindly sympathy she would see in the other's eyes now that she knew the evening Julia had planned with such high hopes had fizzled out.

Once the water splashed over her in the shower and flushed away the last fuzziness of sleep, Julia felt a bit

easier. She had the sudden hope that by the time she got
to the kitchen Birch would already have explained away
their night apart with a plausible lie, thus sparing her the
dear woman's concern.

She pulled on jeans and a T-shirt and tied the laces of
her tennis shoes, at the same time thinking up entrance
lines that would distract Cora from any mention of what
had taken place during the night. The obvious subject
was last night's musical.

Turning to the mirror to comb her hair, Julia saw
herself for the first time since soon after her fall, and was
appalled. The bump on her forehead was the size and
shape of a halved Ping-Pong ball. Her face was pale and
marked with two dark smudges under her eyes.

She looked like Ratso Rizzo's sister, she thought dis-
gustedly, and rummaged through her limited supply of
cosmetics for makeup to camouflage the telltale evidence of a rendezvous that had gone awry. With a face
like this, asking Cora about last night's performance
wasn't enough to keep her from wondering what had
gone on at home while she'd been away.

When Julia had disguised the damage as best as she
could, she dabbed a bit of peach glow on her nearly col-
orless cheeks and sallied forth, hoping that whatever
conversation Birch and Cora were engaged in was en-
grossing enough to distract from her entrance.

Hearing no voices as she approached the open door to
the kitchen, she peered in to find the housekeeper rolling out piecrust on a pastry board, her back toward Julia. Birch must be in the study, Julia thought.

After a moment's hesitation she slipped away without announcing herself and went to explore the house
from study to terrace, looking for him. She dreaded the
dialogue she knew lay ahead, she also knew she had to

make Birch understand that what had happened the previous night was of no consequence. Fear that he might already have magnified it into a real barrier between them hastened her steps.

When she'd prowled the length of the house and found him missing, she burst into the kitchen, everything else forgotten—last night, the lump on her forehead and her decidedly un-together appearance.

Cora turned her head at Julia's arrival and gave her a startled look.

"Cora, where's Birch?" Julia asked. "He hasn't gone off again on his own, has he?"

"As a matter of fact he has, but don't be upset. Nothing's going to happen to him."

"Why didn't you wake me? You know how I feel about him being out on the streets alone. I'm going after him."

She turned to go, but Cora's next words stopped her.

"He's not walking. He took a cab."

"A cab? Where to?"

"I didn't ask. To the blind center, I suppose. There's no place else he goes, is there? He said he had an appointment."

"Who did he go with, Cora?"

"No one. I told you he took a cab."

"Not by *himself*?" Julia wailed and by the look on the other woman's face, knew that he had. "Oh, my God! That's insane. He'll get run down by a car or mugged or—"

"I doubt that, my dear," Cora said calmly. "He's got to start testing his wings if he's ever going to fly again."

"But he's such an easy target!"

"*Let go*, Julia," Cora admonished her almost plead-ingly. "Unless you let go, one way or another you're going to lose him."

It was on the tip of Julia's tongue to ask the older woman to explain what she meant, but the sight of Cora's glance drifting to her forehead and then away and back distracted her. She raised a self-conscious hand to cover the lump. "I . . . uh . . . walked into a door in the dark," she mumbled and was at once ashamed of her childish ploy.

The piecrust finished, Cora moved over to peer more closely at the lump without comment. Her silent scru-tiny was too much for Julia.

"Look, Cora, the evening didn't turn out like I'd hoped, but if you're thinking *Birch* did this—"

Cora laughed aloud. "Oh for heaven's sake! Not Birch! You forget, he's like my own! Much as I doubt that you ran into a door, laying that lump to Birch would be the last thing to enter my mind."

Julia grinned feebly. "Actually it was the corner of a table," she admitted. "I was walking around in the dark and tripped over something. I fell and cracked my head."

Cora gave her a searching look, but the scene leading up to the accident was not one Julia was about to share.

At the moment her sole concern was that Birch had gone out by himself to hail a cab and had taken off to a destination he'd neglected to mention. But if she was looking for a sympathetic ear to pour her worries into, she had the feeling she wouldn't find it in Cora—nor, for that matter, in Matt . . . or Hugh Dryden—and least of all in Birch himself.

Let them call her overprotective, dammit! Birch was too important to her; *she* hadn't forgotten that it was as a victim of a violent crime that Birch had lost his sight in the first place. Nor could she ignore the fact that he was far more vulnerable now than he'd been when he could see. She wasn't trying to "smother" him or "emasculate" him, she told herself defensively. She was trying to do for him what he couldn't do for himself: keep him out of harm's way—not just cabs and trucks and bicycle messengers and careless drivers, but sidewalk barriers and vending carts and the open maws of underground elevators.

Growing increasingly certain that she could expect no understanding from Cora, Julia poured a cup of coffee for each of them and turned the conversation to other things as she fixed a piece of toast for herself. The housekeeper gave a glowing critique of the musical comedy she and her sister had seen and an affectionate report on the sister's grandchildren. Julia imagined she heard a wistful note in the childless Cora's voice.

Breakfast finished, Julia cleared up their dishes and moved away to the study, where she looked up the number of the rehab center and tapped out the digits on the phone.

"Could you tell me what time Birch Cheney will be through at the center this morning, please?" she asked of the pleasant-voiced woman who answered. "This is Mrs. Cheney, his wife, and I'm checking to find out when I should pick him up."

"Just a moment, Mrs. Cheney. I'll have to look at his schedule." In a few moments the woman came back on the line. "Mrs. Cheney, according to my book your husband will be through at four. He's starting on the all-day regimen today." Julia thanked the woman and hung up.

All-day regimen? It was the first she'd heard of it. *Something's going on here,* she thought uneasily. He'd been so sure he'd see again any day that he hadn't gone near the rehabilitation center the first month after he'd come home from the hospital, and when he finally had decided to enroll, he'd never stayed more than an hour or two at a time. Did "all-day regimen" mean he'd resigned himself to being blind for a long time...forever?

Giving up wasn't like Birch, but the question frightened her, nonetheless. The unexpected move to spend more time learning how to live with his blindness sounded ominously submissive to Julia. It aroused in her a new urgency to get him to the ophthalmologist she'd researched weeks ago—a Dr. Burnside, whose credentials were impeccable. Somehow she had to persuade Birch to put himself in the specialist's hands.

It was bad enough that Birch clung to the verdict of amaurosis, but what filled her with a kind of helpless anger was his stubborn determination to poke around in the dark corners of his mind and try to find the answer to his blindness himself. He might at least go to a bona fide psychiatrist. She was sure he'd learn then that there were no dreadful secrets lurking in his healthy, well-adjusted psyche that could cause him to go blind. Once he accepted that, maybe he'd be in more of a hurry to have Dr. Burnside look for a physical cause.

BY THE TIME she pulled her car into a tow-away zone in front of the rehab center, Julia had herself primed to force the ophthalmologist issue with Birch. It was *her* life, too, dammit! He had no right to shut her out. They'd given *his* way a fair trial and were getting nowhere. It was about time they tried it her way....

She turned off the motor, but stayed behind the wheel so she could move on if she had to, not wanting to risk having the car towed away while she was looking for Birch. As she waited for him to appear, a longing for the lovely worry- and pain-free life that had once been theirs overtook her like homesickness. For a moment she saw the two of them as they'd been then, lighthearted, loving, skipping carelessly all over the world.

But the picture hurt too much. Summarily banishing her nostalgia, she turned her attention to a dark sedan that was pulling in ahead of her BMW to share the tow-away zone.

Turning her eyes back to the center's entrance she saw Birch. In a perfect Pavlovian response her pulse leaped for joy, and for a fraction of a moment, before the white cane reminded her, she forgot he was blind. A few steps outside the doorway he paused a moment, as if to get his bearings, and then moved forward. She noticed for the first time that he had conquered the shuffling gait that came with feeling his way, and while his advance was somewhat slow and deliberate, he lifted his feet in a normal, surefooted step that belied his blindness. Watching him cross the sidewalk she was choked with pride.

As he neared the curb, she opened the car door and hurried to meet him. "Birch! Right here, darling," she called out.

He stopped, turning his head toward her voice. "What are you doing here, Julia?" he asked after a moment. There was no welcome in his voice, nor in his face.

She was beside him now, and reached to take his arm, but he pulled away from her.

"I came to pick you up," she said, and when he still resisted, she pleaded, "Please, Birch, don't be difficult.

You know as well as I do that you could be killed stepping out onto the street to hail a cab. You can't depend on that white cane to keep you safe," she said.

"I thought we came to an agreement on this yesterday in the elevator," he said in a strained voice.

"I suppose you mean I'm 'smothering' you again. Well, let me tell you, Birch Cheney, if giving a husband a ride home is 'smothering,' there are men being smothered all over America every day by their wives," Julia said tartly. "The car is straight ahead of you."

"Is ours the only car here?"

Julia looked at him in surprise. "A car service sedan pulled in right in front of me as you came out," she said. And then, as the driver stepped forth to stand on the sidewalk beside his vehicle, his eyes scanning the entrance from which Birch had just emerged, suspicion dawned in her.

"Good. It must be the one I arranged to have pick me up," Birch said, his voice harsh with ill-concealed annoyance. He moved away from her toward the curb, reaching out with his free hand until it came in contact with their car.

Speechless for a moment, Julia watched his hand move along the doorframe and around it until he found the windshield. Taking direction from that, he continued on past the car until he touched the sedan directly ahead. Thus alerted, the driver jumped to attention and opened the door for him.

Julia found her voice. "Birch!" she called, starting after him. "This is ridiculous! I'm not—" She stopped. Birch showed no sign that he'd heard. He stopped for a moment to talk to the driver and then stepped into the back seat of the sedan. A few steps away Julia watched

in helpless outrage as the driver closed the door behind
him, got into the seat behind the wheel and drove away.

As Julia fought her way through the late-afternoon
traffic, she noticed her gas tank was nearing empty and
went out of her way to get it filled. By the time she got
back to her neighborhood and parked the car in its stall,
she had begun to feel less angry than hurt, and she
geared herself for a showdown with Birch.

REACHING THE APARTMENT ahead of Julia, Birch
couldn't remember a time in his life when he'd felt more
physically tired. Or more demoralized. Stretched out
full-length now on one of the terrace lounges, a summer breeze whispering through the leaves of the dwarf
pear tree at his head, he looked back on his day, which
had been filled with multiple frustrations.

The early-morning appointment Matt had made for
him with the psychiatrist, Dr. Shields, had started off
well enough, with Birch giving the doctor a brief history of his own background, an account of the attack in
the park and a description of his injuries, to which he'd
added Dr. Kritzer's opinion that in the absence of physical evidence the blindness had to be psychological in
origin and treated accordingly. But for an occasional
question, the doctor had listened closely, taken a few
notes and said nothing.

And there it had ended. Make an appointment for
next week, Shields had said. No therapy would be un-
dertaken until he had been able to review all the existing
records on Birch's condition himself.

Disappointed, Birch had gone on to the rehab center.
There, according to the plan he'd devised in the last
desperate hours of his sleepless night, he enrolled him-

self in the full rehabilitation program. Unlike the doctor, the rehab center was prepared for him *now*.

He'd attended only short sessions sporadically at the center for the past month and hadn't applied himself to his full capacity. His goal had been simply to learn a few basic skills to tide him over until his sight returned. This brief sampling hadn't begun to prepare him for the intensive workout he had been put through today, nor for the discovery that learning—so easy when he'd had his sight—was far more difficult now. Easy tasks were suddenly hard; hard tasks, demoralizing. The effort it took simply to teach himself to swim in a straight line had left him frazzled and out of sorts.

It turned out there was a hell of a lot more to rehabilitation than Braille and finding one's way about with a cane; there were lessons in communication and socializing, mobility, fitness and the arts. Even the lunch hour was put to mastering table skills.

The eight-hour day he'd just gone through had been as grueling as a decathlon. He realized now that he'd thrown himself into it with the same grim, joyless energy he'd put into his work at the family brokerage firm.

Now he was home, and there'd be Julia to face. Julie. The one he loved. And had hurt. How could he explain to her why he had balked when she came to pick him up? He didn't understand the reaction himself. He'd heard her voice and suddenly something had snapped. All he could think was that she was dead set on making him helpless, and he'd be damned if he'd let her get away with it. But even as the hired car had driven away, he'd known he was being unfair. The same mugging that had cost him his sight had planted fear in Julia. It was as simple as that. She could no more help what she was doing than he could help being blind.

His resentment had turned to sorrow for his joyous, brave-hearted Julia, who feared for him now. He wished to God he'd paid off the car service driver and ridden home with her. He'd had the driver circle the block and come back, hoping to patch things up, but by then her car had disappeared.

Sipping the cool drink Cora had brought to him on the terrace, he talked to Julia in his mind. He told her he was sorry he'd ridden away from her, and at the same time he tried to devise a gentle way to make her realize that her hovering was turning him into someone he didn't much like. And soon she wouldn't like him either if she didn't let up.

Lying there in the soothing warmth of the early-summer sun, his hard day—on top of his sleepless night—caught up with him and he fell asleep.

IT WAS THERE Julia found him a short time later when she got back to the apartment. Still a little undone over his rebuff, she gazed down on her sleeping husband from the open French doors of the terrace with an ambivalence that didn't last. In spite of herself her heart stirred with pleasure at the sight of him. Suspecting he'd slept no better than she had the night before, she wasn't surprised to find him asleep.

She watched him for a moment and then slipped quietly back to the kitchen to ask Cora if she'd mind serving an early dinner. She found the housekeeper already busy with preliminary meal preparations.

Before Julia had a chance to speak, Cora said, "Birch looked tired when he came in a while ago, and if you don't mind my saying so, you don't look all that great yourself. You look like you both could use a good night's sleep. I thought it might be good to have an early dinner tonight."

"You read my mind," Julia said, wondering how much the canny woman had guessed about the night before. "What can I do to help?"

"Go back and keep Birch company. Dinner'll be ready in less than an hour. If you insist upon helping, make that two," Cora said her voice only half-teasing.

"Am I that bad?" Julia asked. Because she knew she was, she added with scant enthusiasm, "Someday, maybe I'll get you to show me how to put together a decent meal without getting every utensil in the place dirty and ending up with most of it on the floor."

Cora smiled skeptically. It was a routine they'd been through before. "You have only to name the day."

With a sheepish grin, Julia retreated to the terrace. She and Birch would have a little time to talk before dinner, and there were issues to be settled between them—not including what had happened this afternoon. She'd be darned if she'd let herself waste these moments with him in a fruitless harangue about why he'd spurned her. Anyhow, she knew why; even understood why, in a way. It all had to do with Birch's childish crusade against her "smothering." Talking about it would only lead to a row.

Standing again at the French doors that led to the terrace, Julia saw that Birch had awakened and was sitting in a lounge chair now, both feet squarely on the floor, his elbows on his knees, his chin resting on both hands. Every line of his body spelled weariness—an inner weariness that she suspected went far beyond any tiredness of the body. It was a Birch Julia had never before seen, and the effect on her was devastating. It was as if Michelangelo's *David* had turned into Millet's *The Man with the Hoe*. In that instant she lost all desire for a showdown.

Dry-eyed, she wept for him within. If she could only make him smile, she thought, and paused in the doorway, searching anxiously in her brain for something light and funny to say that would brighten his mood. But she found that all the fun had left her. She couldn't muster up anything for him tonight but her love. Not even desire.

Stepping over the threshold, she hurried across the terrace and saw him raise his head at the sound of her footsteps.

"Julie?" he said and she dropped down before him. She pushed herself between his knees, circled his body with her arms and hugged him with all her might. The force of the unexpected embrace made him grunt, and Julia, still hoping to lift the pall that hung over him, pulled his head down to rain a storm of kisses over his face.

"There," she said as she let his head slip from her hands. "What I'd really like to bring you, dear one, is something to make you happy, but I'm afraid all I've got for you tonight is my love."

"Julie . . ." His voice broke. Burying his face in her hair, he finished hoarsely, "That's all happiness is to me. Didn't you know?"

She knew—and knew they both knew—that until something changed, what he'd said was true. But there had to be something more.

He pressed her head to his heart and held her close, and she felt, rather than heard, the ripple of a groan in his chest.

"Oh God, Julie, I acted like a lout this afternoon," he said. "I'm sorry. Please forgive me, if you can."

"It's all right, Birch. It doesn't matter," she said quietly. "It's just part of it, I guess. I can't help being afraid for you and you can't help..." She left it hanging. After a moment she finished, "I guess that's the way it's going to have to be until...something changes."

She let herself slip down until she sat on the floor, her head resting on his knee. She sensed there was something more Birch had to say, but it seemed he couldn't decide whether to say it or not. She heard him clear his throat.

"Something *is* changing, Julie—at least I hope so," he said. She lifted her head to look at him curiously.

"I had my first visit to a psychiatrist this morning," he said.

She eyed him without enthusiasm. "Not...?"

"No, not Inzelman. A Dr. Luke Shields. Matt got me the appointment."

"What does Matt know about this man?"

"Matt was given the job of checking him out a few years ago, when the son of someone in the firm had a breakdown, and the father was looking for a psychiatrist," Birch said. He added wryly, "You've got nothing to worry about. If Matt's anything, he's thorough. Dr. Shields comes well recommended, his credentials are excellent, and by all accounts both the cured son and his father swear by him."

Julia drew a sigh and let it out soundlessly, deciding it was not for Birch's ears. A psychiatrist wasn't exactly what she'd hoped for, but at least it was a start.

"Well?" she said curiously.

"Well, what?"

"What did he say?"

"My darling Julia, consulting a psychiatrist is not exactly like lancing a boil," Birch said. "Don't you know it's bad form to ask what I said to the psychiatrist or what he said to me?''

Taking heart from the fact that he was loosening up and sounding more like himself, Julia decided to go with the foolishness. ''Come on, Birch. Don't be a spoilsport. I've always wanted to know what a psychiatrist says to a patient,'' she wheedled. ''Just tell me this once. I'll never ask you again. I promise.''

Did she imagine it, or was there a hint of mischief in the twitch at one corner of his mouth?

''You promise? I'll hold you to it, you know.''

''I promise.''

''I'm not sure I can give you a verbatim report,'' Birch said solemnly, ''but as nearly as I can remember it went something like this: Dr. Shields said, 'What is your birth date?' and I said, 'July 10th, 1952.' And he said, 'Where were you born?' and I said—''

''Birch!'' Julia exclaimed. ''Cut that out. I want to hear the good stuff.''

''You mean like how did I get hurt and when and— Am I boring you?'' There was no question now that there was a grin on his face.

Julia yawned conspicuously and patted her mouth with her fingertips, wondering foolishly why she was putting on a show for him when he couldn't see. ''Not at all. I'm enthralled.''

Birch relented. ''That's all we talked about today. Sorry. Shields won't go any further until he's seen all the medical reports. I've got another appointment next week.''

''Good. You can tell me about it then,'' Julia said saucily.

''You promised.''

''This doesn't count.''

"Nothing doing."

"Oh, well! If you're going to play dirty!"

She'd stretched the routine to its limit, Julia thought, rather pleased with herself. Birch's mood had lightened visibly. His hands rested loosely on her shoulders, and her cheek lay contentedly upon the fleshy part of his thigh. Twilight was upon them, and they sat together in the gathering dusk in companionable silence, Julia wondering idly what would happen if she let her hand stroke the line of his inner thigh upward to the groin . . . and beyond.

But she lacked the will to find out. The night before had taken its toll on both of them. Her hand felt heavy. And she guessed that in the light of last night's frustration, it would be disastrous to start something Birch might be too exhausted to follow through on tonight.

"I'm thinking of getting Cora to teach me how to cook," she volunteered lazily after a while, not because it was true, necessarily, but because if they didn't start talking, they would both fall asleep before Cora called them to dinner.

"You *what*?" Birch chortled, startled out of his lethargy.

"What's so funny about that?"

"Nothing, really," Birch said, but she could see he was struggling to hold back laughter. "I was just remembering the time you fixed canned spaghetti."

Julia grinned, in spite of herself. "It wasn't all *that* funny!"

But Birch was not to be stopped. Laughing now, he said, "Remember? You put the can into a pan of boiling water on the stove to heat? Without opening it?"

Julia was laughing, too. "Do I ever! I went to answer the phone, and it was my mother, with all the family gossip. All of a sudden while we're talking there's this sound like a Molotov cocktail from the kitchen...."

"And I'm out in the hall unlocking the door to come in, and a bomb was the first thing that came to my mind," Birch recalled, in high hilarity now. "And we both tore into the kitchen to see what the hell was going on, and all I could see was spaghetti—bright red spaghetti splattered all over the cupboards, the floors, the counters, hanging from the ceiling, the drawer pulls, the sink. There wasn't a square inch in that kitchen that wasn't polka-dotted with spaghetti." By now they were both laughing too hard to talk coherently. Julia got the hiccups. Tears streamed down her cheeks.

Gradually their laughter subsided. Julia lifted herself to curl up in his lap and to lay her head upon his chest. After a moment she burst forth with a final giggle.

"Something I missed?" asked Birch.

"Have you forgotten? You promised you were going to write a testimonial to the Franco-American people telling them how far your wife could make a can of Franco-American spaghetti go." She added reproachfully, "You never did." After a minute she pulled his head down and gave him a fierce kiss.

"I love you, Birch." she said with sudden intensity.

"Not more than I love you."

Warmed by the echo of shared laughter, she snuggled back into the arc of his body, fitting her head under the curve of his chin, listening to the faraway street sounds as the darkness closed in around the terrace. And when Cora Meigs came to call them to dinner a while later, she found them thus, cradled together in the lounge chair, both asleep....

WHEN SHE AWOKE the next morning, her eyes still closed, Julia's first thought was the usual one: *Birch is blind.* There had been a time when her second thought would have been: *Is today the day for him to see?* But that was in the early weeks when she'd still half believed in the miracle Kritzer and Inzelman had held out. Whether the cause of her husband's blindness was physical or psychological, she'd long ago given up hope that he would recover without professional help.

This morning her second thought was of Dr. Luke Shields. Remembering, she felt a whisper of reborn hope. While a psychiatrist wasn't exactly what she was aiming for, she had a gut feeling that if he was any good, at some point he would see to it that Birch was examined by an ophthalmologist.

Opening one eye, she found the cloisonné clock on her night table and saw it was a few minutes after seven. They'd slept ten hours. She couldn't remember when she'd felt so good.

Running her hand across the sheet she found Birch's arm and stroked it gently, torn between not wanting to disturb him and wanting very much to have him awake. He was turned away from her, his body curved like a question mark, and his shoulders rose and fell with the steady rhythm of his breathing. When the touch of her hand failed to rouse him, she slid across the empty space between them and fitted herself around the curve of his back like the interlocking piece of a puzzle. She slipped her arm around his waist, and the rhythm of his breathing broke. She had disturbed him, she knew, but was he awake?

She held her breath for a long moment, listening, and had the unsettling feeling that now he was only pretending to be asleep. She plucked at a hair on his chest.

Birch's body straightened involuntarily and he let forth a yowl of complaint.

"Damn it, Julie, why did you do that?" he said sleepily as he tried to sit up against the restraint of her arm.

"To see if you were awake," she admitted.

"Well, if I wasn't then, I am now," he grumbled.

She pushed him playfully down so that he was on his back and burrowed her nose in the hollow of his neck. "Mmmm. I love the smell of a good man," she murmured. "Essence of Sleeping Male." She moved her head to nip at his earlobe, bathing it with her tongue. He struggled to break away, and in the next moment, pulled free and sat on the edge of the bed, his feet on the floor.

He's getting up! thought Julia in dismay, too shocked for a moment to feel hurt. She rolled after him, grabbing him firmly around the waist with both arms.

"Stay, darling. It's early. Come back to bed for a while," she said, bewildered as she touched proof of the effect she was having on him.

But he broke away from her and stumbled to his feet. One hand out before him as if groping for support, he moved a few steps away. Julia watched helplessly from the bed as he stopped and turned back again.

"Don't, Julia. Please," he said quietly, his voice anguished. "I'd like to...uh...put this on hold for a while."

She stared at him in disbelief. "You mean you don't want us to make love anymore."

Birch groaned. "That's not what I mean at all," he said, but something fearful inside him wondered if he would ever be able to again. "Just until..." He hesitated.

"Until you can see again?" Julia cried, her voice a heartbroken wail.

"Until I can get myself...together...a little more," Birch said reluctantly. "You'll admit I've got a record of failure up to this point."

"Twice isn't a record," Julia said sharply, but her voice softened as she went on. "Actually, there's no such thing as failure when we make love to each other, dear heart. I thought you knew. I don't mind if we don't always get where we thought we were going. It's the trip that counts."

It was in moments like this that Birch felt, in spite of everything else, that having Julia made him the luckiest man alive. Yet he couldn't help wondering if she would say the same thing if every time meant only the trip.

He knew she lay waiting for him on the bed, but he turned and fumbled his way toward the bathroom and a cold shower.

Stopping at the door, he said, "Give me a little time, love, and put your faith in my new shrink."

"It's *us* I put my faith in, Birch," she said, a spark of fire in her voice. "If we went right on making love to each other every day as if nothing had ever happened, you might be surprised."

For a moment Birch hesitated, but in the end forced himself not to turn back. No more trips, he thought grimly, until he could count on how they'd come out.

WHEN SHE HEARD Birch looking for his clothes in the dressing room, telling her he'd finished his shower, Julia got up and slipped past him to the bathroom, making a point of going quietly so he wouldn't notice her passing. She'd be darned if she'd let him think she was trying again to seduce him, she thought spitefully, a bit ashamed that mean-spiritedness had driven out the good humor she'd felt when she'd awakened only a short time earlier.

Hurrying, she showered and dressed in a sage-green cotton print skirt and shirt, dabbed a bit of color on her lips, slipped on a pair of tan leather sandals and ran a comb through her hair.

She arrived in the breakfast room a few minutes later to find Birch at the table listening to the morning news on public radio. At a counter nearby Cora Meigs was in the act of taking a Belgian waffle out of the iron.

Determined to put up a good front, she greeted them with a bright "Good morning." Birch turned down the radio and reached up a hand to her. She thought of bypassing it but in the end took it, and when he pulled her face down to his she went willingly and gave him a fervent kiss. For all the lumps she'd taken in recent days, she adored him. Sulking didn't make hard times better, she thought.

Having surfeited them with plump, fluffy waffles served with apricot-pineapple jam, Cora joined them for coffee and leisurely table talk.

"I'll get the car and pick you up out in front when you're ready to go to the center," Julia said presently, and was not surprised to see a tightening at the corners of his mouth.

"No need to," he said after a moment with an innocence that denied the subject had ever been a bone of contention between them. "Now that I'll be going fulltime, I've made arrangements with the car service to take me and bring me home. You don't need that kind of a hassle twice a day, five days a week."

"Oh," said Julia dully, suddenly deflated. There was something in his voice that told her this was no longer an arguable point.

He reached and turned up the volume on the radio just as the announcer gave the time as eight-fifteen. Reaching for his cane, Birch pushed back his chair and got to his feet.

"I'd better be on my way. My driver will be here by the time I get downstairs," he said, feeling for her chair, her shoulder and finally, her face. Finding it, he tipped it up for a kiss. "You're about due for some time you can call your own. Enjoy it. You deserve it."——

AFTER HE WAS GONE, Julia shooed Cora off to do her marketing and set herself to work clearing up the breakfast dishes, pausing occasionally to stare blindly at the cabinets in front of her.

"Enjoy," he'd said, and closed her out of his life.

What if she couldn't see all that much in her life to enjoy right now? She'd be damned if she was going to spend her days sitting around feeling sorry for herself and worrying about Birch, who'd obviously decided he didn't need her.

She put the last plate into the dishwasher and poured in detergent. Closing the door on the dirty dishes she picked up the phone and dialed Sid Unger's number.

"Sid, this is Julia," she said when the agent answered. "I just called to tell you that if that magazine, *Metropulse*, still wants me to do those articles, I'd be willing to talk about it."

CHAPTER TEN

"I COULDN'T INTEREST YOU in going to a movie with me tonight, could I, Cora?"

The *Times* entertainment section in one hand, Julia peered in the open door of the housekeeper's room, where Cora Meigs sat, her shoeless feet propped on an ottoman as she watched an afternoon soap opera. Over Julia's protest, Cora hoisted her ample body out of the chair and turned down the volume on the TV.

Julia's approach was cautious. She was uncomfortably aware that their occasional sojourns to the cinema together in the six weeks since she'd started writing for *Metropulse* and Birch had withdrawn into the world of the rehab center hadn't always brought the two women equal satisfaction.

"I'm sorry the last one I picked was a dog," she said, thinking it just as well that they took turns choosing what they were to see since their viewing tastes were so different. For every *A Fish Called Wanda* there was an Andy Hardy rerun and for every Busby Berkeley musical, a *Rain Man*.

"Here are a couple you might like," Julia said, holding out the *Times*. "*Big Business*, with Bette Midler and Lily Tomlin—supposed to be very funny, and there's one called simply *Big*. It says here it's sweetly nostalgic and makes you laugh. You can take your pick."

The housekeeper looked at her and said, without enthusiasm, "Not tonight, Julia, if you don't mind. I'm sorry, my dear, but there's this *Cheers* rerun on TV I missed the first time around. It's when Sam and Diane—"

Julia laughed. "You don't have to explain, Cora. If I had something else to do, I wouldn't be looking for a movie myself. I've got this article for *Metropulse* I should finish tonight, anyhow. I thought I'd get it done this afternoon, but I ran into a solid wall of writer's block."

As Julia talked, she noticed Cora sneaking an occasional glance at the silent screen, and she realized she was keeping the other woman from her "soap." "Go back to your show, Cora," she said. "I might as well try to get more done this afternoon before Birch gets back from the center."

Cora reached down and switched off the television. "Don't go. Sit down a minute," she said sympathetically. "You've been holed up in your office all day. You need a break."

"I don't want to interrupt your show," Julia said.

"Nothing'll happen today anyhow. They're building up to something, so anything I miss I can pick up tomorrow. What they do is keep you in suspense a few days and then let you know what it's about," Cora said. "Sit down and tell me how the job's going."

Having no desire to go back to work, and a latent hope that the older woman's company would boost her flagging spirits, Julia took the platform rocker. Cora settled herself back in the easy chair she'd been sitting in.

"The job's...okay," she said with a noncommittal shrug.

"I read your story about Little Italy last week. It was real—" Cora hesitated, as if groping for a word, then finished "—cute."

And Julia said wryly, "Thanks. That's what it was supposed to be." And it was exactly why she hated everything she'd done for *Metropulse*, she thought. The idea of writing the series on the various cultural and racial enclaves of Manhattan—"warts and all"—had seemed like a good one when she'd agreed to do it. Unfortunately the editors wanted her to make Spanish Harlem seem as charming as Martha's Vineyard. They'd forgotten about the "warts," it seemed.

"You don't sound very happy about it," Cora observed.

Again Julia shrugged. "It's something to do."

Out of the silence that fell between them, Cora said abruptly, "I'm worried about Birch. Would you mind telling me what's going on?"

The suddenness of the question caught Julia off balance. "Nothing you don't know about."

"All I know is, he's blind. But it's more than that. He didn't act this way when you first brought him home from the hospital."

"I . . . Cora, I'm not sure I know what you mean."

"Yes, you do." The older woman's voice was impatient. "If you want me to say maybe this is none of my business, I'm not going to. Regardless of what you think, it *is* my business. Birch's mother and I grew up together. We were best friends—closer than sisters." Her voice softened. "She would have loved you, Julia. As for Birch, I couldn't love him any more if he were my own son. And that goes for Matt, too."

"I'm sorry, Cora. I didn't mean to put you off," Julia said, touched. She tried earnestly to make amends. "I *do* know what you mean. It's just that I don't have an answer. Birch and I don't...talk to each other that much anymore."

"I guessed as much," the other woman said. "He's so touchy! Like the other day—he's gotten so good at doing everything since he's been spending so much time at the rehab center, I made the mistake of complimenting him on how well he's doing, and what do you think he said? 'Save your praise until you see me driving a car, Cora,' and the way he said it had an edge like a knife."

What kind of inner hell was Birch going through to vent his frustration on this devoted woman who'd taken the place of his own mother? Julia wondered sorrowfully. If only she could talk to him about it...but she knew anything she said would send him retreating into his shell. Sometime shortly after he'd started regular sessions with Dr. Shields, she and Birch had ceased to communicate on any but the most superficial level.

"It's not like Birch," she said in weak defense. It wasn't like the Birch she'd married, but it *was* like the Birch who'd emerged in recent weeks. These days he took kind words for pity. Praise was "patronizing." Suggestions or advice meant they were "trying to make an invalid out of me" or "trying to run my life."

Silence fell between the two women. Then Cora asked, "Why is Birch going to a psychiatrist instead of an eye specialist?"

"Because Birch wants it that way."

"Didn't an eye specialist see him in the beginning?"

"As a matter of fact, no," Julia said. "The emergency team patched up all the surface damage, and lacking evidence of eye injury, never called in an ophthalmologist to examine him."

"Why not later?"

"He was in a coma at first and then on painkillers. It was a couple of days before anybody guessed he couldn't see," Julia explained unhappily. "By then he was in the hands of a doctor who'd seen some cases of amaurosis in Vietnam and was quick to jump to conclusions."

"Even so, you'd think the doctor would have consulted an ophthalmologist before calling in a psychiatrist."

"It's probably irrelevant, but Dr. Kritzer has a business relationship with the psychiatrist he brought in to see Birch," Julia said with a touch of bitterness, then sighed. "In fairness, a superficial examination didn't turn up anything wrong with Birch's eyes, but the testing stopped there. The doctors agreed it was hysterical blindness—amaurosis. Birch bought it. I'm still trying to get him to an ophthalmologist."

"Is this the same psychiatrist—the one he's going to now?" Cora asked.

"No, thank goodness. This man's supposed to be very good, but I'm beginning to wonder," Julia said. "I thought the first thing he would ask for would be a report from an ophthalmologist."

Neither spoke for a minute and then Cora said, "I take it Birch balks at seeing an eye specialist?"

"He's never actually *balked*, but when I bring it up he keeps wanting more patience and understanding from me. And I thought all the time I was being pretty damn patient," Julia said resentfully.

"I think he's afraid," said Cora.

Julia jumped immediately to Birch's defense. "You know Birch better than that! He's not afraid of anything."

"Everybody's afraid sometimes, Julia. If not, they're stupid," Cora returned flatly. "I think the reason Birch shies away from seeing an ophthalmologist is he's afraid he'll find out something he doesn't want to know."

"That his blindness is incurable?" Julia asked, shaken by the thought of what Birch must be going through if what Cora believed was true.

"Look at it this way. He's got a choice: hysterical blindness they tell him he'll get over, or seeing an eye specialist who could tell him he's going to be blind for life."

"You think Birch is afraid to risk finding out?"

"Wouldn't you be? Only I don't think he realizes he is."

"You mean *subconsciously* he's afraid?"

"If he realized it was fear that was holding him back, you couldn't keep him from seeing an ophthalmologist, if I know Birch."

"I suppose," said Julia after a moment. "But that doesn't explain why he's been so moody."

"I think the reason is this psychiatrist has started him asking questions of himself," Cora said. "He's been doing a lot of brooding. I think he's begun to wonder if the blindness is physical after all. It scares him."

"And I think he's spending too much time at the rehab center," Julia said disconsolately. "He's shutting himself off from the rest of the world. He comes home and lies down out on the terrace until dinner, and after dinner he goes to bed. It's as if he's settling in to the world of the blind."

"Now that he can eat with people without embarrassment, maybe having someone to dinner would help bring him out of his shell."

"He wants to be left alone," Julia said, a touch of resentment in her voice. "He has too many things on his mind to deal with small talk right now. Anyhow, who would I invite?'' she finished in frustration. ''Since the accident, he's been so withdrawn old friends have quit making any effort to see us.''

Cora sighed and reached down to pick up her shoes beside the ottoman. ''I'd better go start dinner. I thought we'd have meat loaf. That takes a while to make.''

Julia was no more eager to go back to her work than she had been when she'd first sat down. She watched the other woman put on her shoes and get to her feet.

''Were you serious about teaching me to cook?'' she asked, looking up from where she sat.

''Of course. If you want to start now, come on out to the kitchen with me. Meat loaf is as good a place as any to start. First I'll teach you how to chop an onion.''

''That's the best offer I've had all day,'' said Julia, getting up from the chair to follow the housekeeper to the kitchen. ''Birch'll be proud of me. I think.''

''GUESS WHO COOKED dinner,'' Cora Meigs challenged Birch later when the three of them were seated at the table.

''I presume you did,'' Birch said, his tone establishing that he couldn't care less. ''Otherwise one of Julia's takeout places.''

''Wrong. Julia cooked it,'' Cora informed him with a teacher's pride for an apt pupil.

''I didn't exactly cook it all,'' Julia said modestly. ''I cooked the meat loaf with Cora's advice and she cooked the rest.''

''If the meat loaf is because it doesn't need to be cut, may I remind you that's no longer necessary,'' Birch said sarcastically.

''She made meat loaf because it takes a lot more doing than a plain, solid piece of meat,'' Cora informed him.

Deflated, Julia said, "You might at least taste it."

Birch tasted. "It's fine."

"Birch! Is *that* all you have to say?" exclaimed Cora. He heard Julia mutter something about being "damned with faint praise."

Looking back on the scene later from the solitude of the big bed in the master bedroom, Birch was annoyed that the two women had ganged up on him. He'd said it was fine, hadn't he? What the hell was he supposed to say about a plain, ordinary meat loaf? Come to think of it, he wasn't all that crazy about meat loaf anyway.

But the episode nagged at him. Would it have hurt him to wax a little more eloquent, considering the meat loaf represented something of a milestone for Julie?

It occurred to him then that he'd been finding it harder every day to wax eloquent over anything. His words seemed to turn to bile before he spoke them. And the words of others took on double meanings as they reached his ears. Like the meat loaf thing. He knew damn well Julie hadn't made it to remind him that for a time he couldn't cut his meat, but it had come out sounding as if that was what she meant.

Before he'd started with Shields, all he'd felt frustrated about was his blindness, and he'd been able to take comfort in the belief that that would end. Since he'd begun to doubt, everything was frustrating.

From the first day, Shields hadn't given him any encouragement. "Let's get one thing straight, Birch," the psychiatrist had said at the beginning of that first session. "Until I have a report from an ophthalmologist telling me your blindness has no physical cause, I have no reason to believe that you have amaurosis. If you expect me to make you see again, you may as well face the fact that you've probably come to the wrong man."

And Birch had said, "An ophthalmologist just means more testing, and I'm not ready for that just yet. Will you take me as a patient, anyhow?"

And Shields replied, "If you want to risk it. You wouldn't be normal if you didn't have some hang-ups it wouldn't hurt to knock loose. And there's always the chance there *is* no physical cause for the blindness, in which case we'll have a head start."

Every session after that there'd been questions: "Have you ever wondered why you don't want an ophthalmologist to examine your eyes?" And, "Tell me. What do you see that's so good about amaurosis?" And, "Why do you suppose you told your brother about the promise to your father but you haven't told your wife?" Over and over, the same questions were put in different ways until by the time he got home at night after his daily workout at the rehab center, they were all he could think about—they, and his terrible longing for Julia.

Shields wasn't that much help there, either. Before he would even discuss the subject of impotence, he insisted Birch have a physical exam, and referred him to a doctor— the Cheney family physician having retired during the course of his and Julia's travels. When the doctor reported Birch to be in excellent condition, apart from his eyes, Shields had said bluntly, "Okay. So you're not impotent. Beyond that, there isn't much I can say except try to remember you don't have to see to make love. You're the same man you always were."

He didn't *feel* like the same man. That other man had never been depressed in his life. That other man had never been afraid of being blind forever. That other man had never been afraid he would fail Julia. That other man had not been afraid of his fears.

"Someone on the phone wants to talk to you, Birch." It was Julia at the bedroom door. He'd turned off the bell in their room so he wouldn't be disturbed, counting on Julia, who was at work in their office, to answer incoming calls. In the unlikely event that one was for him, he'd instructed Julia to deflect it.

"I'm asleep," Birch said over his shoulder. "I don't want to talk to anybody. Who is it?"

"I haven't the faintest idea. It's somebody who says it's important, and that he's got to talk to you. He seemed very determined. I can't hang up on him."

"Well, I can," said Birch testily, rolling over and reaching for the phone.

"Birch!"

At the sound of protest in her voice he relented with a resigned sigh. "Okay, Julia. I won't hang up on him without fair warning." Then, "Hello?" he said into the phone.

"Mr. Cheney?" The voice had a hollow sound as if its owner were speaking through a mailing tube.

"This is Birch Cheney."

"Your brother, Matt, is getting himself in over his head at Cheney, McCrae. Unless he's stopped, he's going to be in serious trouble," the stranger said. "Suffice it to say, it'll be in your best interests as a major stockholder and Cheney's brother to tell him to back off."

"That's very interesting," Birch said, suddenly alert. "May I ask just what you want me to get him to back off from?"

"That's not necessary. Your brother will know."

The phone went dead.

"Mind telling me what that was all about?" Julia asked from the doorway. A moment later he felt the weight of her body as she sat on the edge of the bed beside him. "Who was it?"

"He didn't say, but I think I can make a pretty good guess," Birch said thoughtfully. "As for what it was about, I haven't the foggiest, except the guy was making veiled threats about Matt."

"Physical threats?"

"If it was Langley, disguising his voice, I don't think there's any danger of its being physical. Langley's a slippery bastard, but I don't think he's got the stomach for violence."

"Besides the fact that you don't like the man, what makes you think it might be Langley?"

"Two things. Something about his voice. And 'suffice it to say.' "

"What?" asked Julia.

"I've never known anybody but Evan Langley who said 'suffice it to say.' "

"Do you think he could cause trouble for Matt?"

"I don't know, Julia. There's something going on at Cheney, McCrae," Birch said. "Matt wanted to tell me about it, and I told him I didn't want to hear."

"Birch! You said that to your own brother?" Julia said, her voice disapproving. "You are going to call him now and find out about it, aren't you?"

Birch lay still for a moment, not answering. "Trust yourself," he'd told Matt. "Do what you have to do.... The fate of the firm's in your hands." So what would it do to Matt's belief in his own judgement to have his brother come investigating? It would be doing to Matt's morale exactly what Julia had been doing to his.

"I don't think so, Julia."

"But this call you just had? You've got to tell him about that!"

"I don't think so."

He felt the bed bounce as she jumped to her feet. "Well, *I'm* going to. Matt's got to be warned that someone's out to make trouble for him. Probably Langley. I wouldn't think of letting your brother's problems interrupt your soul-searching. I'll call him from the office," she said scathingly.

"Julie, darling, come back," Birch called out, hearing her footsteps taking her away. But she was gone. He flung himself out of the bed, seizing his cane as his feet touched the floor. Remembering then that he was naked, he felt his way to the dressing room for a robe, out of consideration for Cora, whom he could encounter.

How could he make Julia see that he wasn't doing what he was because he was so wrapped up in his own concerns he was indifferent to what was happening to his brother? He'd never make her understand that if he started looking out for Matt it would damage the fragile fabric of his brother's faith in himself.

He put the robe back in the closet and found his way back to bed. At least he could be sure that through Julia Matt would be put on notice that Langley was after him. He'd known he'd have to get the word through to Matt some way; better he be told by Julia. Hearing it from her could do no harm to Matt's self-esteem.

IT WAS A FORTUNE COOKIE opened while seeking material for a *Metropulse* article on Chinatown a week later that reminded Julia of Birch's birthday ten days away. In the strange language of fortune cookies, the message inside said, "A good man is as rare as a golden egg. Celebrate him on the day of his birth."

The day of his birth? July 10. On July 10 Birch would be thirty-six years old.

Sipping pale tea from a small, handle-less china cup, she wondered what she could do to "celebrate" Birch on that day. How did one "celebrate" a man? The idea rather pleased her.

With love...what else? she thought and realized it had been a while since she'd told him she loved him. Too long! They were losing each other. Birch had begun spending his days away from home, and she'd started writing those stupid, cotton-candy pieces for *Metropulse*.

He might have started coming home early again if she'd been waiting for him there. Then, he might have talked to her about his sessions with Dr. Shields instead of turning inward and becoming a virtual recluse. She might even have gotten him interested in working with her on the tips-for-travelers book she'd thought about that night she waited in the office for Langley to leave.

Picking up her check, she got up and made her way to the cash register with new resolve. It still wasn't too late. The first thing she was going to do to "celebrate" Birch was turn in the Chinatown article and tell Sid she'd do no more ethnic pieces for *Metropulse*.

IT WAS WITH HOPE of breaking down the barrier that was building between her and Birch that Julia began to look for special ways to gladden his thirty-sixth birthday and remind him of her love for him.

Her work for *Metropulse* finished and all ties severed at the end of the week, she sought to enlist Cora Meigs in her cause.

The two women were sipping iced tea on the terrace when Julia first broached the subject. "Cora, what was Birch's favorite meal when he was a kid?" she asked, apropos of nothing.

"That's easy," said Cora. "Baked stuffed pork chops with mashed potatoes and gravy. For dessert—a toss-up between rhubarb pie and chocolate fudge cake with marshmallow frosting."

"Salad?"

"None, if he could get out of it. The same with vegetables."

"How come he turned out so healthy?" Julia said, amused. "He'd be happy to live on green stuff now. He can eat a bushel of asparagus with hollandaise sauce. That's what we'll have. And lettuce with Green Goddess dressing."

"Are you planning a dinner, by any chance?" Cora asked curiously.

"For Birch's birthday. I want a party that will make him forget how rotten things are for him right now," she told the housekeeper. "It seems to me that some of the smells and tastes he remembers from his childhood might be good for starters."

"How many people do you plan to have?"

"Just family. Birch and Matt and you and me. And I'm going to cook it. Can you teach me how to make baked stuffed pork chops and chocolate fudge cake before next Friday night?"

"I don't see why not. But leave Matt and me out of it. What Birch needs more than anything on his birthday is a gala dinner alone with his wife," Cora said. "You can cook for Matt and me some other time. I'll take the evening off."

The suggestion appealed for a moment, but Julia made a generous effort to dissuade her. She was relieved when Cora stood firm.

"If you're thinking of buying presents, you'd better do your shopping in the next few days," Cora reminded her. "Thursday we'll have to buy groceries, and it'll take most of Friday for you to bake the cake and get dinner ready."

Buying small, special gifts for each other had been one of their favorite delights in what Julia had come to look back on as their "other life". As she fingered the bit of amber at her throat, she thought of the compass she'd bought for Birch in Paris and realized that this was the first time since he was blinded that she'd even thought of giving him a gift.

Looking for birthday presents that weren't dependent upon visual appeal, Julia fantasized a scenario in which Birch became so enchanted with the gifts she'd found for him that he forgot his blindness for a few hours and was once more the passionate, unfettered lover of that other flawless time.

At a small gallery in the East Seventies she found two small sculptures—an alabaster bust of a young girl and a free-form piece—that pleased her. Closing her eyes, she studied them with her fingers again and again, finally putting the bust aside. It was too heavy, the marble too cold to her touch. The free-form piece was agreeably light and awakened a wonderfully sensual response in her as she smoothed her hand over its planes and curves.

Walking out on the street with the wrapped piece in a string bag on her arm, Julia understood suddenly what the intent of Birch's birthday evening should be: to reawaken his joy in the four senses that remained to bring him pleasure—scent, sound, touch and taste.

For taste and smell there would be the dinner . . . and then what? Suddenly she grinned. Molasses taffy! If she slipped a piece of molasses taffy into his mouth after dessert, would he remember how he'd said it tasted like the color of her hair?

And there was the Napoleon brandy. She pictured herself on her knees beside his chair after dinner, warming the snifter between her hands to release the aroma of the brandy, lifting the crystal globe to his face to pleasure his sense of smell.

Touch and taste and smell were easy, but when it came to Birch's hearing, Julia despaired. Music had been almost as much a part of their earlier life as breathing. His tastes were eclectic, and back then, she could have given him any music he didn't have—from Beethoven to Bruce Springsteen—and it would have been accepted with enthusiasm. However, now that Birch depended greatly on his hearing to keep abreast of what was going on in the house, music was an unwelcome distraction. The elaborate stereophonic system he'd put together component by component and had once reveled in, had long been silent.

So Julia haunted book and record stores, looking for a narrated tape—a novel, an essay, a poem—that would somehow tell Birch how much she loved him. Scanning titles in a shop one afternoon, a certain set of words insinuated itself upon her consciousness, and she realized suddenly they had been running through her mind like a haunting tune all day.

Let me count the ways...count the ways...count the ways. Let me count the ways.

She put the cassette of a sound-recorded novel she was holding back on the shelf and stood still in the aisle, trying to remember where the words came from and what they meant. For a moment she was a moonstruck girl again perched in an apple tree in her family's Washington orchard, in her hand a book of poetry from her mother's college days.

"'How do I love thee? Let me count the ways...'" she murmured under her breath. Elizabeth Barrett Browning's *Sonnets from the Portuguese*. She'd been sixteen years old and Bambi-eyed with unrequited love for the young, happily married high school athletic coach. She'd been forbidden to read the sonnets by her mother, who considered them "too sophisticated for a young girl", Julia remembered with a smile.

Something delicious bubbled up in her as she imagined herself, for Birch's birthday, reading on tape the gentle, sentimental lines the Victorian lady had written to Robert Browning more than a century ago. No sooner had the idea bubbled than it fizzled out. The old Birch would have been moved by the sweet power of the words, and pleased and amused that she'd chosen such a confection to reaffirm her love for him.

She couldn't be sure how he would react now.

Still, the idea pleased her too much to let go of it. Moving out of the tapes section of the bookstore, she prowled through shelves of poetry and literature and found a single dusty volume of *Sonnets from the Portuguese*, which she bought and took home to read. There she chose a collection of her favorite love sonnets. Putting her whole heart into the passionate words, she read them aloud into her tape recorder, beginning with what she'd decided was the most romantic poem ever written by a woman to a man: "How do I love thee? Let me count the ways," and ending with the sonnet that read:

...a mystic Shape did move
Behind me, and drew me backward by the hair;
And a voice said in mastery, while I strove,—

"Guess now who holds thee?"—"Death". I said.
But, there
The silver answer rang,—"Not Death, but Love."

UNDER CORA'S KINDLY EYE, Julia produced a perfect
chocolate fudge birthday cake with marshmallow frosting on Friday morning, after the first effort had been
wisely consigned to the garbage disposal. By late Friday
afternoon, what Julia had dubbed "the great cook-in"
was over. Cora had left for the evening with a last warning not to let the water under the hollandaise sauce ever
come to a boil. The pork chops, oozing savory dressing
Julia had chopped and diced and seasoned before stuff-
ing into a pocket cut by the butcher in each chop, were
ready to go into the oven. Each fat stalk of asparagus
had been conscientiously "de-spurred", leaving knicks
from the peeler on Julia's fingers to prove it.

Dressed for the evening in a zippered jumpsuit of sea-
green washed silk Birch could see only with his hands,
Julia felt as skittish as a new bride as she waited for him
to come from the rehab center, where he'd been all day.

Waiting for him, she fretted because he wouldn't be
able to see the fantastic cake she'd created. Should she
decorate it with candles he couldn't see? If she did,
would he think them another reminder that he was blind,
and take offense? If she didn't, suppose he noticed them
missing? Would he be upset?

She couldn't keep walking on eggs like this, she
thought suddenly. Last night, with his still, brooding
body turned away from her on the other side of the bed,
a fierce resentment had dissolved her grief for him for a
while. How dared he quit like this? she'd thought. A
man who'd been blessed with numerous gifts. What

right had he to give up because one of those gifts was lost?

The surge of bitterness had passed, but it had left her feeling shaken and unsure. For three months now she'd waited on him, yearned for him, chattered falsely cheerful trivia to him out of the depths of her own grief. And day by day she'd watched Birch become more and more a taciturn stranger.

If she couldn't renew some flicker of his old zest for life tonight she . . . actually, she didn't know what. She only knew she couldn't go on this way much longer.

In the study she paused by Birch's leather chair. On the table where his hand would touch them were the elegantly wrapped packages—the sculpture, the tape, the brandy, the piece of molasses taffy.

So much hung on tonight, she thought. And then she remembered something she'd forgotten—the beluga caviar for before dinner—the taste for which had not yet been acquired in his pork chop days but in later times that belonged to them alone. It had been an integral part of all their celebrations together.

Glancing at the time, she flew to the bedroom for her purse and sped away. If she hurried, she could get back before Birch got home.

As she stepped into a taxi in front of the apartment building, Birch's car service driver pulled up to the curb and let Birch out.

"Wait for me," Julia said to the cabdriver and stepped back onto the street, intending to walk in with Birch as far as the elevator and let him know she would be back shortly. On second thought, she changed her mind; he might look on her unexpected appearance as "hovering," and the whole evening would be off to a bad start.

She got back into the cab. "Take me to Zabar's on Broadway, please," she said to the driver as Birch disappeared into their apartment building.

LETTING HIMSELF into their apartment a few minutes later, Birch called out to let Julia and Cora know he was home. Moving on into the study he settled into the big leather chair.

He had walked out of Luke Shields's office shortly after eleven that morning and had been walking much of the time since. His tired body, sticky with sweat from hours outside in the muggy heat, cooled quickly in the temperate climate of the air-conditioned apartment. He wondered vaguely where the women had disappeared to but hadn't the energy to find out. His mouth tasted as dry as ashes, but the kitchen seemed too far away to go for a drink.

He dropped his head in his hands. The psychiatrist's words that morning came back to overwhelm him with renewed despair. "We've come to the end of our road, Birch. We've explored your relationship with your father in depth and with your mother, your brother and your wife. Looks to me like you've got your head on pretty straight."

"In other words, you're washing your hands of me?"

And Shields had said, "I've done all I can. The rest is up to you: seeing an ophthalmologist, telling your wife about your promise to your father. I won't go on taking your money when I've nothing much to give you in return."

"What if the eye specialist can't find any physical reason for me to be blind? Do I come back to you?"

"To be honest with you, Birch, as a doctor and your psychiatrist, I very much doubt you have amaurosis.

Should an ophthalmologist find no physical reason for you to be blind, we might want to reconsider amaurosis. I might tell you, however, there's no miracle cure for the syndrome. Patients get over it, sometimes with and sometimes without treatment—sometimes in a few hours or days. Still, hysterical blindness is not necessarily the syndrome of choice. There are cases on record where it has lasted many years without responding to treatment of any kind.''

It was as if he'd been walking down a long, dark corridor toward a beam of light only to discover the light might have been nothing more than a wishful hope. Even amaurosis didn't come with a guarantee that he would see again.

His whole spirit rebelled against blindness and the skills he was being taught at the rehab center.

Outside the doctor's office, he had dismissed the car service driver, who was there to take him to the center, and began to walk. Sweeping the white cane in front of him, he walked on and on with no idea where he was going or where he was until sounds around him told him he had come to Battery Park. In a kind of daze, he realized he had walked unassisted half the length of the island. He felt no pride in his feat. He felt drained—more from the absolute concentration required to stay alive and on course than from the physical energy he'd expended.

He continued along the Battery walkways with no purpose, focusing on the raw demands of moving ahead. The unmistakable ballpark smell of hot dogs led him to a vendor's stand. He bought a frankfurter on a bun with mustard and sauerkraut and ate it sitting on a nearby bench the vendor directed him to. As he ate, he tried to recapture in his mind the long-lost thrill of an afternoon at Yankee Stadium with a batter up, two outs and the bases loaded.

Failing, he tapped around the bench to find a trash can and tossed in his unfinished hot dog and bun. Only then did he sit back on the bench, bow to the inevitable and listen to his own tormented thoughts tell him what he'd refused to believe until now: that a very real possibility existed that he was doomed to be blind for life.

In the wake of the thought came questions he'd avoided thus far: what would there be left for him if he couldn't see? Would he lose Julia? Would their marriage fall apart? If he could never take another picture, what would he do?

They were hard questions. Without answers.

God, if he could only get away from the distractions of the city, of Julia, of the center. Away from the city's miasmic heat to someplace he could be alone until he learned to live with this blind man—this stranger—who used to be himself . . . someplace where he could, in his own way and his own time, come to terms with the endless darkness.

He thought then of the house at Seahampton he'd so seldom visited in recent years but where he'd spent the summers of his childhood. Maybe there, where the only sounds were those of the sea and the marsh birds, he could find the courage he needed to walk into the murky future.

It was late afternoon when at last he got to his feet and found someone to direct him to a phone booth. There he called the car service to send a driver to take him home.

In the car he closed his eyes, and as it crept through heavy traffic on its way uptown, his mind turned again to Seahampton. Cora could go with him to do the driving and look after the place, he thought. Cora knew how to let him be alone. But how would Julia, who thought every problem was to be solved by talking it out, fit in? The dialogue he had in mind didn't include Julia. It was an inner dialogue between himself and himself.

With a new feeling of despair, Birch realized then that he had to go to Seahampton without Julia. Alone was the only way it would work. But how could he make Julia understand he didn't want her along?

CHAPTER ELEVEN

JULIA UNLOCKED THE DOOR and stepped from the bright entryway into the early-evening gloom of the unlighted apartment. Her errand had taken longer than she'd expected. Zabar's had been crowded and she'd stood in a slow line to pay for her single item. In the street again all the cabs had been either full or off duty, and it was several minutes before she found one for her return.

"I'm home, darling," she called out as she walked in and paused a moment on the threshold, waiting to hear Birch's answer to know where he could be found.

From the shadows of the study came his expressionless voice. "Here," was all he said. She hurried to him, turning on lights as she went.

She found him sitting in his big leather chair, a hand resting loosely upon one knee, his body slumped dispiritedly. The lines of laughter in the strong, handsome face had given up to channels of despair. His face was empty and dark. Julia's heart cried out to him.

It was hard to imagine that this man had ridden the wind in a glider and prowled the caverns of the ocean in diving gear. She leaned down and laid her cheek against his before she kissed him. He responded by lifting his hand from his knee to rest for a moment upon her head. In the weight of it she felt great wariness. The hand slipped away and dropped to his lap.

Straightening, Julia said, "Don't go away. I'll be right back."

In the kitchen, she put the pork chops in the oven according to Cora's instructions. Hurrying, she dabbed caviar on triangles of toast, and, after adding sour cream and onions, arranged them on a plate. She took the plate, along with tulip glasses for champagne and a bottle of iced Moët in a silver bucket, to the study and placed them on the table beside Birch's chair. To her disappointment, he seemed hardly to notice until she wrapped a napkin around the champagne bottle to catch the moisture and placed the wrapped bottle in his hands.

"Champagne?" he asked in a tone of mild surprise.

"For a special occasion," she said and saw by his face that he'd forgotten, and had little interest in learning what the occasion was. "You will do the honors, won't you?"

Without comment, Birch grasped the bottle more firmly and pulled the cork with the ease of a wine steward. There was a discreet pop. The wine bubbled up the inside of the neck to stop just short of the opening. He performed the act indifferently now, Julia saw, and held back words of praise she knew instinctively would be ill received. She rewarded him, instead, by slipping a sliver of toast and caviar in his mouth. She poured champagne for them both and put a glass of it in his hand.

"'Happy birthday to you, Happy birthday to you,'" she sang, touching her glass to his. "'Happy birthday, dear Bi-rch, Happy birthday to you.'"

Birch groaned. "Oh, God. I forgot all about it. The birthday game. Who needs it?"

She repressed the gorge she felt beginning to rise.

"*I* need it," she said in a level voice and took a sip from her glass, letting the twinkling liquid roll slowly over her tongue. Birch did not respond.

She couldn't remember a time in the past six weeks when he had started a conversation on his own or extended one beyond the demands of necessity. *Dammit, he might at least try,* she thought.

He sipped some champagne and ate the caviar she supplied with no sign of pleasure—politely at first, then inattentively, mechanically, his mind clearly otherwise engaged.

After a few minutes the silence between them grew oppressive. She hadn't planned to give him the gifts she'd bought until after dinner, but when he set the champagne glass, still half full, on the table beside him, she rose, picked up the box containing the sculpture and placed it in his hands.

He seemed reluctant to come back from wherever his thoughts had taken him. She watched his fingers pick listlessly at the wrappings.

"Open it," she urged him.

He took the lid off the box and lifted the small sculpture from its nest of paper. She watched him touch it half curiously, a hint of interest on his face. He passed his hand over its surface. She felt a stirring of hope.

"What is it?" But she saw that already he didn't care.

"It's a piece of sculpture."

"Sculpture? For *me*?" He gave a small, mirthless laugh.

"It wasn't made to *look* at, Birch," she said, steeling herself against a growing sense of futility. "Visually, it's not especially exciting. It's made to be touched."

She saw his face darken. He pushed the piece of sculpture back into the box and rose to his feet, thrusting the package into her arms as she jumped from her chair to rescue it.

"Just what I need today," he said bitingly. "Some new thing to remind me I'm blind."

Like a physical blow, his words knocked the breath out of her. She stood still, hugging the box to her body.

"I'm sorry, Julie," he said after a moment. "I didn't mean to say that. It's just that it's been a lousy day and you have a way sometimes of—" He broke off, then finished helplessly "Oh . . . hell."

Waiting for her inner trembling to subside, Julia still didn't speak. He reached for her, but she was beyond the range of his arms and made no effort to move closer.

"Where are you, Julia? Speak to me," he said in the face of her silence. "You know I can't see."

"No. You really *can't* see, dammit! And it isn't only with your eyes," she said, anger welling up within. "If you could see, you'd know I would never purposely give you anything I thought might make you feel more blind. I love you, Birch. I thought of it as a . . . sort of celebration, maybe. A celebration of ways you can see without your eyes."

She stopped, shocked at the cruelty in what she'd said. The words she'd used—*see, blind, eyes*— were words she hadn't spoken in his presence since he'd lost his sight. She saw him flinch, but now that she'd started she couldn't stop.

"You have all your other senses. What you've lost are color and light."

He'd turned his face to the sound of her voice. His expression resentful, he fumbled for his chair and lowered himself into it. After a moment he said defensively, "I can't see form."

"You could see it with your hands if you tried." She dropped to the floor beside him, took his hands in hers and lifted them to her face. She held his palms on her cheeks, then moved them over her brow and her hair; finally she placed them back in his lap.

"I'm form, too," she said unsteadily. It had been so long. She got to her feet, suddenly embarrassed, ashamed of the pleading tone in her voice. She heard a muffled sound from him.

"Don't, Julie," he mumbled. "You don't know what it's like. You don't know—"

"Oh God, I wish I did," she cried. "All I know, Birch, is that we used to be alive, and now we're not. We don't even talk to each other anymore. You've given up your friends, pleasures that could still be yours. One of these days there'll be nothing left but your blindness."

"Julie, for God's sake—"

"What do you want us to do, Birch? Give up living because you're blind?"

"It might have been better if the bastards had finished the job," he said bitterly.

There was a new sound in his voice that sent a cold wave of fear through Julia. It was the sound of self-pity, never heard until now from Birch through all the weeks of his blindness—a sound that burned into her like a brand.

"Stop it, Birch!" she cried. "It's *my* life, too, in case you've forgotten. If this is what six weeks of psychotherapy has done, I'm making an appointment for you tomorrow to see an ophthalmologist."

"Please, Julia, let me—"

But Julia had reached the breaking point. What Cora had said flashed into her mind. "You're afraid, Birch Cheney," she said accusingly. "You latched onto the diagnosis of hysterical blindness because you're afraid an ophthalmologist might tell you you'll be blind for life. You'd rather look for a nonexistent hang-up than take a chance on the truth.''

"That's not true," Birch broke in angrily. "I had a damned good reason to believe in the diagnosis."

"You, Birch Cheney, the best adjusted person I've ever known? This notion that your psyche is so messed up it caused you to go temporarily blind is absurd. Don't you see, darling? Subconsciously you're afraid of what an eye specialist might find. Amaurosis gives you an easy out.''

Maybe it was the gently reasonable tone of her voice that sent a flare of resentment through Birch. Suddenly he was no more in control.

"Would you call a deathbed promise to give up photography and go back to work at the family business absurd?" The words burst out of him unbidden. For a moment he couldn't believe he'd said them. But he knew he had. The terrible stillness that settled in around them confirmed the fact.

"Julie! Julie, dearest. That wasn't what I meant to say."

"You promised your father . . . ?" Her voice was little more than a whisper; the words seemed to catch in her throat.

"I did, but it wasn't like it sounds," Birch protested. "I promised, but I never expected to have to go through with it. I—"

"A lie won't do, Birch. I know you too well for that."

"Listen to me, Julie. You've got to listen!"

"There is nothing you could say that would make me believe the Birch Cheney I know would make a promise he didn't intend to keep," she said coldly, the words cutting into him like an icy blade. He heard her moving away and started to follow, calling after her, knowing only that somehow he had to make her understand.

"Julie. Wait."

"Let me go, Birch. I don't want to say something I'll regret," she said fiercely, still walking.

He stood listening after her, longing to go to her—swiftly, unerringly—then seize her in his arms and hold her until she'd heard him out. But such was not his to do. He'd lost his swiftness along with his sight. Simply by staying out of his reach she could evade him for as long as she wished. With a groan at his helplessness, he moved on down the hallway toward their bedroom after her.

As he went, he heard her quick footsteps, caught the light scent of Antonia's Flowers in the air and reached out, too late. In the next moment he heard the click of the front door and realized for the first time that she was leaving the apartment.

"Julie," he called out. But she was gone.

FIGHTING HER WAY OUT of the ruins of her destroyed world, Julia walked from the apartment building into the gathering dusk outside, and kept walking. Dazed by the unexpectedness of Birch's admission, she paid no attention to where she was or where she was going; all she could do was explore the facets of his betrayal with growing bitterness.

He had made a promise rejecting everything they'd built together—Birch, to whom the word *promise* was synonymous with *honor*. And it had been more than a simple promise; it had been a *deathbed* promise; crowning the betrayal by having made it to his father—

the man who had held Julia and their marriage and the work she and Birch did in open contempt.

Heedless of the passage of time, she walked on until she gradually became aware that outside the periphery of the brightly lighted streets lay darkness. It had grown late. Too late for her to be wandering aimlessly along city streets by herself, she thought, not really caring.

The deep feeling of hurt within her left no room for anything else. Until tonight, home had been Birch. Now suddenly she was alone and lost. She needed someone to help her find her way. She needed Birch.

Oh God, could she ever trust him again?

She thought of going to Cora, but knew at once how wrong it would be to pour out her bitter sorrow to the older woman. Birch was as dear as a son to her. One by one Julia thought about their few friends who lived in Manhattan. She couldn't appear on the doorstep of any one of them at ten o'clock at night without an explanation, however close the friend.

In the end she waved down a cab and gave the address of someone with whom she'd never shared a confidence and whom she scarcely knew in any real sense. When he rose to her mind, instinct told her to go to him. She wondered if he knew yet that if Birch were to recover his sight, he, too, would be a victim of his brother's promise.

In his midtown loft Matt sighed in satisfaction and rolled his chair back from his desk. It had been a good night's work, he thought, taking off his heavy-rimmed glasses and rubbing his tired eyes. It was all there. Just as he had suspected, Langley had been dealing in inside trading secrets for the past year.

He had a sudden urge to call Birch. He wanted his brother to know that the problem he'd wanted advice on six weeks earlier looked as if it was going to work out just fine. As he reached for the phone, he noticed the date on his desk calendar and realized it was his brother's birthday. Feeling glad that he'd remembered in time for an eleventh-hour greeting, he was about to dial Birch's number when the buzzer from the ground floor sounded to announce a visitor. He put down the phone and went to the vestibule to answer the buzzer.

"Matt, it's me. Julia."

"Julia! What the devil are you doing here?"

"Can I come up?" There was a sound of desperation in his sister-in-law's voice that set off an inner alarm.

"Is there something wrong with Birch?"

"No more than usual." The acid in her voice was unlike Julia, he thought.

On a sudden suspicion Matt asked, "Did he know you were coming here?"

"I didn't know myself. I'm not sure he gives a damn. Look, Matt, if you'd rather I..." He imagined he heard a tremor as her words broke off.

"Don't be foolish. I'll send the elevator down for you and unlock the door," Matt said. "I'm on the phone, so walk in when you get here."

When he'd dispatched the elevator, he went to the phone and called Birch's number. "Matt here, Birch," he began when he heard his brother's voice.

But Birch didn't let him go on. His words exploded in Matt's ear. "Julia's gone! I've called everyone I can think of and half the hotels she might—"

"Calm down, Bro. She's here. I sent the elevator down for her just now," Matt told him.

He heard a deep sigh of relief at the other end of the line and then a long moment of silence. He waited.

"Thank God," Birch said quietly. "I've been going out of my mind."

"What's going on?"

"I told her about the promise," Birch said. The sound of defeat in his brother's voice told Matt all he needed to know. He heard the elevator door opening in the vestibule and knew Julia would be in the room in a minute.

"Wait. She's at the door," he said hurriedly. "I'll talk to you later. I'll see that she gets home safely. You sound beat—try to get some sleep."

He hung up as the door opened and Julia walked in.

"That was Birch I was talking to," he said matter-of-factly. "I called to let him know you were here. He was worried about you." He could see by the drawn look on her heart-shaped face that the past hours had taken their toll.

"That's nice to hear," she said sourly. "Lately he's hardly noticed I'm around."

At a loss, Matt changed the subject. "I just finished working and was getting ready to send out for a pizza when you buzzed. Care to join me? Or have you eaten?"

She looked at him blankly for an instant before letting out a gasp of dismay. "The pork chops!" She turned as if to leave, but changed course and walked to the big window overlooking midtown Manhattan. Her back to him, she stared out at the lighted towers of the city in silence.

After a minute she said in a shaky voice, "Would you mind calling Birch again and asking him to turn off the oven? Tell him to turn the right-hand dial at the top clockwise until it stops." She added dully, "And I guess you'd better count me in on the pizza. I just remembered that all I've had since breakfast was a sliver of toast and a spoonful of caviar.''

Curious, but of no mind to ask questions, Matt delivered her message to his brother. Birch's only response was to ask if Julia had said anything to Matt about why she was there. A negative answer brought the brief conversation to an end, and Matt called in the pizza order. When he was through at the phone, he moved to join Julia, who continued to stare silently out the window almost as if she'd forgotten he was there. By the straightness of her back and the uplifted tilt of her chin, he could see she was fighting some inner battle.

The breach between his brother and his beautiful, obviously heartbroken wife troubled Matt deeply. He doubted Julia had come to confide in him or to seek his advice. He guessed, typically, that he'd been the proverbial port in the storm.

The window where Julia stood took up most of one wall of the main living area of Matt's loft. The loft itself consisted of one huge high-ceilinged room that had once been half a floor of a garment factory. Now, screens and movable partitions divided the area into smaller spaces that accommodated a kitchen, a bedroom, an office and a bathroom.

When Julia showed no sign of wanting to converse, Matt retreated to his office. With an occasional glance out at her still figure at the window, he left her alone and set about clearing his desk of the papers he'd finished working on a few minutes before her arrival.

When she turned around at last, he left his desk and went back to the living room.

''Sorry,'' she said, her voice thick as she made a feeble attempt at a grin. Tears glistened on her cheeks and she sniffed. "I . . . could use some tissues, if you've got any."

Sending her to the bathroom, he went to answer the buzzer and let the pizza delivery man in.

"What'll you have to drink? Beer or wine or a glass of milk?" he asked when she appeared a few minutes later in the kitchen area where he'd set out plates and was about to cut the pizza.

"Beer'll be fine," she said. "I'm not very hungry. Don't give me a lot."

"All that caviar spoil your appetite?" he asked laconically and was rewarded with a weak grin. Even when her heart wasn't in it, Matt thought, his brother's wife's smile was worth working for.

As much as anything he'd ever wished for in his life, Matt wished he could make her understand about the promise. He wanted her to see that Birch had been trapped. Even if his brother hadn't been too fuzzy-headed from lack of sleep that day to lock horns with their father, he would have *had* to make the promise. Surely Matt could make Julia see that Birch couldn't have taken the chance of causing their father another heart attack. . . .

Would she bring up the subject? he wondered hopefully as they carried their pizza and beer into the living room and settled themselves on floor cushions across from each other at the low, round oak table.

Looking out at the lighted spire of the Empire State Building in the near distance, Julia showed no sign of doing so.

"Great view," she said conversationally.

Much as he wanted her to talk about the promise that was shaking the foundations of a marriage he considered near-perfect, Matt couldn't screw up the courage to bring up the subject himself. Suppose he made a mess of it? He was such a damned bumbler, he thought dourly. If he'd been Birch, he'd have known how to draw her out, known how to make her see the picture the way it was. Birch was the one—

The thought came to a surprised halt. If Birch had known how to handle it, then why was Julia here in his apartment looking grim?

"For God's sake, Julia! Stop looking on that promise Birch made Dad as a mortal sin!" The rough words were blurted before he knew he was going to say them; they were words he would never have let himself say if he'd taken time to think.

Julia stared at him for a moment, speechless, her cheeks blanched. "So you know about the promise," she said, her voice strained.

"I even know a little of how you feel, maybe," Matt told her. "I heard about it first from our father, and I was madder than I'd ever been before in my life. Dad let me think Birch had sold me out."

"Well, didn't he?" asked Julia hotly. "If Birch could still see, he'd be running the family business right now instead of you."

"That's what I thought, Julia, until I talked to him in the hospital and found out how wrong I was. Birch was so woozy from lack of sleep at the time and his thoughts were a long way from crystal clear. All he could see was that if he refused it could bring on another heart attack that might kill Dad," Matt told her. "It was a promise he never expected to keep."

"I don't believe that for a minute," Julia said, her voice rising in anger, "and if *you* do, you don't know much about your brother's distorted code of honor."

"Wait a minute, Julia!" Matt began, his own voice rising in his brother's defense, but he stopped abruptly.

He knew suddenly it was up to him to set things straight with Julia for Birch. It was something he could do for Birch that Birch couldn't do for himself. Julia's unexpected arrival had given Matt a onetime chance to square things for his brother, and he couldn't blow it by losing his head.

When he spoke again it was quietly, and he let his genuine brotherly affection for Julia sound in his voice for the first time. "All I *really* know about Birch's code of honor is how he came by it. After you've heard the story, Julia, I don't think Birch's principles will strike you as distorted anymore."

She gazed at him with suspicious eyes.

When she didn't speak, Matt went on quickly, "First, though, let me fill you in on the conversation Birch and I had at the hospital the day before Inzelman diagnosed Birch's blindness as amaurosis."

Once into it, Matt had no trouble arguing his brother's case. He soon discovered that Julia was too full of her own hurt to have an ear for reason at first; but gradually her mood gentled. In time he found her listening avidly and with an occasional nod of understanding.

The turning point came when Julia asked, a lingering trace of disbelief in her voice, how Birch could have imagined his father would ever release him from the promise once it was made.

And Matt said, "After Birch's head cleared it didn't take him long to see the promise for what it was—a promise he'd been trapped into making under duress. One way or another, it no longer mattered."

"Why didn't Birch tell me?" she asked at last. They were drinking coffee Matt had brewed, and had deserted the living room floor cushions for a butcher-block counter in the kitchen.

"Because he was afraid you'd be so upset you'd never give him a chance to explain," Matt said.

"I wouldn't—" Julia began in protest.

"You *did*," Matt said bluntly.

She blinked and after a moment gave him an abashed grin.

It was after midnight when she got to her feet, yawning, and announced that the "encounter session" was over. They'd been at it for more than two hours; strenuous hours for both—hours in which Julia learned for the first time the full extent of Horace Cheney's tyranny over his wife and sons, and got a full history of the infamous promise that had hung like a dark cloud over her marriage from the day it was made.

And through the course of it, Matt welcomed a growing kinship with his sister-in-law, whose perfections he'd found somewhat intimidating in the past. Under the beauty, the warmth and the intelligence, under all that self-assurance, he'd found another vulnerable person not too unlike himself.

Over Julia's protests, Matt insisted on going downstairs with her to hail a cab and then got in and rode uptown with her to the apartment. There he told the driver to wait while he saw her to the elevator inside.

"I promised Birch I'd see you home safely," he said when she protested that she'd taken care of herself in more dangerous places than New York City.

"You Cheney brothers are a stubborn pair," Julia said.

To his surprise, when the elevator door opened to take Julia on, she turned and put her arms around him and gave him a warm hug. "Thanks, Matt," she said. "It's good to have you as a brother."

The door closed and Matt walked away with a bemused hope that the frustrations forced on him by his blindness would never cause Birch to forget he was a lucky man.

FOR THE FIRST TIME in the years she'd known and loved Birch, Julia had been given a look into the home he'd grown up in—so different from the cheerful, loving, warmhearted surroundings that had been hers. It no longer surprised her that Birch insisted upon looking for emotional damage hidden away in his subconscious to account for his blindness. After listening to Matt tonight she could almost believe in an emotional cause herself—if they had been talking about anybody but Birch, she thought as the elevator carried her up to her floor.

But part of the reason she'd fallen in love with him in the first place was that he was so in tune with himself and the world around him. It was this inner stability that made the diagnosis of hysterical blindness incongruous, made her *know* that a physical injury of some kind had to have made him blind. To have him under the care of a psychiatrist instead of an ophthalmologist now—after more than three months—made her a little crazy. Especially since he came home from each session with Dr. Shields a little more withdrawn, a little more touchy, a little more depressed.

She shouldn't have let the situation go on so long, she thought as she left the elevator and resolved that tomorrow, once and for all, she would talk him into quitting Shields and putting himself in the hands of an ophthalmologist.

Opening the door quietly, she felt a momentary alarm at finding the living areas of the apartment lighted, but remembered at once that Birch wouldn't know the lights were on. She'd been in too much of a state to think about turning off lights when she'd flounced out into the night in her fury of righteous indignation.

Flicking switches as she went, she walked down the hallway and came to a stop at the study door, drawing in a quick breath at the sight of Birch sprawled in the big leather chair sound asleep. She stood for a moment watching him, wishing she could take back the bitterness she'd poured upon him a few hours before.

Evidence before her of the disrupted birthday party plunged her into remorse. How could an evening she'd wanted to be so right have gone so terribly wrong?

She wrinkled her nose at the faint smell of onion and stale caviar still on the plate, which remained just as she'd arranged it, barely touched. On the table by Birch's chair the open champagne bottle sweated in the bucket of melted ice. Beside it the two half-finished glasses of champagne had gone flat. The sculpture, nested in tissue paper, was still where she'd set it down with the unopened presents on the table across the room.

Some birthday party! she thought and walked softly across the room to stand near Birch's chair and look down upon him. Even in sleep his strong, handsome face looked worn. She was surprised and a little sad to see some silvery strands in the dark sandy hair. They hadn't been there the last time she'd paid attention.

"Birch," she said softly.

He gave a start and came struggling to his feet, moving his head as if to get his bearings and reaching a hand in the direction of her voice. "Julie!" he said, his voice thick with sleep. "Thank God you're here. Tell me I'm awake."

She slipped under his arm and clung to him fiercely. Wrapping his arms around her, he drew her to him in a single violent movement that pressed her breasts and the full length of her thighs and belly against the hard, muscled planes of his body.

Her voice shaky, she said, "You're awake."

"You came back," he said as if he found it hard to believe.

With his hot breath fanning her head, she was suddenly overcome with wild desire. A laugh bubbled up from deep in her throat. "Of course I came back, dear fool," she said, teasing. "I love you. Take me to bed."

She felt him stiffen and begin to pull away. Her rising passion faltered in a cross fire of new resentment. He wanted her, too, dammit! She'd known him too long, too intimately not to recognize it. His body didn't lie.

"Not now, Julia. We've got to talk."

Struggling against the feeling of rejection that threatened to overtake her, she said in a level voice, "You're darned right, we've got to talk. We've done precious little of that since you started seeing the psychiatrist."

"Today was my last day with Shields, if that's any comfort to you," Birch said. "I could have saved the fee by listening to you. He doesn't think I have amaurosis either, and will see me again only if an ophthalmologist can't find anything physically wrong with my eyes."

For a moment Julia was too overcome to speak. After all her fears, it had come so easily. At the same time it was clear to her that Birch didn't consider Shields's dismissal a cause for celebration. She tried to keep the sound of relief and gladness from her voice.

"I've looked into ophthalmologists and have been told there's a Dr. Paul Burnside who's one of the best," she said. "I'll arrange first thing in the morning to get you in to see him, since Dr. Shields—"

"Never mind that, Julia," Birch interrupted. "I'm not ready to see anybody right now."

"Not *ready*?" she cried out in disbelief. "What are you going to do?"

"That's what I want to talk to you about," Birch said quietly. "Before I tackle anything more there are some things I need to work out. I'm thinking of going out to Seahampton for a while."

"Seahampton?"

"It's peaceful and quiet and away from the noise and confusion of the city. Maybe there I can find out who I am again," Birch said. "I'll ask Cora to drive me out in her car and stay with me while I'm there, if you can get along without her, and she's willing."

The message implicit in what Birch was saying struck Julia with the force of a battering ram. He was politely telling her he didn't want her. He didn't need her. He wasn't inviting her to come.

Still Birch continued to explain. "It'll do us both good to get away from each other for a while, love," he said gently. "We've been doing some upsetting things to each other lately, and at the bottom they're all my fault. Maybe out there with nothing but the gulls to listen to..." He left it hanging.

Her bruised spirit lashed out. "Go on, then. Go on out to Seahampton and atrophy!" she cried angrily. "I never thought that you—the great Birch Cheney—would deal with the only devastating problem you've had in your life by giving up. You've given up on your friends, you've given up on me, and you've given up on life. Well, *give* up if you want to, but I'll be damned if I'll give up with you."

Silence followed her explosion. Finally Birch said, "I don't want to hurt you, Julia, but lately every time I open my mouth it seems I do. I love you, my darling. The hope of my life is that you love me, but if we keep on lacerating each other the way we've been doing, we're going to leave wounds that will never heal."

All Julia's anger collapsed like a punctured balloon. He was right, she knew.

"I do love you, Birch. You know I do," she said in a choked voice. "Now good night. Please go to bed."

Turning away from him she dumped the flat wine from the glasses into the champagne bucket, heedless of the water level that was very near to overflowing.

"Good night, my love," he said.

Her heart heavy, Julia watched him move off toward their bedroom before she loaded up the remains of the ill-fated party and carried everything to the kitchen.

She spent a long time cleaning up all evidence of uneaten food and airing out the odor of burned meat to keep Cora from suspecting that dinner had been a fiasco. Feeling deeply apologetic to the hungry of the world, she cut two pieces from the chocolate fudge cake and fed them and all the asparagus and hollandaise sauce down the garbage disposal along with the charred pork chops.

With a last look around for telltale signs that might have been overlooked, she turned out the light and went to their bedroom, where she could see by Birch's breathing that he'd fallen asleep. Crawling into bed a short time later she slipped close to him and fit herself around the curve of his body, laying her face against his back. He stirred but didn't awaken.

She would feel better, she thought, if she could cry, but no tears came. She felt empty of everything.

CHAPTER TWELVE

THE FIRST MORNING at Seahampton, Birch awakened with a fresh breeze blowing across his face through an open window. It brought in the smell of the ocean, and for an instant he was a boy again, poised to spring out of bed and go racing half-naked down the path through the salt grass to collect whatever wonders the sea had spilled onto the beach overnight.

An instant later he was a man who had come here hoping to find again the man he had been before blindness had turned him into a brooding recluse.

He lay still, trying to recall more from those glorious summers of his boyhood, remembering, instead, those last constrained days before he'd left the city. Nothing he'd said had made Julia understand that coming here alone wasn't a rejection of her. The more he'd explained, the worse he'd made things.

Would she ever forgive him? he wondered drearily, and knew the answer lay in how successful he was in curing his own malaise.

Even Cora and Matt, who both understood why he'd felt it imperative to come here, disapproved of his leaving Julia behind. Cora was too discreet to say so, but when Matt had come over to the apartment, ostensibly to help pack—Julia had found an excuse not to be around—it hadn't taken long for Birch to see that his brother's real purpose in dropping by was to tell him he was making a big mistake not taking Julia along.

Understanding that he was here at the cost of alienating everyone close to him, Birch was uncomfortably aware that he hadn't come with any preconceived program. He didn't even have a clear notion as to how he expected Seahampton to heal the inner torment that was destroying him. He felt only that being here alone would somehow make him begin to feel whole again.

He pushed the covers aside and sat up slowly. Putting his feet on the floor and without bothering to reach for the cane at his bedside, he found his way to the open window and breathed in the fresh salt air. He was home. A wonderful sense of security came over him—something he hadn't felt in a long time.

THE DAY AFTER Birch and Cora left for Seahampton, Julia remembered the birthday presents she'd set out on the study table to be opened by Birch the night her world collapsed. She went looking for the open box with the piece of sculpture in it she'd last seen on the floor by Birch's chair. She noticed then that the other gifts had been removed from the table, too. A search of the house yielded only the brandy, unwrapped and put away in the liquor cabinet. The taped reading of the love sonnets was nowhere to be found, nor was the bit of molasses taffy.

The three days before Birch had actually left had been miserable for Julia, and no better for Birch, she guessed. It would have been easier if he'd taken Cora and gone the day after things blew up, but Cora had had matters to take care of before she left the city, and the caretaker at the Seahampton house had needed time to get the place ready for their arrival.

In spite of her deep feeling of rejection, she'd managed a good show of amity for the sake of Cora, and in
fairness, so had Birch. They'd hardly spoken, however,
and she'd managed to find reasons to stay away from the
apartment a good part of the time. Thinking back as she
searched the empty apartment for the missing gifts, Julia saw that what little conversation had occurred had
been cautious and formal. Too much anger had spilled
out between them.

Had he taken the piece of sculpture he'd rejected on
some last-minute whim? she wondered, toying with the
thought a moment before deciding the act highly im-
probable considering Birch's state of mind. Her real
concern was not the sculpture but the tape. Her wounded
spirit did not thrill to the possibility that her voice might
now be pouring out Victorian love sonnets to an indifferent Birch.

Laying the disappearance of the gifts to Cora's or-
derly nature—she had insisted on giving the apartment
a thorough housecleaning before she left—Julia finally
gave up the hunt. She'd ask Cora later where she had
stashed away the presents. She'd feel more comfortable
when the unfortunate tape was back in her own hands.

The apartment had an echo of emptiness, as if it had
been stripped of pictures and furnishings, she thought
gloomily, sinking into the big leather chair that bore the
imprint of Birch's body. A chill sense that their marriage was on the edge crept over her.

Whatever had happened to Julia Cheney, the inde-
pendent, liberated career woman? she asked herself
suddenly. With a sense of shock, she tried to think how
long it had been since she'd seen herself as anything but
Birch's wife; certainly long before he was blinded. Except for her brief, defiant fling with *Metropulse*, she'd

abandoned her career to be with him after he lost his sight. She'd given up every last vestige of independence, only to have him complain that she was smothering him. In outraged afterthought, she realized that in becoming Birch's willing appendage she hadn't even noticed she was losing herself.

She was as unliberated as the Victorian woman who wrote the sonnets, she thought—and Birch didn't need her. Didn't want her. He'd said he loved her, and with the next breath, had said he was going to Seahampton to find out "who I am," and would she do him a favor and stay in New York!

"So who are *you*, Julia Cheney?" she muttered to herself scathingly. "Liberated career woman, or Birch Cheney's wife?" And what was she going to do about it, now that Birch was gone? Well, she knew for certain one thing she *wasn't* going to do. She wasn't going to wait around in the joyless confines of the apartment, drowning in her own resentment, for Birch to decide he wanted her again.

IN THE KITCHEN at Seahampton that first morning, Cora was clearing up their breakfast dishes when Birch started along the well-worn path he remembered led from the house to the breakwater and then to the beach. Wearing jeans to protect his bare legs from the sharp-bladed grass, and a faded sailcloth jacket and cotton hat pulled far down over his face to shield his city skin from the sun, he moved forth cautiously. Feeling his way with the cane, he was pleased to find the old path was as he remembered.

He'd known he wouldn't be able to manage his cane and carry shoes at the same time once he reached the sand, so he hadn't worn shoes, and his tender feet suf-

fered from every sharp twig along the way. But the boy
in him whispered that barefoot was the only way to walk
in sand, so he bore up and forged stolidly on.

Confident the path would take him to the breakwater
he could follow down to the beach, he moved rapidly on,
pausing at one point where the path seemed to converge
with another only to decide it was nothing but a wide
spot in the single path. Pushing on, he expected any
moment to reach the breakwater.

After a while he began to sense he was moving in the
wrong direction. By now the sound of the tide should
have been straight ahead, not off to the right.

A few steps farther, and he lost the path completely,
to find himself unexpectedly plodding through clumps
of salt grass as he groped around for smooth ground.
Completely disoriented, he beat the grass, striking
around him with his slender cane. With a sense of panic
he realized he was lost. Tasting bitterness, he realized,
too, that he couldn't be more than two city blocks from
the house. Cora, doing the dishes, could probably see
him from the kitchen window if she looked out. It was
all he could do to keep from waving his arms to catch her
eye and bring her to his rescue.

The light cane was of no use in the deep salt grass.
After a few steps he pushed the cane down into a quarter of its length and shoved it into a rear pocket of his
jeans to free his hands. With his hands and feet he felt
his way through the grass, with only sound to guide him.
After taking a few steps he stopped to listen. The low
rumble and splash of the ocean suddenly seemed to
come to him from all around. Fear washed through him,
and he stood paralyzed, not knowing which way to go;
at the same time he was frighteningly aware that he

would never find the path again if he continued to stand still.

Terrified by his helplessness, he saw himself in a dark, alien world of nothing but salt grass. Then a remembered sound fell upon his ears. A raucous chorus of seagulls swooping down on a school of sardines told him that the ocean was straight ahead, and he began to laugh, shakily at first, and then in a derisive hoot.

Knothead! he muttered aloud. He was lost and ready to panic within sight of the house he grew up in! The situation struck him all at once as hysterically funny. The worst thing that could happen would be not finding his way back before Cora sent out a rescue squad.

He took time now for some cautious planning, determined to avoid that particular embarrassment if it was humanly possible. If he steered a reasonably straight course, keeping the gulls and the sea to his right, there was no way he could miss the breakwater. With this in mind he started forth again, only to catch his foot on some large, heavy barrier he imagined to be a length of driftwood. Fighting for balance, he plunged forward and landed facedown on the ground.

He cursed, and fumbled frenziedly around him. He'd lost the damned cane! If he didn't find it, Cora would have to send out the troops for sure. He tried to remember the last time he'd felt the cane poking him in the butt and realized at once it didn't matter. If he hadn't dropped the cane here where there was a possibility of touching it, it was as good as gone.

The sound of some large creature bounding through the grass nearby suddenly caught his attention. He sat up in alarm just in time to have himself flattened back on the ground by the biggest, most exuberant animal he'd ever encountered. A heavy-haired monster he presumed to be a dog dropped the missing cane on his chest and barked excitedly, letting Birch know he was expected to do his part and pitch the cane away again to be retrieved.

"Sorry, Barkis," Birch told him, grasping the cane tightly. The animal smelled rank, but in his relief to have the cane back Birch was willing to forgive him for having recently rolled in something that had either been dead too long or not long enough.

"Hey, get off me, you mutt," he said an instant later, giving the animal a shove when it appeared the beast was about to take up residence on his chest. He heard the rattle of a leash hook on a collar and was suddenly inspired. He coaxed the dog down beside him. Slipping the web belt off his jeans he attached it to the collar.

Rising gingerly, he gave the dog a pat on the head and said, "Come on, Barkis. Let's find that breakwater, old boy. If you're going to hang around me, you're going to have a bath in the Atlantic Ocean."

He braced himself against the dog, who, in his eagerness to go, threatened to drag Birch off his feet. Holding back, he listened to the sounds around him for guidance. When he was reasonably sure of his ground, he set off again, stumbling through thick clumps of salt grass in the wake of the dog. After a few yards the animal came to a sudden stop in front of him, and Birch took an unexpected dive over the big, shaggy body and landed in a heap against the breakwater.

Again he got to his feet, the dog beside him, and started along the breakwater once more until after frequent collisions with each other and yet another spill for Birch when he became entangled in the improvised leash, they reached the water's edge. There, with the full cooperation of Barkis, Birch gave him the promised dunking. Both of them soaked to the skin and dripping, they started back up the breakwater to the path at the end, which took them home.

This time, as he'd grown accustomed to doing in the city, Birch counted his steps all the way to the house. There he found Cora on the back porch waiting for his return.

"My, if you aren't a sight! Where in the world did you get that dog?" the housekeeper asked, her voice both astonished and amused.

"He picked me up on the beach."

Cora sniffed. "Seems to me I've heard that song before!"

"What's he look like, Cora?"

"He's the biggest, ugliest, shaggiest dog I ever saw. About as big as a small pony, and a mixture of most of the colors dogs come in except black." He heard her come down the steps, to get a better look at the dog, he guessed. "At least he's clean."

"Little does she know, eh, Barkis?"

"He's got a collar but no license tags," Cora said. "Looks like I'm going to have to go into the village and see if I can find out who lost him, if he won't go home by himself."

Birch laughed aloud. They were words that had been repeated more than once in the years of his and Matt's boyhood, when they'd had an affinity for every stray animal—some of them not so stray—that had crossed their path.

Birch remembered his lines. "Aw, c'mon, Cora. Do you have to?"

"Of course I have to," she said sternly, but then she laughed. "Birch, honey, you sound almost the way you're supposed to. Maybe you were right about coming to Seahampton to be by yourself.''

A HEAT WAVE HAD DESCENDED over the city and the air was already beginning to thicken with smog the next morning when Julia arrived at the Central Park reservoir dressed in workout gear. She hadn't run for a while, and her muscles felt tight.

After a few minutes of warm-up exercises she started off at a fast walk. Halfway around the track she broke into a slow jog she could feel in every muscle of her body. Approaching the wooded spot near where Birch was attacked, she thought of the mugging and broke stride, breathing heavily. When her breath returned to normal, she began to run again and did so steadily, until she noticed a shoelace was coming untied. She stepped onto the grass, out of the way of an approaching runner, to retie the lace.

"Julia! Julia Cheney," the runner cried as she drew near. Breathing heavily, she came to a stop beside Julia.

Julia looked up to see the lithe figure of Marian Koski, the senior editor of *Flair* magazine, wearing the latest in running togs. She was as colorful as a tropical bird.

"Marian! It's great to see you," said Julia in pleased surprise. She finished a double knot on her shoes and stood up. "I didn't know you ran."

"Every day," Marian assured her, still puffing. She grinned sheepishly and confessed, "Well, maybe not every day. A couple of times a week. Anything new on Birch?"

"Nothing new," Julia said tightly. "Cora drove him up to his family's place at Seahampton a couple of days ago to get out of the heat."

"What about you?" But before Julia could answer Marian interrupted herself. "Julia, I've got to get a move on. I'm running short of time, but I'd like to visit with you later if you have time. Let's do lunch. I don't think I have anything on my calendar today from twelve to two."

"Me, either," Julia said, hoping Marian hadn't caught the doleful note she heard in her own voice.

"Come up to my office just before twelve, then. There's a good little restaurant a couple of blocks from there. They serve marvelous low calorie lunches that taste like real food. I'm a very good customer. I can get them to save a table for us."

"Sounds wonderful," Julia said, and meant it more profoundly than the editor could possibly have guessed.

Sitting across from Marian at the restaurant some time later, Julia became aware that the *Flair* editor had been eyeing her speculatively while they ate.

"So, Julia," Marian asked bluntly at last, "what are your plans?"

Julia remained quiet while a waiter cleared away plates of what had been chicken salad with fruit, glad for the respite; but even after he was gone she still was unsure what she wanted to say in return. Seeing that Marian still expected an answer, she stalled. "Plans?"

"I gather that Birch—" Marian hesitated, then went on "—might conceivably not be doing any more pictures. I'm really sorry, Julia—more sorry than I know how to say." She hesitated again, but continued forthrightly, "I don't mean to sound brutal, but I have to say it. Watching Birch do *blind*, old friend, isn't exactly a career."

Julia bridled. "Birch has needed me, Marian. When I brought him home from the hospital he could hardly dress himself."

"Does your housekeeper help him dress at Sea-hampton?"

"Of course not. That was more than three months ago. He's been going to a rehab center for the blind. He can do everything for himself—short of threading a needle," Julia said with a wry laugh and, she realized unexpectedly, a feeling of genuine pride.

"Exactly my point," Marian said. "If Birch can get along without you at Seahampton, either you're writing the great American novel in the closet or you're going crazy looking for something to do."

Julia's defence collapsed. "Well, I don't write books," she confessed. "Got any bright ideas?"

"How about going back to Paris and finishing that fashion assignment you were doing for *Flair* when Birch got hurt?"

Julia looked at her friend with sudden interest. "I thought you'd given it to someone else."

"When you asked to be released I decided to wait a while," Marian said. "You and Birch put a lot of work into this already, and all of us at *Flair* like what we've seen. Timing isn't too important when the articles are basically background and biographical sketches with pictures, and our inventory is fat right now, so it didn't cause any problems to hold off."

"But what about the pictures?" Julia asked. "Birch did some beautiful portraits and photographed some of the fashion houses in production, but by the time the series comes out in *Flair* the material will be going on two years old. It won't work without some new pictures to bring it up-to-date."

There was a moment of silence before the editor said, "Look, Julia, Birch is one of the best photographers in the business. Don't think I'm not in complete agreement with you about that, but we aren't going to have Birch any more for now. You were in this business before you met Birch. Who did your camera work then?"

"The man who taught Birch," Julia said. "I'm sorry to say, he died more than two years ago." As she spoke, her mind raced. Birch had already done all the important camera work for the fashion series; for the rest she could get Meg Mooney, or—

She cut herself short. How could she think of going back to Paris without Birch? Paris had meant so much to them together. She felt somehow guilty, remembering it was a Paris Birch might never again be able to see.

Aloud she said to the woman across the table, "It's very inviting, Marian, but I couldn't do that to Birch."

"I don't see how it could hurt Birch, Julia. But then I've never figured out the secret of this perfect marriage we all know you two have going for you. Worse luck! So who am I to talk?" Marian said. "Think about it a few days and call me. I've got to run."

AT THE HOUSE in Seahampton that early afternoon, Birch came downstairs in dry jeans to find that Cora had packed sandwiches and pickles and fruit in a paper bag, which he tucked into the pocket of his windbreaker before taking off again. A friendly, snuffling sound outside notified him that the dog had waited for him. The two started down the path together.

Not wishing to wander off the track again, Birch moved with more caution this time, and counted. He had retrieved his belt, and the dog walked beside him now, the huge body taking up more than half the path.

Where they'd been continually in each other's way that morning, knocking against each other and stumbling around, the animal seemed more of a stabilizer now.

After a while something began to dawn on Birch. The damn fool dog had elected himself pilot! He wanted to run the show. Amused by the discovery, Birch decided to humor the animal. He found at once that moving with the dog's weight when he pushed against his legs prevented Birch from veering to the right, which was his natural tendency and was causing him to stray from traveled ground. He found, too, that when the dog planted his bulk solidly in Birch's way it was time to watch out for an obstruction.

Dog and man shared Cora's sandwiches, and when Birch fell asleep on the beach, he awakened to find the dog lying quietly by his side.

"He's no Seeing Eye dog," Birch said, telling Cora about the animal's exploits later. "That's about the extent of his expertise. If some passing kid throws a stick, he'll leave me flat and not come back for an hour. He's about three parts hippie and one part Good Samaritan."

For lack of any other name, Birch continued to call the dog Barkis, the first name that had popped into his head when the animal had come barking up and dropped the cane on his chest. He and Cora didn't encourage him to hang around, but when Barkis settled down on the back stoop that night, showing every sign that he intended to stay, neither had the heart to let him go unfed.

By the third day Barkis had become a fixture, and Birch, like the boy Birch, was in no hurry to send him away.

"We ought to get that fool dog home, Birch," Cora said that evening as they were having dinner. "I'm going

in to the village tomorrow and see if I can't find out who
owns the beast."

"I suppose you're right," Birch said reluctantly.
"What are you going to do? Take him up to the village
in your car?"

"I should say not!" Cora said indignantly. "I'm not
letting that moose in my car. When I find out who owns
him, I'll let the owner figure out how to get him
home...."

SEAHAMPTON WAS little more than two hours away, and
though relations between them had been strained when
Birch left, Julia had half expected him to call to let her
know they'd arrived. When she didn't hear from him,
she started thinking about Cora's car—a ten-year-old
Chevy with a shine like the Fifth Avenue face of Trump
Tower. Knowing Cora and her habits, Julia had to believe the Chevy was in as good condition as the day it
was purchased.

But she should have checked into Cora's driving
ability, she thought. Cora wasn't one to go around telling her age, but Julia guessed she was nudging seventy.
Which didn't mean she couldn't be a perfectly good
driver, Julia amended guiltily, remembering that her own
mother was close to seventy. She had been driving all
over the state of Washington most of her life, and had
never gotten a ticket.

She decided to call Matt.

"Have you heard anything from Birch?" she asked
anxiously when she had her brother-in-law on the phone.

"Should I have?" asked Matt.

"Well, no, but I haven't heard a word since they left,
and I was wondering—"

"You're not worried about them, are you?"

Julia came to the point. "Matt, how good a driver is Cora?"

She thought she heard a politely suppressed snicker at the other end of the line. Darn Matt! It wasn't funny!

After a moment Matt said, "I'd say Cora's a pretty good driver for an old gal."

"I'm going to pretend I didn't hear that chauvinistic answer, brother-in-law," said Julia. "What I really want to know is, would *you* drive out to Seahampton with her?"

"I most certainly would," Matt said stoutly. "Cora Meigs is a hell of a lot better driver than most of the maniacs tooling around out there on the Long Island Expressway."

"Thanks a bunch. I'm glad I knew who to come to for comfort!"

"Quit your worrying, Julia. If they'd gotten into any kind of trouble you'd have heard about it within the hour."

Julia sighed. "I suppose," she said. "It's only—" She changed course abruptly. "Listen, Matt, how do you think Birch would feel if—" She stopped, not sure what she was going to say—not even sure she wanted to tell Matt about Marian's proposal.

"Julia? Are you there?"

"I had lunch with Marian Koski, the editor of *Flair*. Birch and I were doing an article for her when Birch got hurt," she said, starting cautiously. "She wants me to go back to Paris and finish it. It doesn't seem like a very nice thing to do to Birch." She added quickly, "I said no."

"Why did you do that? It's just what you need, Julia. Tell her you changed your mind. Birch will want you to go when he hears about it. It'll do you both good."

"You think so?" Julia asked weakly, not completely happy with the answer.

"Of course I'm sure," Matt said with enthusiasm. "You've been hovering over him like his guardian angel since you brought him home from the hospital. To tell you the truth, Julia, I've been worried about you."

"Worried?" Julia repeated uneasily.

"Worried that you were going to suffocate Birch with all that pity and loving attention. And not do yourself any good, either."

There was a long moment of silence before Julia said, "You thought...that?" Her voice broke, before she could finish.

At the other end of the line she hard Matt groan. "Julia! Oh, my God, I'm sorry. I didn't mean that the way it sounded. I only wanted to say that sometimes too much...oh, hell! It can make a man feel...diminished."

"It's all right, Matt. Birch has said as much. I didn't like it any better coming from him," she admitted painfully, struggling to regain her composure.

"I should have kept my damn mouth shut," Matt said. "It's just that I would hate like hell to have the best marriage I've ever seen go on the rocks because a couple of bastards blinded my brother."

"Thanks, Matt. You're a sweetheart. I'd hate it like hell myself. I can promise you this much—if it ever happens it won't be because Birch is blind."

When she'd hung up, Julia sat back in the chair. There was a great emptiness inside her. It wasn't fair. She could probably go to Paris and back, and Birch wouldn't even notice she was gone.

After a while she reached for the directory, and when she found the Seahampton number she dialed.

"How are things going, Cora?" she asked when she heard the housekeeper's voice.

"They're just fine," Cora replied, but before Julia could ask more, she said, "Hang on. I'll get Birch."

Julia panicked for a moment. What was she going to say that wouldn't sound reproachful...or self-pitying...or overly concerned? There was a knot in her stomach by the time his voice came on the phone. Her palms were moist.

"Julia! Is something wrong?"

For an instant she melted under the magic of the warm, baritone voice she loved so dearly, now filled with anxious concern. In the next a wave of anger and hurt swept over her. It was about *time* he showed a little concern! *You don't have to worry about my suffocating you anymore, lover,* she promised in bitter silence. *From now on I look out for Julia.*

Steadying herself, she echoed Cora's words, "No, everything's just fine." Aiming for a tone of cool amiability, she went on. "Since I haven't heard from you, I thought—"

"I couldn't think of anything to say to you, Julie," Birch interrupted her gently. "I did such a lousy job of explaining myself the other night, I thought calling would only make things worse. I should have known you'd worry if I didn't let you know we got here safely."

"Me worry?" Julia said with a quick laugh. "Don't be silly. I just thought I'd call and tell you I'm thinking about going to Paris. Marian Koski wants me to go back and finish the fashion series for *Flair*."

There was a scarcely noticeable silence on the line before Birch said, "That's great. That's wonderful. It'll be good for you to start working again on something you really like. You've always had a love affair with Paris."

"Yes," she said. *But not without you,* she thought. Paris without Birch was just another city. After a moment she went on. "You've already done the most important camera work, if you don't mind my using it. I can get someone to take some current shots that should bring what we've done up-to-date."

A small, scarcely discernible sound—like the sound that came with a wince of pain—reached Julia's ears, and suddenly what she'd just said seemed unforgivable.

"I'm sorry. I didn't mean to..." she said sorrowfully, her voice hardly more than a whisper. "Forget I said it, Birch."

"Not at all, love. It was a perfectly reasonable request, and of course I don't mind," Birch said, but she knew him too well to miss the strain in his voice. "Hold on, maybe I can think of a cameraman for you."

They talked on as professionals for a few minutes, Birch mentioning photographers she might be able to use. Then suddenly they had no more to talk about, and there was silence again on the line, broken after a few uncomfortable seconds when both tried to speak at once.

Birch said, "Give my regards to the Ritz," and she recognized the note of pain in his voice again. For a moment she wavered.

"I haven't said for sure I'd go," she said.

"Of *course* you're going, Julie. It'll get you back in the swing of things, and there's nothing to keep you here," Birch said, his tone cheerful again.

"No," she agreed in a level voice. "There's really nothing to keep me here."

Silence again. Then Birch said, rushing the words as if suddenly in a hurry to get them out, "You'll be seeing Hugh?"

And Julia said, "I hadn't thought of it. I could give him a call, I suppose." Silence.

Both started to speak at once again, ending in an awkward agreement to "keep in touch"; and Birch hung up.

Something ached in her chest. Had she wanted him to protest? Even ask her not to go? Did he *want* her to see Hugh Dryden after the brouhaha he'd caused when Hugh was in New York?

If only he hadn't sounded so darned hearty about her going!

Maybe a bit *too* hearty?

Thinking over the exchange, she sighed. She didn't know what to think anymore....

FOR A MOMENT after Birch hung up, he imagined he caught a fleeting whiff of Antonia's Flowers. Fear spread through him; fear that she was to become no more than a passing fantasy in his life—here and then away, finally to be lost to him forever.

He'd wanted to cry out, "Stay! Don't go to Paris!" or even, "Wait for me!" but something wouldn't let him. It was wrong for her to be trapped in New York while he retreated to his childhood haven and licked his wounds. It was right for her to listen to the cry of her natural spirit. It was right for her to finish their work in Paris; inevitable that she should get someone else to finish taking the pictures he could no longer see to take.

Saying to Cora that he was tired, he climbed the stairs to the bedroom that had always been his in the rambling clapboard house. He missed Julia with an intensity that racked his being. After a while he got up from the wicker rocking chair where he'd slumped disconsolately, and found the box containing the sculpture she'd given him the night of his birthday. He'd carried it with him from the apartment, not knowing why, only that it represented something of Julia, and he felt somehow impelled to bring it along.

Lifting the free-form piece from the box he'd placed on the dresser, he settled back in the rocker and explored the surfaces of the sculpture with his hands. There was something about the artwork that was strangely comforting and reminded him of Julia in some indefinable, disturbing way.

God, how he loved her!

Sitting there in the chair with the piece of sculpture in his hands, he remembered the gift-wrapped tape Matt had found with the bottle of brandy on the study table.

"It's hand-labeled and says 'E.B.B. by Julie,' whatever that means," Matt had said when he unwrapped the tape. He'd dropped it in Birch's pocket and sent a cassette player along in case Birch decided to listen.

The player was on the dresser, but it took Birch a while to feel through the closet for the denim jacket he'd been wearing that day and retrieve the tape. In the same pocket his fingers touched and picked up a small, wrapped lump. His mouth curved into a slow smile when he found it to be molasses taffy. Darling Julie! What a unique collection of gifts he'd snubbed on his birthday night. He couldn't begin to guess the significance of the brandy Matt had put away in the liquor cabinet at home. He didn't even much like the stuff. But he was sure that, coming from Julia, it was neither meaningless nor picked at random.

The taffy he understood. He was something of a molasses taffy maven, and he'd told her often that her hair was the color of molasses taffy, though it wasn't; it was more the color of polished pecans.

Thinking of the strange assortment of gifts his wife had assembled, Birch was suddenly curious for the first time about the tape. With the taffy melting deliciously in his mouth, he settled back in the chair and turned on the player. The tape rolled in silence for a few moments and then the lovely, slightly husky voice that haunted his spirit day and night when they were apart, began to speak.

"I'm borrowing words that Elizabeth Barrett Browning wrote to her husband and lover, Robert, to tell you what you mean to me, dear spouse. Even after more than a hundred years, her sonnets say it all more truly than I ever could in my own words."

There was a pause, and then, her voice, as sweet and lyrical as a bird's, began: *"'How do I love thee? Let me count the ways....'"*

The tape rolled on through her reading of selected sonnets, all variations on the same theme—everlasting love—coming at last to the final selection: *"'...a mystic Shape did move/behind me...'"* And with the final words, *"'The silver answer rang,—"Not Death, but love."'"* Birch understood Julia had meant this sonnet to remind him that her love would never let him turn his blindness into a living death.

When her voice ceased, Birch sat still for a moment, his eyes moist. An ache in his throat would not let him swallow. Then, he rewound the tape and heard it through again.

CHAPTER THIRTEEN

PARIS, THIS TIME, held none of its earlier enchantment for Julia. She'd taken a room in a small, pleasant hotel within walking distance of most of the places she would be working. She passed with hardly a glance the landmarks and monuments that had enchanted her in the past. Her mind was occupied with too many other things, and not the job she was here to do. Thoughts of her and Birch's marriage, their future and most of all, Birch's health—physical and mental—consumed her.

His escape to Seahampton after six weeks of moody indifference had left her shaken—for escape it had been...escape from her, though he hadn't said it quite that bluntly.

Almost as disturbing as the stark fact that he didn't want her with him anymore was her own discovery after he'd left that the feeling was mutual. She'd realized guiltily all too soon that it was a big relief not to have to measure every thought and every word against Birch's state of mind.

She kept a lid on her personal concerns as much as she could and concentrated on her work. She had little enough time to finish what she needed to accomplish before the August hiatus three weeks away, which annually sent most Parisians out of the city for a month.

With Meg Mooney substituting for Birch at the camera, Julia spent her days in the workplace of one couturier or another. At night she plodded her way into mindless exhaustion, turning voluminous notes into rough copy, or planning the next day's camera schedule with Meg.

But always, just below the surface, was the pain. She missed Birch. She sorrowed for him. She loved him. She railed at him. She wrote him brief, noncommittal letters, mostly about her work, and received in return crudely typed notes addressed in Cora's florid hand.

Julia almost wished he wouldn't bother. For the most part the notes were so indecipherable they didn't give her the satisfaction even of knowing whether their tone was affectionate or impersonal. Her efforts at translating left her feeling more frustrated than if he had never written.

Still, she decided, communication between them wasn't much worse than it had been in the last weeks they were together. At least he was learning to type.

In the most readable of the notes she'd deciphered a garbled reference to a dog, which disturbed her. She wondered if he'd gone the whole distance and become owner of a Seeing Eye dog; and if he had, what did it signify? A final acceptance of blindness that ruled out any intention of seeking further professional help?

When the possibility had gnawed at her until she could no longer stand it, she called Matt in New York.

"Have you heard anything from Birch?" she asked directly, when greetings were out of the way.

"Only that he's bought a typewriter. Don't tell me he hasn't written!" Matt said impatiently.

"Oh, he's written all right," Julia said in disgust. "The problem is, he can't type!"

"I thought he *knew* how."

"Hunt and peck, which doesn't work unless you can see. To say he has a rudimentary grasp of touch typing would be an exaggeration. Half the time he gets his hands in the wrong position on the keyboard and there isn't one single readable word in the whole blasted letter," Julia said crossly. A laugh from Matt across the ocean hardly improved her humor.

"It's not funny, Matt. How can I know what's going on? I wish he'd let Cora check his notes."

"You know Birch better than that, Julia. He wouldn't think of showing Cora something intended for you alone."

"I *don't* think there's anything that intimate in them," Julia said acidly. "If I wasn't afraid he'd think I was trying to manage him from afar, I'd suggest he have a bit of tape stuck on the home keys of his keyboard to tell him where his hands should be."

"Good idea. I'll tell him myself."

"You aren't thinking of going out to Seahampton soon, are you?" Julia asked hesitantly after a pause.

"Well, I'm pretty busy right now," Matt said. "Besides—stop me if I'm wrong—wasn't the idea for him to get away so he could be by himself to think?"

"The idea was to get away from *me*, Matt. I thought you knew."

"Julia, that's not true. Birch loves you."

"It *is* true, and you know it. And yes, he loves me. He just can't stand to have me around," Julia said, her voice suddenly quiet. "I remind him of something he doesn't want to be reminded of."

"Like what?"

"Ophthalmologists."

"Yeah...uh...well..."

"Matt...listen," Julia said anxiously after a pause. "There was something about a dog in his last note that

I couldn't make out. It worries me. He hasn't said any
thing to you about a Seeing Eye dog, has he?"

"I haven't really talked to him, Julia. He doesn't call
and when I call I always get Cora," Matt said. "Birch
spends most of his waking hours out on the beach, she
says. Come to think of it, I believe she did mention a
dog. Have you got something against Seeing Eye dogs?"

"Of course not. If Birch has to go through life blind
it might be good for him to have one, but at this point
a Seeing Eye dog is no substitute for an ophthalmol
ogist."

"Well, hardly."

"It's like he's settling in for a long, hard winter, Matt.
If Birch has gotten himself a Seeing Eye dog, it means
he's sticking with amaurosis to the bitter end. It means
he's grabbing at anything that might make being blind
more tolerable while he goes on hoping the blindness will
go away."

"You don't think he has any intention of going to an
ophthalmologist . . . *ever*?"

"Not if he has a Seeing Eye dog," Julia said despair
ingly. "An ophthalmologist might burst the bubble and
tell him he'll always be blind."

"On the other hand, an ophthalmologist might find
he has a physical injury that could be corrected, and he'd
be able to see again."

"Exactly! And if it should turn out the other way,
we'd at least know what we had to deal with and start
accommodating ourselves to the reality."

"Maybe if we give him a little more time. . . ."

"It's been nearly four months, Matt!" Julia pro
tested desolately. "Putting our life on hold to wait for a
miracle that doesn't show any sign of happening is

what's destroying our marriage. And me." In spite of herself, her voice broke, and she came to a stop.

When she could speak again she said into silence from the other end, "I'm sorry. I didn't mean to dump on you."

From far away she heard Matt clear his throat. "Hey, Julia honey, it's all right. Anytime." There was a pause. "Maybe I can find time to take a ride out to Seahampton over the weekend and see what's going on."

THE FOLLOWING FRIDAY afternoon Matt took the Long Island Expressway and headed out for Seahampton ahead of the summer weekend traffic. His mind was on the upheaval that was looming in the bastions of Cheney, McCrae. Maybe he'd sound Birch out on the action while he was there, he thought. Birch might be glad to hear that Matt had taken his "Do what you have to do" edict to heart and gone digging into what had been going on at the family firm.

But the conversation with Julia a few nights previously stayed with Matt like his own shadow, and it occurred to him that his brother's problems meant he couldn't be all that "glad" about anything. Matt hadn't heard many glad sounds from Birch since he'd lost his sight.

When he arrived at the house, Matt pulled his car into the gravel driveway that ran along one side of the house and led to a parking yard behind it. Once he'd parked, he took the back porch steps two at a time and ran headlong into Cora, whereupon he swung her off her feet in a hug and planted a kiss on her cheek.

"Well, if isn't my favorite lady! And looking absolutely smashing, if I may say so, in a red-and-white-checked apron, and not a hair out of place," Matt greeted her exuberantly.

Cora gave him another hug. "You're a dear boy, Matt, even if you *are* a little too cute for your own good. Are you staying for dinner?"

"I may even spend the night, if you invite me."

"Then you're invited, love. Knowing you were coming, I bought six ears of sweet corn fresh from the farmers' market this morning, and I'm in the middle of making your favorite—coconut cream pie."

Matt grinned at her teasingly. "I guess I can make do with six ears. If not, I can make up for it with the pie. Where's Birch?"

"He's out on the beach. Go find him. I've got to get back to my pie."

Matt turned serious. "How's he doing?"

"Go see for yourself."

He'd known when he asked that the discreet Cora would tie her tongue in a knot before she'd answer that kind of a judgmental question, but he'd seen a certain look of satisfaction in her eyes that whetted his curiosity and boded well.

"Dinner'll be ready in half an hour," she called after him as he left the house.

He loped along the path toward the breakwater and the beach. Where the dune began he stopped abruptly to gaze at a tall, loose-limbed figure far up the beach moving at a low-keyed jog along the edge of the tidewater on the heels of an enormous dog. Uncanny, he thought, how much the jogger reminded him of Birch.

When his eye first caught the twosome they were heading away from him. As if they had reached a predetermined point, they came to a stop a minute later and turned to jog back toward the breakwater. As they drew nearer, Matt was startled to realize that the lone figure was indeed his brother.

If this huge, unkempt creature lumbering along ahead of Birch with Birch's collapsed cane in his mouth was Julia's dreaded Seeing Eye dog, the Seeing Eye people were scraping the bottom of the barrel, he thought with amusement.

Watching Birch now at closer range, Matt had an eerie feeling that the blinding had happened in a dream. His brother ran surely along the tide line, his head up, his face turned to the breeze that ruffled his sun-streaked hair, looking so completely like the brother he'd once known that Matt had to stop and reorient himself. For a single crazy instant he wondered if the "miracle" Julia had spoke of so sourly over the phone had in fact occurred, and Birch could see where he was going.

"Birch! Hey, Birch!" he called, heading across the sand to intercept them, and was horrified to see the big dog turn his head and come to a stop to gaze curiously his way, leaving the unwarned Birch to somersault over him and go sprawling across the sand.

"My God, Birch!" Matt cried, racing to get to his brother now. "Are you hurt?" But he saw at once that his brother was already scrambling to his feet, laughing and trying to catch his breath.

"Where the hell are you, Bro?" Birch said, still laughing as he reached one sand-covered hand into the empty air for Matt to grab hold of. "Glad to have you back in the neighborhood."

"That's some Seeing Eye dog, you've got," Matt said, accepting his brother's hand. "I thought for a minute he was going to kill you."

"Sometimes I think that myself," Birch said. "I've gotten pretty good at diving over him when he does what he just did. Once in a while I manage to come up on my feet, but usually I ram my face in the sand."

"You mean he does that often?"

"Often enough," Birch said with a rueful grin.

"Where the devil did he come from?"

"He's the town dog."

"Has he got a name?"

"When he hangs out with me, his name's Barkis, but he's got other names, too," Birch said and proceeded to give a ludicrous account of his first encounter with the dog. Matt roared with delight.

"He more or less belongs to Seahampton village, and is the unofficial lifeguard here at the beach," Birch continued. "I'm told his first master was a descendant of one of the town's old whaling families and had a drinking problem. Barkis's mission was to steer the cap'n from tavern to tavern and make sure the old boy got home. Since the cap'n's demise he's been every-body's dog and lives at the firehouse except when he takes up with someone such as me for a while."

"How come *you*?"

"Maybe my ragged gait and falling-down ways re-mind him of the cap'n," Birch said easily. He paused thoughtfully and went on. "I've learned a few things with old Barkis...and remembered a few that had slipped my mind."

"Like what, for instance."

"He taught me that I pull to the right and tend to end up walking in a circle unless he's around to keep me on the straight and narrow. Thanks to him, I've learned to compensate," Birch said cheerfully. "For a fellow who can't see, it's a handy thing to know."

Matt chuckled. "Looks like he's restored your sense of humor."

"That, too," Birch said quietly.

After a moment Matt said, "Cora's about ready for dinner. Maybe we'd better start back to the house. If we roll in late, she'll figure we're up to our old tricks. Remember when..."

One "remember when" led to another as they trudged up the dune and on to the house where Cora was putting dinner on the table and waiting with her own store of "remember whens." Sitting at the round oak table where she had served them meals through all the summers of their boyhood, they slipped back into that half-forgotten age when troubles were inconsequential and no problem so great it could not be lost in a good night's sleep. They were a pair of rowdy siblings again, arguing over the extra ear of corn when Cora ate only one of her allotted two. In keeping with the spirit of compromise she'd instilled in them, the housekeeper broke the ear carefully and gave each of them half. Between them they scarfed down half a pie.

When Cora rose to clear the table, Matt echoed a time-honored challenge, certain, in that other time, to raise an instant argument: "It's Birch's turn to do the dishes!"

The words were no more than out when he realized they might better have been left unsaid. He turned a stricken glance to Cora and, encouraged by the bland unconcern in her eyes, looked at Birch and was relieved to find him grinning.

"Wrong, Elephant Brain," Birch countered. "I distinctly remember I did them last. Furthermore, I don't do dishes."

On solid ground again, Matt said brashly, "Hear that, Cora? Up to his old tricks!"

"Don't think I couldn't learn to, Bro," Birch said, clearly only half-joking. "One thing I've discovered out here—I can do about anything I want to, if I put my mind to it. But why give up a good excuse when I've got one not to do something I never did like?"

"Get out of here, both of you," said Cora. "Neither one of you were ever much help. I'd just as soon do them myself."

"How about walking down to the beach?" Birch said to Matt.

"Are you crazy! It's black as the pit out there," Matt protested again, not thinking. Realizing at once it was no darker now to Birch than it was at any other time, he added quickly, "It's easy for *you* to walk around in the dark, dammit, but I could break my neck, you know."

Birch chortled. "Sorry. I forgot. Borrow a flashlight from Cora. Remember how we used to sneak out to the beach at night after we were supposed to be in bed? The tide still sounds as good as when we were kids."

Outside, ready to start off, Matt asked, "Where's Barkis?"

The dog was nowhere to be found, and after a few perfunctory calls, the brothers started along the path. Matt elected not to use the flashlight he'd borrowed from Cora until Birch threatened to send him back to the house if he didn't stop bumping into him and straying off the path.

From the top of the dune they could hear the gentle rumble and swish of the tide as it rolled out across the sand and in again in a steady, hypnotic rhythm that Matt found infinitely soothing. They sat quietly, each in his own thoughts.

Matt's mind was busy with the changes he'd seen in Birch. He thought of how this brother, the hero of his growing up, had let blindness turn him into a stranger by denying the courage, the humor, the personal cachet that had been his hallmarks and withdrawing into himself like a land turtle. To find that in the short time since they'd last seen each other Birch had accomplished a complete reversal was almost more than Matt dared believe. He wanted to hear from Birch how the transformation had come about, but felt unexpectedly shy about probing his brother's inner reaches.

After a while Matt asked, "Have you got what you came for, Birch?"

"Well . . . I've finally figured out there's a lot more to life than just being able to *see*," Birch said slowly. "And I've run across a few occupations I think I could handle that I might like about as well as the one I can't handle anymore."

Quiet fell between them again. Matt didn't press.

Presently Birch continued. "Talking to people on the beach and browsing around Seahampton checking out Barkis's seafaring master, I discovered something, Matt. I discovered I relate to people about as well as I ever did if I give them a chance. They just have to get used to being chatty with a blind person. It takes a little time before they discover there's more to me than just *blind*. It's up to me to let them see what else is there."

"You're saying people hold back when they know you're blind?"

"It depends. Sometimes it's kind of an icebreaker. People who are not known to be friendly will often accept a blind stranger more easily than they will a stranger who sees."

When he could no longer contain his admiration, Matt said after a while, "I have to say you've really got it together, old Bro."

"If I just knew how to work things out with Julia," Birch answered, his voice suddenly bleak. "Until I started going to your friendly psychiatrist, Luke Shields, I never even entertained the possibility I could be permanently blind. I honestly believed that because we had an unloving father, some kind of buried psychological problem was at the root of this escape into blindness. Uncover the problem and deal with it—ergo, I would see again and things would go back to the way they were."

"Sounds reasonable, having known Dad."

"Luke started me doubting, almost from the first. Between our mother and Cora, we seem to have had enough good going for us in our formative years to counteract Dad's heavy hand."

"Well, that's encouraging," Matt said with heavy irony.

"That was when I began to realize I'd been using amaurosis as a crutch. That's when I knew I had to see an ophthalmologist and face the fact for the first time that I could be blind forever."

"Which brings us to the point when you decided to come out here to Seahampton and think things over? Right?"

"I might never see again, and I didn't want Julie to find out before I was sure I could cope with the blindness myself," Birch said.

"And now you're sure?"

Birch sighed. "I know I'm ready for whatever the ophthalmologist has to say, but the possibility of losing Julie scares the hell out of me. There's no future for us together, Matt, if the guy says I'm going to stay blind."

"The *hell* there isn't! Julia doesn't give a damn if you're blind, you jerk!" Matt burst out. "What I mean is she does, of course, but it doesn't matter. She loves *you*! She loves the man you were when she married you. She didn't marry you because you could *see*, for God's sake!"

"Love isn't the issue. It's not love that holds two people together, anyhow. It's compatibility," Birch said, his tone dreary as if repeating an accepted truth.

"It's love," Matt argued stubbornly. "That moody character in the leather chair you were those last weeks before Seahampton didn't offer much in the way of compatibility, if you ask me! What do you think kept you two together, Birch? Julia stayed with you because she loves you. She'd be here right now instead of in Paris if you hadn't shut her out."

He heard a choking sound beside him, but he went on. "But you're all right now. You've got back the man you've always been—the guy she married. That's what you've got to give her, old buddy. It's all in the world she'll ever want."

Once again quiet settled between them. Within, Matt groaned. God! He'd talked too much. He got to his feet and turned on Cora's flashlight.

"Sorry," he said wearily. "I'm going back to the house."

"Do you *really* believe what you just said, Matt?" Birch asked softly.

"Believe it? I *know* it, Birch!"

"Thanks, Bro," Birch said. "Go on. I'll be up soon."

THE TWO BROTHERS spent the early part of the following day—before Matt left for the city again—on the beach. Together they jogged along the tide line a mile or more and back. Barkis, who hadn't appeared at the house since dinnertime the night before, came out of nowhere to run a short distance with them but soon lost interest. Matt saw him chasing sticks for a group of children a while later. Families there for the weekend had sprouted like mushrooms across the sand.

Neither Matt nor Birch made any attempt to resume the debate of the night before or to reopen the subject.

On the way back to Manhattan in the late afternoon, Matt remembered that he hadn't mentioned the concerns of Cheney, McCrae to Birch, and was unexpectedly glad he hadn't. If they'd gotten into the whodunit brewing at the family brokerage house, they might never have had that debate on the dune....

As AUGUST APPROACHED, Julia's assignment in Paris was winding down. Her days were still busy, and there remained work to be done, but she had free time now in the evenings for homesickness. Not homesickness in the sense that she missed what she had left behind in New York, or her parents and relatives in the state of Washington, or even Birch, who had vanished into a shell that contained nothing but blindness. She was homesick for the near-perfect life that she and Birch had built together. She yearned for the lost man she had shared it with.

The occasional notes from Birch had improved. They still took some deciphering and blossomed with typos, but it was evident that Matt had passed on her suggestion for positioning his hands correctly on the keyboard.

They were easier to read, but no more informative— except the most recent. From that one she learned that Matt had spent a night at Seahampton, that Birch and Cora would be going back to the Manhattan apartment the following week and that the dog she had worried about was no Seeing Eye dog but a fickle stray who had now attached himself to someone else.

A veritable *New York Times*! she thought dourly. The note dutifully sighed, "Love, Birch." No "Hurry home," or "Miss you, Bride." Just "Love, Birch."

Factoring in how long the note had taken to reach her, Julia realized that he and Cora were now back in New York, and for a moment the only thing that kept her from picking up the phone and calling the apartment was the thought that the phone service ran both ways. If he wanted to hear from her, he could do the calling.

Besides, what did she have to say to him? "Is it all right for me to come home?"

A wave of anger washed through her and dissolved in a new feeling of hopelessness. Nothing had changed. While there was no Seeing Eye dog, neither was there any ophthalmologist. She could see Birch as she imagined he was at that very moment, sitting in the big leather chair in the study, his face expressionless, every line of his body a picture of defeat.

And if she went back when she finished her work, he'd get depressed, too. By trying to avoid driving him crazy, she would, no doubt, become half-crazy herself.

One evening Hugh Dryden called. With Birch's suggestion in mind, she'd thought several times of calling Hugh when she was no longer working so much at night. Then, figuring there would be no way to avoid discussing the most obvious subject they had in common—Birch—she'd put down the phone without dialing.

"What do you mean not calling me, Julia!" Dryden scolded her. "I understand you've been over here most of the month."

"I've been tied up with an assignment, Hugh, and didn't want to call until I had time to talk," Julia said glibly. "How did you know I was here?"

"It's a long story," Hugh said with a laugh. "I just got back from a conference in New York last week. When I couldn't raise anybody at your place, I called Matt and he said Birch was at Seahampton, so I called there and got Cora. Birch was out on the beach, but Cora told me you were here and gave me the name of your hotel."

"If I hadn't watched you butter Cora up that night at the apartment I wouldn't have believed that information could be pried out of the discreet Cora Meigs by *anybody*," Julia said, laughing now, too. "I'm delighted she gave it to you. It's good to hear a familiar voice. It's good to hear *English* . . . spoken by an American!"

"An American who would like nothing better than to fill your ears with English any time you have to spare for me for the rest of your stay in Paris," Hugh said gallantly, and Julia felt better all at once.

She'd forgotten what fun it was to have a man favor her with nonsensical flattery. She felt suddenly lighter of heart, and was quite delighted when he suggested they start on the spot. It was night and the hour was nearly ten o'clock, but Julia didn't even consider saying no.

A short time later, they were sipping wine at a sidewalk table at a boulevard café where Dryden regaled her with bits of amusing and amazing international gossip. From that evening on, hardly a day passed that wasn't brightened by an effort of some kind from Hugh. With him she made the rounds of Paris's most brilliant night spots and four-star restaurants. On the nights when they didn't see each other he sent flowers or sweets or other small gifts.

Starved for small attentions that had been hers in the halcyon days before Birch was hurt, Julia sparkled under Hugh's special treatment. For the first time in months her life contained laughter and foolishness.

There seemed almost a tacit understanding between them not to mention Birch, and though Julia found this puzzling, she accepted it with relief. It had been a long time since a man had made her feel good about herself. Still, she was plagued with a guilty fear that she was becoming dangerously attracted to Birch's charming friend.

She was loath to bring the interlude to an end. It was innocent, lighthearted play, quickly forgotten and soon to be over, she told herself. Harmless. Meaningless.

Dammit, didn't she deserve a little harmless play? For many weeks play had been in such short supply she'd felt sometimes as if she'd begun to wither. With Hugh she felt herself in flower again.

When she finally realized that Hugh thought she and Birch had separated, Julia was shocked. Shocked mostly by her own reluctance to bring the truth out in the open and tell Hugh frankly that his gossip lines had it all wrong.

From the beginning, her relationship with him had been no more than casually affectionate. He'd made no covert move in the direction of intimacy, but she now recognized in his gifts and attentions a subtle, ongoing reminder that if her marriage had indeed become untenable, Hugh Dryden was waiting in the wings.

Just a few more days of innocent pleasure, she begged herself, knowing she had to set Hugh straight and say goodbye before he could take any more for granted than he already did. But she put it off. What harm could there be in a few days more when she'd be gone for good by the end of the month?

And then came a night when Hugh suggested for the first time that they finish an already provocative evening with champagne sent up to her hotel room. Mellowed already by wine and the romantic ambience of a dinner cruise on the Seine, Julia hung in a state of ambivalence for a moment. Then, having convinced herself that the suggestion meant no more than a reluctance to put an end to a delightful evening—with which she was in full accord—she agreed.

In the room they toasted each other once more with champagne, then Hugh took her in his arms and kissed her with unexpected passion. One hand drifted expertly to unfasten her front-buttoned dress and curve his fingers around one lace-covered breast. The force of her own throbbing response shocked her out of the world of pretend she'd floated in since the night she'd first sipped wine at the café with him.

"Let go of me, Hugh," she said quietly, pulling herself away and rebuttoning the opened front of her dress.

"Julia! What the devil . . ." Dryden began heatedly.

"Forgive me, Hugh. I'm sorry. This is entirely my fault, and I'm ashamed. I should have told you that Birch and I are not separated when it finally dawned on me that that was what you thought," she said contritely. "I knew it would put an end to all the lovely attentions you were giving me, so I kept putting it off. I salved my conscience by telling myself there was nothing wrong in enjoying a few innocent pleasures with Birch's old friend. That may or may not be true, but what we're getting into here doesn't come under the category of 'innocent pleasure,' and we both know it."

Unexpectedly, Dryden laughed. "Julia, my darling, don't be ridiculous! You are a cool, sophisticated young woman who has been around. *You* know better than that! We're attracted to each other. There's no reason in the world for us not to make love. Birch doesn't have to know."

He reached to take her in his arms again. Julia eluded him with a hard push.

"I'm glad you said that, Hugh. I've been feeling guilty because I thought I wasn't playing it straight with *you*," she said, a note of contempt in her voice.

"My dear, Julia, this is no time for self-righteousness," Dryden said loftily. "You wanted to make love with me just now. Don't deny it."

"Wrong, Hugh," Julia said in a level voice. "If I ever imagined I did, that kiss just now convinced me I definitely don't. The only person I've ever wanted to make love with is Birch. Now, please go."

WHEN CORA CAME BACK from shopping in the village the Monday morning after Matt's visit to Seahampton, she reported that Barkis was sleeping at the firehouse again.

"Why, the ingrate!" Birch said. "Do you suppose he didn't like Matt?"

"Maybe he's telling you it's time to go it alone," Cora said sensibly.

A short time later Birch started along the path to the breakwater, this time by himself. Counting his steps and bearing to the left instead of the right, he arrived at the top of the dune and the breakwater. Starting again with a new count, he made his way on down the breakwater until his feet felt the hard, wet sand at the edge of the water. Newly pleased with himself, he thought that maybe Barkis was right. It *was* time to go it alone.

In the absence of the dog to carry his cane, he was undecided what to do with it. When he held it in his hands as he ran it put him slightly off balance. He took a minute to secure the cane upright in the rocky structure of the breakwater; then, counting again, he took off up the beach in a slow jog. When he had run a thousand steps, he turned and ran back.

With a quarter of the return still to go, a raucous bark announced the arrival of the dog, who stayed with him the rest of the way to the breakwater. A moment after that, Birch found himself alone once more.

Back at the house Birch called Dr. Shields, the psychiatrist.

"I've been thinking about what you said on my last appointment with you, Luke," he said without preliminaries when the doctor was on the phone and Birch had identified himself. "I want to get an appointment with an ophthalmologist by the name of Burnside. What would be the quickest way for me to go about it?"

"I'm glad you're doing this, Birch. I'll be happy to set up an appointment for you with Burnside. I happen to know him, and he's one of the best," Shields said.

"Well, you didn't leave me much choice," Birch said wryly. "It's all right, isn't it, to tell my shrink that I'm scared as hell?"

"That's normal. You'd be psychotic if you weren't scared," Shields told him. "I'll get back to you as soon as I have something arranged."

In the early afternoon, the psychiatrist called to say that Dr. Burnside would see Birch first thing Wednesday morning.

As Birch was about to hang up Shields said, "By the way, what's become of your brother? I haven't seen him out at the marina for quite a while. Somebody told me he was thinking of selling his sailboat. If you happen to see him, tell him I'm interested."

"I didn't even know he *owned* a sailboat," Birch admitted with chagrin as he realized he'd been so preoccupied with himself he hadn't given much thought to his brother's interests for a long time.

"He's got a beautiful boat, but they say at the marina that he hasn't done any sailing since your father died. Too busy at the office," Shields said. "We used to do some sailing together. You might tell him I said to hang loose."

Birch hung up thinking not about his coming appointment, but about his brother. "Beautiful boat," sounded all Matt. "Too busy to sail it" did not. For the first time since Matt had approached him for advice, he wondered what was really going on at the family brokerage house and hoped his brother was all right.

Everything he'd said to Matt that day was true, but Matt had to *believe* it. Otherwise, he'd let that bastard Langley ride roughshod over him. He should have *listened* to Matt, dammit! He should have let his brother tell him the whole story and then made sure Matt understood that he was as capable of handling whatever was going on as any man.

The first thing he had to do when he got back into the city tomorrow was see Matt—and find out what he had wanted to tell him two months ago....

CHAPTER FOURTEEN

IT WAS NO IDLE PROMISE Birch had made himself. His new concern for his brother shared his attention almost equally with his coming appointment. He was no sooner back in the Manhattan apartment than he was on the phone trying to reach Matt who, it developed, was tied up in conferences and couldn't be reached.

The thought of having neglected Matt, the uncomplaining listener who had opened his ears to Birch's endless lamentations out on the dunes a few nights before, fueled Birch's bottomless self-reproach. If anybody ever had a right to say, "Knock it off, brother! I've got troubles of my own," it was Matt.

It was late afternoon before Matt called back.

"This is a surprise," he said in greeting. "You must not have read the heat and humidity predictions for this week here in the city or you would have stayed at Seahampton."

"It's about time to come back to the real world," Birch said. "Out there the other night all we talked about was how things were going with me. I let you get away without hearing a damn thing about what's with you and the firm."

"You didn't have Cora bring you all the way into Manhattan for that!" Matt said in disbelief, remembering that this was the brother who had refused to listen weeks ago when he'd gone crying to him for help. Matt had been sore about it at the time. Sore and over-whelmed by his own sense of inadequacy. He knew now that when Birch had said, "The firm's in your hands," it had been the making of Matt Cheney.

Thanks to his brother, he'd pulled it off alone. After having succeeded with no one but himself to rely on, he knew he never again had to back off from something because of a fear that he wasn't good enough.

Aloud he asked, "Are you back to stay?"

"I expect to be. At least for a while. I called Shields to see if he could expedite an appointment with Dr. Burnside, the ophthalmologist Julia's been touting. To my surprise, he can see me tomorrow morning."

"Now that's good news," Matt said. "I think that will make Julia very happy."

"I'd like to get it all settled one way or the other before she comes home at the end of the month," Birch said.

"Like I've said before, it'll be all right."

"Thanks. If you hadn't said it the other night there on the dune, I would probably still be out playing Hamlet on the beach—*to do or not to do!*" Birch said. "But that's not what I called you about. Luke Shields says he might be interested in buying your sailboat. He thinks you're not sailing much anymore. What's going on down there at Cheney, McCrae?"

Unexpectedly, Matt laughed. "Talk to me later, Birch. You've just got time to catch the first of the nightly business news," Matt said. "Turn it on and you'll find out."

The line went dead. Curious at once, Birch reached for the remote control for the TV. The news was just coming on.

"Good evening, ladies and gentlemen," the male half of the reporting team began. "A new stock scam was uncovered today when Evan Langley, stock analyst for Cheney, McCrae, one of Wall Street's most prestigious brokerage firms, was indicted on charges of participating in an insider trading manipulation. He is accused of having profited by in the neighborhood of a million dollars at the expense of stock investors."

Birch drew a long breath. "Wow!" he muttered.

The announcer continued. "'Small potatoes,' you may say, in light of the multimillion-dollar scandal that erupted on the street in '86. What's different this time is that Langley's alleged million-dollar pilfering of the public pocket was first brought to the attention of the Securities and Exchange commission by the head of Langley's own firm.

"According to a spokesperson for the SEC, Matthew Cheney, son of the late Horace Cheney, chief executive officer of Cheney, McCrae until his recent death, first suspected Langley some weeks ago. He confronted Langley with his suspicions, whereupon Langley started garnering proxies in an unsuccessful effort to remove young Cheney from the board, while continuing to take illicit profits on price movements. Cheney took his findings to the SEC."

"That's my Bro," Birch murmured and felt a moment of inexplicable sorrow for Matt because their father wasn't here to know about his coup.

But if their father were still alive, the coup would never have happened, Birch realized immediately. Their father would still be running the show, still holding the top spot in the firm for Birch, in stubborn expectation that eventually his oldest son would come back. At this point Matt might even have been working for some other brokerage firm....

"WHAT A BASTARD!" Julia had muttered aloud after she'd closed the door behind Hugh Dryden that last evening she spent with him in Paris. She trembled inside with anger and contempt for the man who'd charmed her up to a few minutes before, clouding her mind.

He'd been ready to violate every concept of honor and decency, damn him! He had no qualms about making love to an old friend's wife. It hadn't mattered that he'd be betraying a friend and taking advantage of a man who had the misfortune to be blind.

In a fury she peeled off her clothes, leaving them in a pile on the floor, washed her face and her teeth and, without even troubling to take a shower, climbed into bed, still fuming. But as she lay there, unable to sleep, her mind cleared, and she began to see that she had no right to heap all the blame on Hugh. She'd been playing fast and loose with her marriage by giving him no reason to think she would be unwilling to go along when he made his move.

In her nocturnal anguish at how near she had come to letting herself destroy what was most precious to her, she began to reexamine her thinking of the past months to discover what had brought her to this state. It was then that she saw herself and Birch's blindness in a new light.

It was then that she understood she'd been doing all the things he'd accused her of from the day she'd learned he was blind. She'd smothered him. She'd done her best to turn him into an invalid. She'd tried to run his life. She'd nearly destroyed him with her pity. And all because of her own neurotic notion that simply by *being* with him she could save him from harm. Everything she'd been doing in the months since his blindness had cried out, "Poor Birch", "poor, pitiful Birch". And along with those sentiments, she'd been crying, "Poor, poor *me*!"

It was a different Julia who stepped out into the Paris sunshine the following morning— a humbler Julia, a bit hung over, but filled with a tenuous joy at the thought of the reunion that lay ahead.

Hurrying to finish the work that kept her from Birch and home, a part of her was preoccupied with finding a way to show him that being blind didn't make him any less a man—the only man in the world for her. She wished she could find a way to assure him that Hugh Dryden didn't even come close.

And then suddenly her work was done, the month of August was just around the corner, and she was packing to go home. Still she was at a loss to find that special something that would tell Birch without words that to her he was still the man she had married.

In a taxicab, about to leave for the airport, she suddenly thought of the Ritz Hotel and directed the driver to take her there.

"Ah, Madame Cheney," the concierge greeted her with instant recognition. "It is a pleasure to see you again. Are we to have the privilege of your company?"

"Soon, I hope," Julia said. A flush of happiness warmed her spirit at the thought of what she was about to do. "You may recall that my husband and I were here in the early spring to celebrate the fifth anniversary of our marriage."

"Oui, madame," the concierge said. "Your stay was interrupted by an emergency, if I recall. I hope it was satisfactorily resolved."

"I believe it will be," she said and hastened to cover her ambiguity by asking, "I'd like you to reserve the same suite for us for a week, beginning a week from tomorrow."

All the way to the airport in the taxi, a picture of the lovely rococo room with its splendid marble bath played in her mind. In the face of the room's romantic ambience and the urgency of her own immeasurable love, how could Birch *not* understand how insignificant his blindness was to their love and marriage?

The realist in her told her that Birch might never put himself in the hands of an ophthalmologist, but it was a subject she would never try to promote again. It was Birch who had to live with the blindness. The decision was his to make.

In her mind, she knew their life together might never be easy, but in her heart, she knew that together they could make it work.

THE ONLY TIME he could remember being more apprehensive was during the twelve hours Julie had been held hostage on a plane, Birch thought as he waited in Dr. Burnside's office. Two long days and nights had passed since the morning of his first appointment with the ophthalmologist—days in which he'd been painstakingly examined not only by Dr. Burnside, but by a second ophthalmologist and a neurologist, and had undergone a variety of arduous tests. Today he'd returned for the verdict.

He'd spent his nights yearning for Julia in all the old, familiar ways, wanting her as much as he'd ever wanted her in his life, listening to her voice on the birthday tape time and again, as he had every night since the first time he'd set the tape rolling. The sonnets had become a part of him; the words sang in his mind through the waking hours of his lonely nights.

All week long he'd fought a driving urge to call her in Paris and beg her to come home and hear with him whatever the doctor was about to tell him. But the battle for his renewal was his own, and something inside forced him to go the rest of the way by himself.

If Burnside were going to walk in now and say, "Sorry, Cheney. You're blind. There's not a thing we can do for you," he wanted to hear the truth first and alone. If he was going to be blind for the rest of his life, *he* wanted to be the one to tell Julia. He wanted to be able to show her and make her believe, even as he told her, that in every other way he was a whole man and the man she married.

The sound of an opening door brought him out of his thoughts and back to the moment.

"Well, Mr. Cheney, I believe we have found the cause of your blindness," the pleasant, slightly nasal voice he'd come to know as Dr. Burnside's informed him briskly.

A sudden tightness gripped his throat, and Birch realized he was holding his breath. He let it out, waiting.

"We've determined that this is cortical blindness, undoubtedly caused by a blow near the base of the skull, which, curiously enough, seems to have been overlooked when you were in emergency," Dr. Burnside said.

His heart pounding, Birch remained silent.

"The lesion is operable, and so situated as to present no more than the usual surgical risk," the doctor went on.

"Are you telling me you can operate, and I'll be able to see again?" Birch asked tensely, unwilling to wait longer for the answer to that all-important question.

There was a moment's pause before Dr. Burnside said, "I'm sorry I can't promise you that, Mr. Cheney. Had the condition been discovered shortly after your... uh...accident, we could have told you almost certainly that an operation could restore your sight. But the condition has prevailed for several months. That, unfortunately, does not rule in your favor."

Something snapped for an instant in Birch. He'd gone through all this, for *this*? To find out what he'd feared all along was true?

An angry expletive—the curse to fate—died on his lips. What had all the soul-searching out at the beach been about, except to prepare himself for this?

"I guess that's what I've been expecting you to say," he said and realized that what he'd just tossed off without any real thought was true.

"Which doesn't mean the prognosis is necessarily negative, you understand," Dr. Burnside hurried to explain. "Surgery is indicated and could very well make it possible for you to see again, but the longer the condition goes untreated the greater the possibility treatment will not cure the blindness."

Having come prepared for a yes or no answer, Birch felt let down, but only for the moment it took to perceive that an equivocal answer was still to be preferred to a definite no.

"How soon can we get it over with?"

"My nurse will take care of scheduling the surgery. If you don't mind waiting in the reception room, she'll be able to let you know in a few minutes."

As he entered the reception room, Birch was surprised to feel a hand on his shoulder and hear Matt speak his name.

"Matt! I was just about to find a phone and call you."

"Well, what's the verdict?"

Birch could hear the stress in his brother's voice. "Nothing final yet," he said and told Matt what the ophthalmologist had said. "What are you doing here?"

"I knew you were coming this afternoon to hear the findings, so I called and asked what time your appointment was," Matt said. He added apologetically, "I wasn't going to get anything done until I heard, anyhow. I've got to see an attorney at four in connection with Langley's indictment, but I thought maybe we could meet someplace for dinner later."

It would be the first time Birch had eaten outside the confines of his own territory since he lost his sight, and he hesitated.

"Why not?" he said, experiencing an unexpected sense of freedom at the realization that there was nothing to stop him now that he was comfortable with himself again.

With the surgery set for the following week, Birch and Matt left the eye clinic where Dr. Burnside had his office and proceeded to Matt's loft a few blocks away for a beer.

"Are you going to wait till you get home to tell Cora?" Matt asked as they drank their beer.

"She's at her sister's for a couple of days, so I'll call her," Birch said. "Her niece is having a big wedding this weekend, and she didn't want to miss any of the excitement. It was a good excuse for me to see how well I can make it by myself."

"How about taking a ride down to the financial district with me?" Matt suggested as they finished their beers. "You've still got some friends down there you can visit with while I talk to this fellow from the attorney general's office. We can go on to dinner from there."

Again Birch hesitated and thought again, "Why not?"

At home in the empty apartment hours later, a reaction to the emotionally packed day set in. Still keyed up from sharing congratulatory champagne with old friends at the firm in recognition of Matt's victory in the Langley affair and having dinner later at Tavern on the Green, Birch was acutely aware of a new restlessness. The date of the operation—only five days hence—seemed unbearably far away, somehow. He was worried; he'd been blind too long not to fear the operation might fail.

Until now he'd thought he needed time to arrive at his own acceptance of his blindness before he saw Julia. He realized now that if he and Julia were going to share their life again fully, as they had until he'd shut her out, she should be with him when he learned the outcome of the surgery. He needed her; he wanted her. He could take anything with her at his side....

Overtaken by a great loneliness, his whole being aching with desire, he went through the mechanics of undressing and getting ready for bed with the meticulous care he'd learned at the center. He put his coat and pants on a hanger, his tie on a rack and everything else in the hamper. He brushed his teeth and showered. All acts were performed absently, his mind fully occupied with thoughts of Julia.

Naked, still moist from the shower, he reached a decision. According to her letters, Julia was all but finished with her work in Paris and would soon be home, though she hadn't yet said when.

Moving to the bedroom he sat down on the edge of the bed and felt for the phone on the night table, intending to call Julia in Paris. He realized then that he didn't have the hotel's number, and as he tried to recall the digits that would give him international information, he remembered that it was far too early in the morning in Paris for Julia to be awake.

He lay down and covered himself with the sheet, planning what he would say to her when he called her first thing tomorrow—about the ophthalmologist and the surgery, and how desperately he wanted her to be there when he woke up, and could she find it in her heart to come back?

Hearing in memory the silvery huskiness of her voice that could turn a sentence into a love song, Birch fell asleep.

TAXIING IN from Kennedy field shortly after midnight a while later, Julia thought she must have been crazy not to wait until the next morning to leave Paris. It was the time she least liked to arrive in any city; everyone appeared only half-awake and grumpy at having their stupors encroached upon.

Still, she was glad that in her eagerness to be with Birch she'd taken the first plane out after she'd finished her last bit of research on the world of haute couture. If she had waited until tomorrow, she thought, she would be just getting up after lying awake most of the night, too excited with thoughts of their reunion to sleep, anyhow. Now she was here, and Birch was only minutes away; and at least on the plane she'd had a movie to watch when sleep eluded her.

Letting herself into the apartment a short time later, she paused in the entryway and breathed in the familiar air of home. Hearing no sound, she slipped off her shoes and tiptoed through the apartment, not wanting to disturb Cora and at the same time pleased with the thought of slipping into Birch's bed, unexpected, while he was still asleep.

Entering the hallway, she was surprised to see the door to Cora's room open. Hurrying quietly, she peered in the open door and saw the room empty, the bed unslept in. Her spirit slumped in disappointment. They must not have come back from Seahampton. Or they'd come back and left again. Or maybe she'd misread Birch's scarcely decipherable letter—or he'd fouled up on the keyboard and written it wrong.

Turning away, she moved on to their bedroom, already having decided to get a few hours' sleep before starting out in the early morning for Seahampton. Flipping up the light switch at the door of their room, she stopped short at the sight of Birch, sound asleep in bed, his lips upturned slightly in a smile. The sudden thrust of her pulse sent a shock through her whole body.

Stepping to the side of the bed she stood for a long time, looking down on the splendid, hard-muscled figure stretched out on top of the tangled sheet. In his nakedness, she saw Michelangelo's *David* again.

She loved him. She loved him because he was Birch. He would always *be* Birch, even if he couldn't see. It wasn't surprising that in the shock of blindness the man he'd been had been lost for a while. Together they would find that man again.

After a time, when the rise and fall of his chest assured her he was sleeping soundly, she slipped away to the bathroom and showered. Afterward, she crawled into bed and moved next to him. Wrapping her arms around him she pulled her own naked body close to his.

"Julie," he murmured heavily. "Julie." Then, his voice pulling away from sleep, he said, "Oh my God, you're here. You really are here."

His hands reached and found her head, her face, her lips and the curves and valleys of her body—not sensually at first, but as if to remember.

"Julie," he said again, then took her mouth with his in a love dance that anticipated the fulfillment promised ahead. From her mouth, he moved to her breasts and then the soft triangle where her legs began.

Except for small murmurs and cries of love, they came together in silence and with a rapture and passion beyond any they'd ever known. And afterward, as their breathing grew quiet, Julia realized for the first time that her face was wet.

Idly caressing her now, he touched her cheek with his fingers and, finding it wet, bathed her tears away with his tongue. Then, holding her close, he rolled over, carrying her with him until she lay on top of him, her bare breasts hugging his chest. She felt his passion stir and grow inside her, and with a cry of rapture she began to move.

"Julia...my Julie...my Juliet...Bride," he murmured into the palm of the hand he kissed. They lay beside each other now, their passion sated, bathed in their mutual love.

"Guess what I brought you from Paris, darling," Julia murmured after a while.

"If I'd known you were coming," Birch began defensively, but Julia interrupted him with a giggle.

"I know, I know. You'd have baked a cake! It's just as well you don't have a present for me. No matter what it was, mine would be better," she said teasingly. "Besides, mine is as much for me as it is for you. It's a week in our honeymoon suite at the Paris Ritz beginning a week from today."

There was a moment of silence, and then Birch burst out laughing. "Come to think of it, I have a present for you, too. The only trouble is that my present voids your present," he said.

"Mind telling me what that means?" Julia asked, deflated.

"I saw Dr. Burnside this afternoon," Birch began.

Julia interrupted in an excited voice, "Dr. Burnside, the ophthalmologist?"

"The same. I believe he might take a dim view of my being in Paris three days after eye surgery. Even at the Paris Ritz."

"Birch! Oh, my dear!" She felt the tears rolling down her cheeks again, but it didn't matter. She wiped them away and blew her nose, as Birch told her what had been going on with him since they'd last seen each other.

And all at once it was as if they were back in the days before Birch's sight had been so brutally stolen from him. They talked honestly, openly about whatever came into their minds, whether trivial or important. Julia told him about Paris and the oddities of the fashion houses, and Birch spoke proudly of Matt's triumphant acceptance at Cheney, McCrae, Cora's niece's wedding, Seahampton and Barkis.

"Did you happen to see Hugh Dryden?" he asked at one point, and Julia let out a derisive snort.

"Did I ever!" Julia said. "I don't care if I never see Hugh Dryden again as long as I live."

Birch laughed. "So he tried to seduce you, did he?"

"How did you know?" Julia exclaimed.

"Typical Dryden. If you said he hadn't, I would have been sure you were trying to protect me from the sordid fact. I trust you put him in his place."

"You might say that. Don't you mind?"

"I would have minded like hell if I hadn't been sure of my Julia," Birch said calmly. "As it is, I rather like the idea of old Hugh getting his comeuppance."

Julia waited an uncomfortable moment before she said, "I can't put all the blame on Hugh. I was feeling pretty sorry for myself, and I enjoyed his attention...at least, I didn't do anything to discourage him until he finally came on so strong I came to my senses and lowered the boom. I can't blame Hugh for expecting more than he got."

Birch was quiet now for a moment. "It's all right, Bride. Dryden's not easily damaged, so don't feel guilty. Maybe we both owe him a dinner next time he comes to town."

Long afterward, after they'd made love again and lay together on the edge of sleep, Julia had a last moment of dreamy foolishness.

"When I crawled into bed with you it's a good thing you said, 'Julie,'" she said drowsily. "I really would have hated it if you'd said, 'Stephanie' or 'Laurie' or 'Patty Ann.' How did you know it was me?"

Through the window she could see the first predawn light that marked the beginning of a new day. Birch pulled her closer into his arms and began to speak:

...a mystic Shape did move
Behind me, and drew me backward by the hair;
And a voice said in mastery, while I strove,—
"Guess now who holds thee?"—"Death," I said.
But, there
The silver answer rang,—"Not Death, but Love."

EPILOGUE

"YOUR HUSBAND IS AWAKE now and asking for you, Mrs. Cheney. Come with me."

The nurse had no more than spoken from the doorway of the room where Julia waited with Matt and Cora Meigs when Julia was on her feet.

The anxiety that had been temporarily cooled by word that Birch's operation had been a surgical success, sprang up inside her again. For a moment her legs threatened to let her down. She reached out her hand for support, and Matt jumped up to put a steadying arm around her shoulders.

"You all right, Julia?" he asked.

"Yes," she replied, moving away from him to go with the nurse.

This was no time to get wobbly-legged, she told herself impatiently. The lesion had been removed without complication. Birch was in the recovery room waking up from the anesthetic.

Now for the real test. Could Birch see?

Her legs moving solidly under her now, she joined the nurse, too fearful of the answer to ask the question. Twice as she followed the formidably starched young woman, Julia tried to muster the voice to ask, but each time, apprehension silenced her.

At the end of the hallway the nurse turned a corner and opened a door, stepping back for Julia to proceed

ahead of her. In the bed across the room lay Birch, his
face looking a trifle drawn under its healthy Seahampton tan. His eyes were closed, but as she moved
toward him she saw his lids raise slowly, heavily; and for
an instant she was back in that other time in that other
room and Birch was gazing at her out of two perfectly
normal-looking eyes that moments later she would discover were incapable of seeing.

"Julie!"

Julia caught her breath, not daring to hope he saw her.

"Please raise the head of my bed," he said to the
nurse. "It's been a long time since I've seen my wife."

On wings of joy, Julia flew across the room to his
bedside and leaned over to kiss him while the nurse elevated the bed a fraction and slipped quietly out of the
room.

"Julie...Julie...you are so beautiful...so beautiful." His voice drifted off and Julia crooned his name,
and pressed her face upon his, and held him until the
muscles of her neck and shoulders complained. She
kissed his cheek and straightened.

"Hate to go back into...dark, but...can't keep m'eyes
open," Birch murmured.

Opening her shoulder bag, Julia took out a small
package. "Cora and Matt are waiting outside to hear,"
she said. "Before I go, I have a present for you." She
handed the package to Birch but as he began to slip off
the wrappings, she said, "Wait, Birch. Save it until
you've slept a while. I want you to be awake."

"I'm wide-awake," he insisted with a heaviness that
belied his words. Pushing aside the bits of paper and
ribbon, he gazed with interest on the ebony case inlaid
with ivory that he'd uncovered. "What is it?" he asked.

"See for yourself," Julia said.

Lifting the lid of the case, Birch emitted a soft sound of appreciation. "A compass. A beautiful old compass," he said. Aloud, he read the words she had printed on the card: "'To Birch, to keep us on course from now on. Julia.'"

Harlequin Supermromance

COMING NEXT MONTH

#390 A PIECE OF CAKE • Leigh Roberts
Lucius Donovan was shocked to discover he was the
father of a bouncing baby boy. Thea Willits hadn't
said a word when she'd abruptly ended their live-in
relationship. Determined to set things right, he
moved in next door. But winning Thea back would
be no piece of cake....

#391 CATHERINE'S SONG • Marie Beaumont
The Cajun motto, "Let the good times roll,"
signified only *wasted* time to restoration architect
Catherine Nolan. But then she met Blackie
Broussard, who valued the dreams he wove in song
more than any bridge he'd engineered. Soon
Catherine began questioning her own values, because
being held in Blackie's arms somehow felt like
coming home....

#392 RINGS OF GOLD • Suzanne Nichols
Tori Anderson just wanted Michael St. James to do
what he did best—help her recover from her injury
so that she could get back on the ski slopes before
the next Olympics. But racing again might put Tori
in a wheelchair for life. Could Michael convince her
to accept a gold ring instead of a gold medal?

#393 WITH OPEN ARMS • Suzanne Ellison
Stockbroker Camille Blaine had a great job, a slick
condo and a designer wardrobe. Then she met Linc
Stafford, a dead-broke widower with a passel of
kids, a senile grandfather and a sizable collection of
rescued animals. Suddenly, life in the fast lane no
longer seemed so appealing....

**A compelling novel of deadly revenge and passion
from Harlequin's bestselling international
romance author Penny Jordan**

POWER PLAY

Eleven years had passed but the
terror of that night was something
Pepper Minesse would never
forget. Fueled by revenge against
the four men who had brutally
shattered her past, she set in
motion a deadly plan to destroy
their futures.

Available in February!

 Harlequin Books ®

HPP-1A

HARLEQUIN Temptation

The Pirate
JAYNE ANN KRENTZ

At the heart of every powerful romance story lies a legend. There are many romantic legends and countless modern variations on them, but they all have one thing in common: They are tales of brave, resourceful women who must gentle and tame the powerful, passionate men who are their true mates.

The enormous appeal of Jayne Ann Krentz lies in her ability to create modern-day versions of these classic romantic myths, and her LADIES AND LEGENDS trilogy showcases this talent. Believing that a storyteller who can bring legends to life deserves special attention, Harlequin has chosen the first book of the trilogy—THE PIRATE—to receive our Award of Excellence. Look for it in February.

AE-PIR-1